DELAYED RECKONING

Sterling Young

ACKNOWLEDGMENTS

Many friends have given me support and advice during the writing of *Delayed Reckoning*. Those same friends also listened as I went on and on while outlining upcoming sequences of the book. If at anytime I bored or drove someone to the brink of tears with my droning on about this book, I apologize.

I'd like to thank Sheriff Jeff Sidles and Coroner Kevin Hatchett for providing me with insight into the workings of their jobs. I'd also like to point out that I adapted some of what they told me for the purpose of writing *Delayed Reckoning*.

This book is a work of fiction. Names, characters, places and incidents are a product of the author's imagination or are used fictitiously. Any similarity to actual people wandering about in various Kentucky counties is entirely coincidental.

Most importantly, my love and gratitude goes to my wife, Cindy. She, more than anyone else, put up with me while I wrote this book. She patiently listened to all my various scenarios and offered plenty of recommendations as to whether or not my ideas were any good. Probably the most difficult task for her, was editing the book. Did I mention that I wasn't a stellar English student? Needless to say, Cindy spent hours reading and re-reading the book while in correction mode. To my wife, I'm forever grateful.

CHAPTER 1

Late July

Jack Estep knew that what he was doing was wrong. How he actually ended up this way, was at times hard for him to remember. He thought, if only I could start out fresh, then some of the things I've done, would never have happened. Yes, he still knew how to distinguish right from wrong, but sometimes addictions are just too strong. He glanced sideways in the mirror as he walked down the hallway. This caused him pause, so he stopped to take a closer look. The man Jack saw in the reflection disturbed him. He studied the face of what he had become. Mirrors tell it like it is. They don't lie. In that mirror, hanging on the naked wall of his mother's trailer, the truth was painfully obvious.

He looked more closely at himself. His eyes were bloodshot and tired. They were buried deep within his face, like they belonged to someone else, someone much older. His cheeks were sunken, like sinkholes in a farmer's neglected field. The stubble of beard on his cheeks and chin was sparse. It seemed to have stopped growing in spots. He remembered how full it had been. His forehead exhibited the tell-tale signs of premature old age. He looked like an exhausted, wrinkled old man played out from years of labor, even though Jack had just turned twenty-seven. He seldom smiled now, because his teeth were rotting. He thought back to his glory years. He remembered being an all-right looking guy. His reflection was pleasing then. It hadn't been that many years ago. But, that wasn't important to him now. His most important goal in life now was to get his next fix. As Jack scrutinized his reflection, he couldn't accept the despair he saw. He vowed, I'm going to beat this thing, and I'm going to beat it real soon.

Jack continued up the hallway and found his mother lying in a drunken heap on her favorite afternoon spot, the couch. He wondered, which one of us is the biggest loser? At least his mother received legitimate income. That is, if food stamps, Medicaid and low income heat assistance could be considered legitimate, or even be considered income. Hell, he did earn some money. Maybe his job wasn't totally honest, or on the up and up. It wasn't easy peddling drugs on the street. The job was very difficult, harder than most people could imagine. He watched as his mother restlessly turned over again and again, seeking a more comfortable position.

Jack stopped a moment and looked around the living room of his mother's run down trailer. Over the dining room table hung old photos of Jack and his siblings. Of the four children, only two of them were still living, just Jack and his older sister. Supposedly, she lived someplace in Lexington. Jack couldn't remember the last time he'd seen her. His brother was killed a few years back, driving drunk. He was just nineteen at the time. But, at least his youngest sister died from natural causes. She had pneumonia, only four years old. At the time, both his parents were either too drunk or stoned to realize that his sister was terribly ill and that something was very wrong. Jack congratulated himself. He figured he must be doing something right. At least he'd managed to survive to adulthood.

He was thankful that his mother allowed him to stay with her. Otherwise, getting by would be even tougher. He recalled some of the lessons his mom had drilled into him while he was growing up. She'd slur her words as she delivered her same stern message, "Jack, study hard. Get that college education and make something of your life." She constantly warned him, "Jack, you don't want to end up working at some underwear plant that one day just up and closes its doors. Yeah, basically saying, screw all you people." That last piece of advice still resonated in his head, almost as if she had said it yesterday. Hell, for all he could remember, maybe she had. When the Jockey plant closed, both his mom and his step-father lost their jobs. That was when his family started to crumble. His step-dad left to find work, and never returned. Mom found booze to be good company, and government aid kept her afloat.

Before his family had collapsed, Jack's mother pushed him very hard. And, for what it was worth, it had worked. He remembered receiving his acceptance letter from the University of Kentucky. His mom had been as much, if not more excited, than he was. He graduated from Nicholas County High School with a 3.6 GPA and scored extremely well on the SAT exam. His grades, coupled with his SAT scores, earned him a partial scholarship, amounting to $3,000 per year. Jack reflected back and remembered how he loved to brag to everyone in town about his acceptance to UK. That's right, UK, the College of Engineering!

Jack's thoughts quickly returned to reality as he heard his mother tumble from the sofa. She struggled to reclaim her bearings. He bent down on his knees and helped roll her back into position on her afternoon sleep-it-off spot. He did it, despite her incoherent ranting mumbled in his direction. After a moment, she once again appeared comfortable, so Jack stood, brushed off his pants, and whispered in his mother's ear, "Mom, I'll probably be late. Don't bother waiting up for me." She belched loudly, sending whiskey laden breath Jack's way, and then closed her heavy eyes. He looked at her a moment longer, then turned for the door.

It was nearly the end of July and it hadn't gotten hot, very unusual for this time of year, and for that, Jack was appreciative. He closed the trailer door softly and descended the steps, leading to the back yard. His Polaris ATV sat where he'd left it only a few hours earlier. He studied the exterior of the trailer with great attention to detail, and joked to himself, it's not much, but location, location, location. His mother's trailer was situated on a half-acre lot and adjoined a large expanse of woods in eastern Nicholas County. As a result, there were no nosey neighbors. Not a soul lived close by. Jack felt the location was absolute paradise. It enabled him to come and go as he pleased. In his line of business, privacy was paramount.

He checked the oil, making sure his machine was ready. He turned the key and the ever dependable Polaris roared to life. Jack loved that sound. It made him feel that the ATV was an almost invincible method of transportation. He exited through a gate in the fenced in-yard, and followed the narrow blacktop road toward the gravel lane, where he turned off into the woods. Jack ignored the "No

Trespassing, Private Property" posting because he knew for a fact that the owners rarely visited. The old road wound into the woods for at least four miles. Though the road was closed to vehicular traffic, ATV traffic wasn't uncommon. Usually, there were hunters or just people messing around on the trails. Jack wasn't messing around. This was serious. This was his livelihood.

Jack always took his time. He examined the trail while he crept along on his ATV. He habitually scanned the woods, and looked for signs of anyone that didn't belong. The non-maintained county road had been closed to traffic for at least seventy-five years, and it showed. Ruts eight to ten inches deep were common. They only added to the four-wheeling challenge. Directly ahead, a large branch from a dead red oak tree partially blocked the trail. He didn't have time to mess with that. It must have fallen earlier in the day, when the front that carried hard wind and rain blew through. Jack pulled a machete from the Polaris and hacked a temporary route around the obstacle. He never looked forward to traveling the trail to his getaway, especially if it was muddy. Unfortunately today was one of those days. The Polaris spun its wheels in a rut. This would make it more obvious that someone had travelled through recently. But, today, he had no choice. He sure as hell wasn't about to hike the three plus miles to get in here. No way was he about to trek all the way from the paved road.

He slowed as he approached the thicket. This was where he always hid his ATV. He turned to regard the tracks he'd left while entering. They were hardly discernible. It really helped that the last two-hundred yards were covered by rock. Jack smiled, happy that this section of trail, probably an old river bed, hid most of his tracks.

After the Polaris was concealed in the thicket, Jack relaxed and had a smoke. He was generally edgy after arriving, especially until after he'd hidden his machine. The cigarette helped to calm his nerves. His cigarette of choice was Camel. Jack felt smoking helped clear his head. He intently listened to the woods around him, while he inhaled deeply. Quiet, he loved the tranquility. He took one last draw before putting the cigarette out. Ok, it's time to get to work. He began the task of pushing his way through the briars that covered the game trail, which led to his hunting cabin. It felt good out this afternoon. Not too warm, and not too cold. It was damned near perfect.

Jack was always apprehensive when he arrived at the cabin. He always preformed a cursory look around to see if anything appeared out of order. Today, he was satisfied that things were ok. He undid the padlock that secured the hunting shack. He entered the cabin quickly, and then pushed the door closed behind him. Even though the hunting shack was well hidden, you could never be too sure that someone wouldn't have stumbled upon it. Fortunately, within the hunting community, hunters left others hunters' stuff alone. Jack felt if they truly knew his hunting ritual, they might just make an exception. He allowed a rare, rotten-toothed grin as he pulled the camouflage tarpaulin away from his gear.

Inside, the cabin was almost cozy. However, there were no hunting supplies. No buck lure, no tree stand, no turkey call, no skunk scent, and no camo paint to be found. Jack folded the tarp and placed it out of the way in the corner. His cabin was roughly sixty-four square feet, and had windows that opened on the east and west ends. He opened the windows, to check that the seals on the frames were intact. The seals made the cabin nearly airtight with the windows closed. He hung a battery powered Coleman lantern from the rafter and clicked it on. His hideout in the thicket-covered woods was already in shadow. He glanced out the window when he heard a twig snap and watched a doe and her fawn amble by, only giving him a brief look.

Jack lifted the wall mounted table, and locked it into position. It was time to get busy. Most of the ingredients he needed had been hidden under the tarp. He remembered how many trips on the Polaris it had taken to originally stock the lab. Now, he only had to bring a few miscellaneous items whenever he came out. Of course, more cold medicine was always needed to concoct his recipes. As Jack set up his chemistry lab that afternoon, he remembered some of the tricks he'd learned from his abbreviated stint at UK years ago. One of his experiments had resulted in his expulsion from the program. Say goodbye to the scholarship and his mother's dreams, and an honest way of life. But, that was still time well spent, because now he made some of the most sought after, potent methamphetamine in Nicholas County.

The next afternoon

Jack slowed as he entered the thicket where he always hid the ATV. He felt confident that he hadn't been seen or followed. The old county road he used to gain access to his little hideaway was getting woollier each day, but, as opening day of hunting season approached, it would receive increased traffic. But, that was still weeks away. This afternoon, there were no hunters, no open seasons, so the four to five hundred acres of woods belonged solely to him. He loved feeling like a land baron.

Still, he sat motionless after killing the engine and listened for any unexpected noises in his surroundings. Jack knew the people that frequented these woods were few. But, he also knew from experience, you should never let your guard down. He dismounted the Polaris and lit his customary Camel. He inhaled deeply and pondered the batch he would cook tonight. He really enjoyed these moments of solitude. It was another good looking afternoon, once again almost perfect. He smirked as he thought about the dumb asses who cooked meth in the privacy of their own homes. Jack had a few chemistry courses under his belt. One thing the courses had taught him was that you could cook meth almost anywhere. So, why risk doing it at home?

His hidden cabin had served him well over the years. Most addicts didn't want to work hard in order to get their fix. That was the primary reason they got caught. Jack still retained enough brain cells to understand that caution was of the utmost importance. He constantly checked for signs of any visitors. Stubbing out his cigarette, he looked around once again before he began the three-hundred yard trek over the thicket covered trail that led to his cooking hideaway. Maybe he should become a hunter, especially in light of all the wildlife he spooked that afternoon as he made his way to the cabin.

Jack paused several feet from the cabin. He wasn't sure why he felt uneasy, but something wasn't right. He stood motionless and observed the area around him. He turned his head slowly, perusing the setting before finally stepping closer. He carefully studied the ground around the perimeter. He also checked to verify that the windows were still tightly sealed. There were no footprints, or nothing out of the ordinary, that jumped out at him. He was probably being overly paranoid. Tonight, for sure, he definitely needed his fix. Let's put these negative feelings to bed with a little pick me up.

He quickly removed his keys from his pocket, but hesitated once again while he closely scrutinized the padlock. After examining the lock, Jack felt confident it looked as it always did. There were no visible scratches or pick marks. He was quite anxious to get inside now, especially after he'd wasted precious minutes with needless worrying. He unlocked the padlock and quickly pushed the door open. Many thoughts passed through his mind as he watched the door swing inward. It seemed to move in slow motion. A strong smell of propane registered in his mind. He reflexively glanced at his feet and watched as sparks trailed behind the moving door as it dragged over some kind of homemade ignition device. He instinctively closed his eyes and felt the explosion. Jack had been found out.

When consciousness returned, he sensed that it was the middle of the night. He had no memory of what had happened. He had no idea where he was and was clearly confused about why he couldn't move. There was one thing that he was well aware of, and that was the pain that now consumed him. His withdrawals had never felt this bad before. He thought maybe he was in a state of anhedonia, which would account for his extreme state of depression. Maybe he was having a very bad dream. Was it real or was it a dream? He couldn't tell. He had come down hard before, but it'd never been nearly this intense. If he could just scrounge up a fix, everything would work itself out.

He lay on his back and stared at the brightly shining stars. Unknown to Jack, the explosion had blown him backwards several feet from the cabin. It was possible he had suffered some kind of spinal damage, which was why he couldn't move. He lay motionless in a thick briar patch, which now served as his bed, and suspended him inches from the ground. The front of his body was severely burned. Even his eyelids were charred away, leaving his eyes exposed. He still retained his ability to smell and sensed that something was burning nearby. He didn't realize that what he smelled was his own burnt skin and clothing, commingled with the smoldering remnants of his cabin.

Jack managed a slight noise, which sounded like a frightened whimpering dog. Realizing what he heard was his own whimpering, he silently cried out in desperation. Why was it so dark? Why were his eyes so dry? He attempted to move his eyes from side to side, but they seemed locked in position. He had never stared at the stars for so long. Tonight, this gave him no joy. Was he awake or was he asleep? Jack had never experienced withdrawals of this severity. For the first time in his life, Jack prayed. He prayed to waken from this hellish dream.

Jack continued to cry and whimper through the night. As he stared at the stars, he began to distinguish tree branches appearing at the edge of his vision. He thought that maybe his eyesight was improving. But he was still unsure. He wished the pain would end and he could sleep. In addition to the intense pain, pus oozed from his badly burned face and found its way into his lidless, immobile eyes. This caused even more excruciatingly painful stinging and burning.

Morning came

The sun rapidly cleared the trees. Jack realized that it was going to get hot. He had visions of meat searing on a grill. Insects now began to flit around his eyes. Jack prayed harder. Maybe they won't land. Hundreds of flying things quickly learned of his defenselessness and converged on him. They began crawling, nibbling, and biting. It suddenly dawned on Jack that he was lying in the woods near his cabin. He found little comfort in this. Unfortunately for Jack, the remoteness of it guaranteed that he wouldn't be found, at least not anytime soon.

Suddenly, the bright sun broke free of a cloud that had shaded it, and hit Jack squarely in his fixed, motionless eyes with all its intensity. He screamed out as the brilliant light burned his exposed retinas. Delirious, he managed to round up a sense of calm, and some of the pain began to lessen. What Jack couldn't have known, was the decrease in pain was the result of his approaching death.

He sensed movement above and Jack wished he could yell. He could now barely see the large flock of turkey buzzards that were circling overhead. He still had twinges of pain, but nothing like before. He could hardly feel the movement of the things that crawled, tugged and pecked on his body. Although things moved in and out of his ears, he noticed that these feelings and sounds were also fading. He was slipping away.

If Jack Estep's heart hadn't stopped beating, if his brain hadn't stopped sending electrical pulses to the rest of his body, he might have wished to be a student again, to be a freshman, entering the University of Kentucky, with plans to bust his ass studying for a degree in engineering.

As Jack's pain ceased, so did his life.

CHAPTER 2

Beginning of July

Tom Padgett paced the floor of his office. He was trying to get a handle on how to deal with the current situation. He had been around politics for a long time. He could read the writing on the wall, especially how the politics worked in Mt. Sterling. He had 30 years service with the city police, most of those years doing detective work. For some unknown reason, the newly elected Mayor, Bud Blankenship, seemed to hold a grudge against him. Tom was attempting to understand why this was the case. But, in his mind, he'd drawn a blank.

He had two years remaining 'till his planned retirement. He understood the necessity of getting along with Bud. He toyed with an idea. Maybe it would be better to retire sooner rather than later. Tom realized that he would go crazy if he didn't have some sort of job, or something meaningful to do. He was smart enough to realize that spending all his waking hours at home with his wife Darlene would prove difficult, maybe even impossible.

He recalled all the rumors which had floated around the station during the Mayor's campaign. Tom tried not to dwell on the political jousting that seemed to always surround Kentucky politics. Bud was at least ten years his junior. Yes, could that be part of the problem?

Tom had been promoted to Captain a year earlier. He missed the action that working the streets offered, but he managed to stay engaged with his men. Over the years, he had proven himself a top detective. It always came natural to him.

Suddenly, the terrible memory of that fateful day invaded his thoughts. He heard the shots, but he didn't know who did the shooting. It was as if he was there and not there at the same time. He pushed the memory aside, back into the archives of his mind. Tom, *focus on the positive, focus on the now.*

Tom's office was simply adorned. He was appreciative that it at least had a door. Now, when the door was closed, people would knock before entering, not always, but most of the time. There were other advantages to being Captain. One of them was that he didn't carry all the weight of the day home with him. He assumed that Darlene appreciated that fact. However, lately it was hard to tell whether she did or not. Surprisingly, much like the Mayor, lately Darlene even seemed to take issue with him. Tom thought maybe he was being overly paranoid. He felt something was going on with his wife, but he couldn't put a finger on what it was. He couldn't solve all the issues that were floating around in his head, anyway. It was quitting time and he was looking forward to a nice cold beer.

As he left the station, Tom couldn't remember how much beer he had at home. He'd address that problem. He walked over to Big Red's Liquor, which was conveniently located across the street from the station. He grabbed a twelve pack of Budweiser and headed home.

He and Darlene had a place in town, and had for the past five years, much to Tom's displeasure. When they'd met twenty-five years earlier, he was living out in the country off Highway 60. Prewitt Glassy Lick Road, what a fantastic place to have been a bachelor. The first time Darlene visited the somewhat remote home, three miles out of town, she claimed that she loved it. After they married, she went wild decorating the small two bedroom home, making it her own. Tom remembered coming home to find a concrete goose standing on the porch. He really hated that goofy thing, especially when Darlene insisted on dressing it in different outfits. She loved lots of things that he felt were silly.

After nineteen years of marriage, Darlene wanted more than their quiet place in the country. She told Tom she needed to be in town, in order to be closer to her friends. He unsuccessfully argued for the advantages that the getaway offered over a home in town. Darlene was insistent in her demands, maybe even relentless. Eventually, she got her wish. Now he found himself caged up in the heart of town. He had to admit that it was convenient, less than a half-mile from the station.

The Pines on Main was a small neighborhood in Mt. Sterling. Actually it was tiny, there were only two streets. On one road, all the homes were duplexes. On the other, they were all single family homes. Luckily for Tom, they'd purchased a single family. He knew living in a duplex would have driven him crazy.

Lately, nightlife with Darlene was far from exciting. That was greatly dependent on whether or not she was even home. Tom realized that he probably fell short in both the romantic and adventuresome departments, but it did take two to tango.

He felt lucky to have gotten Bella, his golden retriever/yellow lab mix. He found her on a farm near Mount Sterling. She was the runt of the litter, with eight brothers and sisters. When Bella was a pup, she was quite timid. On the drive home, Bella managed to climb onto his shoulders. Then, she wrapped her body around the back of his neck, which surprised him. It really made it difficult to drive. She was shaking like a leaf.

Tom spent hours training her when she was a pup, and as a result, now she was definitely his girl. He wondered where Darlene had been all those days and nights while he was training Bella. God only knows. It was becoming painfully obvious to Tom, that Bella was a far better companion than his 'soul mate' of twenty-five years. The only reason he looked forward to going home, other than beer in the fridge, was to see Bella.

He sat on the porch and sipped his beer while he absentmindedly scratched Bella's ears. He was thinking about tomorrow, Wednesday. He really wasn't looking forward to it. Wednesday was the Mayor's weekly staff meeting. The thought of watching the squatty little man strut around the conference room, could easily put Tom in a foul mood. The Mayor was constantly looking for ideas from his staff. Ideas about doing things better. Tom knew better than offer recommendations, because the Mayor seemed to perceive any ideas from Tom as a deliberate threat to his authority. He'd just be quiet and concentrate on keeping his mouth shut. The Mayor didn't really want input, anyway. The meeting was just Bud's way of making his staff feel needed.

Tom woke early as usual. He lay motionless and stared at Darlene's profile, while he listened to her snore. He wasn't sure when she'd come to bed last night. But, for some reason she was there now. He remembered when they'd first married, Darlene wouldn't have dreamed of climbing into bed, just to go to sleep. And she surely wouldn't have pointed her backside so deliberately in his direction.

He quietly snuck out of bed, not wanting to wake her. He didn't feel up to sharing coffee with her this morning. He really didn't care to hear about any of her plans. He could wait 'till this afternoon for that report. That is, if she was even home. He didn't know what she did all day, or where she went. Maybe he wasn't the sleuth he believed, or maybe he just didn't care. At least Bella would be happy to see him this afternoon, especially if she got to come inside and have some treats. Darlene never allowed her inside.

Tom stood and stretched. He listened to his body pop and crack. He slowly walked into the kitchen, then turned on the coffee and made his way back to the master bath to shave and shower. Why was he so tired? Last night he'd only had four or five beers. He slumped up the hall. This morning, he felt every bit his age. Tom was six feet, but didn't feel that tall this morning. As he looked in the mirror, he thought, man, I'm getting grey. Maybe he needed to change the vanity light bulbs, opting for lower wattage. Not only did he see grey hair, but also wrinkled skin, and teeth that seemed to get more yellow every day. It's terrible to get old, not that fifty-seven is old, but it's not young either. At least I still have a full head of hair, grey, sort of thick, and when it's wet, it still looks dark. He looked at his profile; my jaw line's still fairly strong. Not sagging as much as other guys my age. He stepped from the shower and noticed the size of his love handles. They were bigger than he remembered. Who named these damned things love handles anyway? Thank God he still had his wits about him. He felt as sharp as he had when he was younger. He knew that exercise would delay some of the aging process, but the psychological pain that exercise couldn't cure, could be eased by drinking a few beers.

He dressed, returned to the kitchen, and found Darlene drinking her coffee. She looked up and scowled at him. Good morning to you too, smiley, he thought. She slowly sipped from her coffee and stared at Tom as he poured himself a cup.

Darlene snapped, "I probably won't be here when you get home tonight. My friends and I are having a girls' night out."

He wondered, so, what else is new? But, he refrained from saying anything except, "Hope you all have a good time."

Tom thought, so this is what happens after twenty-five years of marriage? What's the name of that Ray Charles song? *The Thrill Is Gone.* He looked at his wife a moment longer, before he turned and carried his coffee into the living room to catch the news.

● ● ●

The Mayor's entire staff was in attendance. Everyone always sat in the same chairs. It was almost as if they'd been given assigned seating. Tom sat at the opposite end of the table. He was farthest from the Mayor. He glanced around the room at everybody's blank stares. They all listened as Bud droned on and on about some nebulous crap. Tom wasn't sure what Bud was talking about. That was fine. Thoughts of Darlene's plans and his own future were flitting through his head. The Mayor finally finished his lecture. Tom hadn't realized the meeting had ended. He continued staring blankly at the floor. Bud called his name a second time before Tom snapped from his trance-like state.

The Mayor grinned, "Tom, could you come by my office for a few minutes?"

Tom wasn't sure he'd heard correctly. What could Bud possibly want? He tried to come up with an answer. Unable to, he finally gave up. What's the worst that could happen?

"Yes, Mister Mayor. I'll be right in. I just have to make a quick call," Tom lied. Tom had no problems with Bud. Why does the Mayor have issues with me? He really didn't need a confrontation with the Mayor today. Why was Bud in such a damned good mood anyway? He's never in a good mood. He couldn't remember the last time he'd seen Bud smile so broadly, except when he had gotten elected. He had a feeling this meeting was going to be painful, but wasn't sure why. Tom put the handset down after receiving no answer from his make-believe phone call. Well, might as well go meet, *The Man.*

Tom paused, and then reluctantly knocked on the Mayor's door, hearing Bud yell. "Come on in." He stepped into the office and wondered if he should close the door. Before he could decide, Bud strolled over and began pumping his hand. This only added fuel to his level of apprehension. The Mayor closed the door and motioned for him to have a seat.

Bud spoke, "Hey Tom, how about a cup of coffee?"

"Sure, why not, I'm not driving," Tom laughed.

The Mayor punched a button on his intercom, "Barbara darling, could you bring us a couple cups of coffee?"

Tom glanced around the room and noticed all the photos and awards that adorned the walls. He futilely tried to understand why he was here for this impromptu meeting.

The Mayor leaned way back in his leather wingback chair and got comfy. "So, how's Charlene been doing?"

"It's Darlene and she seems to be doing well." Actually, he was kind of wondering the same thing.

"What about your daughter? Ana is it?"

"It's my son and his name is Andy." Tom was anxious to bring this worthless small talk to an end.

Bud paused, then steepled his hands as he considered Tom. Before he could speak, Barbara entered carrying two cups of hot conversation-stalling coffee.

They both took long apprising sips as they each stared into their cups. After several moments, the Mayor lowered his cup and cleared his throat.

"Well, I'm sure you're wondering why I've called you in here."

"Yes sir, to be perfectly honest with you, I'm more than a little curious."

"I believe you'll be pleasantly surprised with what I have to say," Bud beamed.

Tom was positive he'd heard correctly and he was again on high alert. It just wasn't in the Mayor's nature to be 'this nice'. Tom's hands began to sweat and he was quietly thinking, let's finish this babble. Clearly Bud was enjoying this conversation a lot more than he was. The Mayor continued his contemplation.

Bud tilted his head, feigning thoughtful consideration before he continued, "Tom, you've been with the department a long time; a very long time."

Now sweat was forming on Tom's upper lip. This was beginning to have a bad sound to it.

"You've also earned a service record that has been unsurpassed in the history of Mt. Sterling's Police Department."

It sounded like the Mayor was getting wound up. He was preparing to get into one of his typical long winded spiels.

"You've also held every position in the department; that is, with the exception of chief. You exemplify precisely what it means to be a Mt. Sterling peace officer." Bud paused to catch his breath and get a better handle on his thoughts before he continued. "Tom, I'm prepared to make you a generous offer. The offer is for you to replace retired Chief Bryant. I'm promoting you to chief, Chief of Police. Yes, chief of all Mt. Sterling. Now what do you think about that?"

Tom was unprepared for this. He hadn't expected such a turn of events. He was suddenly at a loss.

Bud once again took the opportunity to buzz his secretary, "Barb honey, I think we're going to need some fresh coffee." The coffee diversion gave Tom some time to better collect his thoughts.

"Mr. Mayor, can I be frank?"

"Sure Tom."

"Everything you've mentioned is true. But, there's a reason I've never aspired to be chief. To be perfectly honest with you, I believe the chief position equates to nothing more than that of a glorified manager. I feel if I was chief, I would be alienated and totally out of touch with the men, and what's going on in the rest of the department."

Once again Barbara ambled in and replaced the empty mugs with fresh ones. The Mayor wore a grave expression on his face. He slowly sipped his coffee and stared at his desk. Finally, he spoke very softly, "Let me make sure I totally understand what it is that you're saying. What I believe I heard you say was, you're not interested in the promotion to chief?"

"Yes sir, that's a very good assessment. Mayor, let me further explain my position. If I was forced to take a job that required me to sit on my ass all day long doing paperwork, that job would probably kill me."

Bud offered a hint of a smirk, "Tom, maybe I didn't make myself clear. The promotion I'm offering you happens to be non-negotiable. The job is basically a take it or leave it proposition." He continued, "I'm moving John Stamper into your vacated position of Captain." He once again leaned back in his chair and smiled directly at Tom.

Now utterly confused, Tom needed clarification. "Mayor, you mean that if I refuse your generous offer, I'm finished in the department anyway?"

"Yes, that's it in a nutshell. Reorganization has been long overdue."

Tom glanced over at the Mayor who smiled widely. He felt like reaching over to knock the smirk from his face. He had definitely had his fill of coffee. "And when do you need my decision?"

"Let's see now, it's Wednesday, so why don't you let me know by the day after tomorrow?"

The meeting was apparently finished. Tom rose from his seat and started for the door. The Mayor nimbly moved into position and greeted him halfway to the door. Bud vigorously shook his hand, "I'm sure you'll make the right decision. Why don't you go ahead and take the rest of the day off? That way you can talk things over with Charlene."

Tom slowly walked from the building en route to his car. Normally, he wouldn't have driven the short distance to the city building. It was only a two block walk. So, maybe his intuition was working after all. He felt himself slouch as he climbed into the car. Yeah, he'd take the rest of the day off, alright. He could definitely use a drink or two. It was eleven o'clock; the perfect time to tie-one-on.

When he arrived home, he noticed that Darlene's car wasn't in the drive. That was just as well. She was probably getting an early start with girls' night out. He grabbed a beer and stepped out onto the back porch. He was greeted by a wild, high jumping, tail-swinging Bella.

"How's my big girl?" Bella never argued; never talked back; hardly ever made a sound. It would've been great if I could've taught that trick to Darlene, years ago, when she was much younger, and more malleable. He sat in a lawn chair and absentmindedly stroked Bella's head. At the same time, Bella incessantly scratched her stomach. Tom let out a sigh and thought back to when she was a pup.

You were a lot less work when you were younger, too. Now, it seems I have to take you to the vet every month. Maybe it's a girl thing; or maybe it's just living in this sub-division.

He wondered whether or not he could handle the chief assignment. It would only be for a couple more years. He just didn't know. Thoughts of being locked in a cell came to mind.

●　　●　　●

After Tom left his office, a victorious 'yeah' erupted from Bud's lips. He was a very happy man. His plan was progressing like clockwork. He felt convinced that the ultimatum he'd just given Padgett would produce the desired results. Bud had been Mayor for only two months, but in that time, he'd already grown to despise Padgett. He really couldn't put his finger on the reason why. Padgett hadn't actually done anything to him. He just didn't like how the man carried himself. He was so damned sure of himself all the time; standing tall with his chest all puffed out. Well, Bud had deflated Padgett this morning.

He let out a low belly laugh from the depths of his gut. Laughing more loudly now, he recalled the surprised look on Padgett's face. Padgett, the son of a bitch, didn't know what hit him. The Mayor continued laughing at the thought.

He was completely satisfied with his efforts. Hell, he thought, I wouldn't be surprised if Padgett doesn't turn in his resignation tomorrow. That would be just fine. I could shuffle some manpower around to cover the workload. I could readily approve any overtime that was needed. The only thing that concerned Bud was Padgett's damned popularity. Padgett was well respected around town, but he couldn't let that stop him. Besides, he had nearly four more years to mend those constituency fences.

The Mayor waddled down the hall to the bathroom. He needed to freshen up a bit before lunch. He smiled at his reflection, moved his face from side to side as he approvingly checked out his profile. His double chin was quickly becoming triple. Maybe he'd better lay off dessert today.

After lunch he had one more item of business to attend to, then, maybe he'd take the afternoon off. He remembered some of the things that had been said about him during the election campaign. Things like him having *a Napoleon complex*. Maybe that was so. But, he still managed to walk softly and carry a big stick. He laughed. He had just shown some of his power to Padgett. I'm a force to be reckoned with.

The Mayor was still gloating after he returned from lunch. Comfortable at his desk, he buzzed his secretary. "Barbara honey, could you get a hold of John Stamper and tell him to be in my office at 2pm?"

"Yes, Mr. Mayor."

Mr. Mayor, now that was how he liked being addressed. It made him feel important. Yes, he thought, that's another thing about Padgett that irks me; the fact that Padgett usually refers to me using my first name. That makes it sound like we're old friends. We aren't friends. Padgett doesn't seem to have the respect he should for a man in my position. I deserve respect. As a matter of fact, I demand it!

• • •

John Stamper sat at his desk and scratched his head. He wondered what was up with the Mayor. He was curious why he had an appointment to see him. John recalled the Mayor asking Tom to come by his office after the staff meeting. Now that he thought about it, where was Tom? John was busy working on a case. He really didn't have a lot of free time, but the Mayor beckoned. Maybe he should give Tom a call to find out what was happening. He reconsidered after glancing up at the wall clock. It was 1:45. He'd better go meet with Bud. He'd call Tom after his meeting with him.

Stamper was nearly to the Mayor's door when it swung open. "Come on in, John. Have a seat, take a load off." " Can I get you anything?"

"No thank you, Mr. Mayor."

The Mayor beamed at the reply. Now, here's a man that knows how to show respect.

"So, John, how long have you been with the department, anyway?"

"It'll be twenty-two years next month, Mr. Mayor."

"Twenty-two years. Now, that's commendable, very commendable."

"How's it been working with Tom Padgett over the years?"

John wondered where this conversation was heading. "Working with Tom has been great. It's been one of the most invaluable experiences of all my years in the department."

"Good, good. That's my assessment also. But, it's good to hear that sentiment echoed by one of his peers. It just gives it added justification." Bud carried on, "Listen, I'm sure you're wondering why I called you in here this afternoon."

"Yes, Mr. Mayor, I am."

"I'd like to offer you a promotion, to that of Captain of the department."

"Excuse me, but, that's Tom Padgett's position. Has something happened that I'm not aware of?"

"Why yes, I promoted Padgett to chief earlier today." The Mayor beamed.

This turn of events shocked John. "And he accepted the offer?"

"Let's just say that he's thinking about it, he's mulling it over."

"Mr. Mayor, I welcome the promotion, but I can't in clear conscience consider a job that's still Tom's."

Bud studied Stamper a moment. "Believe me, John; the position of Captain is available. So, if you're interested in the position, I'd like to have your answer as soon as possible. We can go over all the details, once you officially accept the position." Bud stared at Stamper as if willing him to get up before finishing, "Let me know your decision; the sooner the better."

"Yes, Mr. Mayor, thank you." John sat without moving for a moment, before getting up to leave. The Mayor remained seated.

Stamper was stunned. What was all that crap about Tom supposed to mean anyway? The part about him mulling the job offer over? He stepped out into the parking lot and gave Tom a ring.

Tom answered on the second ring, "What's up, John?"

"That's what I'm calling you about, hoping to find that out from you."

Tom released a sigh, "Hey, why don't you come by after you get off. I'll treat you to a couple of beers. Then I can fill you in on what I know."

"Yeah, maybe I can fill you in about my role in the drama, also."

They both clicked off.

•   •   •

Tom got himself another beer and grabbed a few treats for Bella. She loved treats, especially when she didn't have to do any tricks or work to earn them. It was a sunny afternoon; not a bad day for some comp time. He wondered whether or not the Mayor actually had the authority to fire him. But, was he really being fired? He was being offered a considerably better paying job, but unfortunately for Tom, it wasn't a job he necessarily wanted. Should he seek legal counsel, or just accept the position and ride it into retirement? Lying back in the lawn chair, he decided to close his eyes, only for a moment.

A few minutes after five, Stamper wandered around the gate to the fenced-in back yard. He knew this was where he'd find Tom. He held the twelve pack of Budweiser up for Tom to see. That should guarantee access into the gated community. "What's happening old man?"

"Who the hell's calling who an old man? You're only two years younger than me, aren't you?" Tom laughed. "Why don't you put that beer in the fridge and grab us a couple of cold ones?" Fortunately, Tom had closed his eyes for an hour or so. Now he was rejuvenated and thirsty again.

John bent down to pet Bella. She paid little attention because she was busy licking herself; here and there, nonstop. He returned with the beer. "Where's Darlene?"

"It's girls' night out. Oh, that reminds me, where's your wife?"

"Oh, Kathy's home, I told her not to bother holding dinner for me."

Tom gave John a telling look, "So what's the story from Mt. Sterling's grapevine?"

"No grapevine Tom. I believe our little exchange has been relatively hush, hush. The only people that seem to know are you, me and the Mayor."

Tom took a healthy swallow. "Ok, so what opportunity has the Mayor offered you?"

"Bud offered me your old job."

"He told me that part of the plan. So did he tell you the rest of it?"

"Yeah, he told me somethin' about you considering the chief position. I told him I found it hard to believe that you'd be interested in that job."

25

"Why, that's very astute of you. You keep working at this and someday you'll end up being one hell of a detective. Where'd you receive your training anyway?" They both laughed.

Their beer drained, John, the gopher, went to grab a couple more. When he returned, Tom had a somber expression on his face. "Did the Mayor let you know that he'd given me an ultimatum, which was either take the chief position or else?"

John sat down. "He can't do that, can he?"

"He may have overstepped his authority, but I'm really not sure."

"Doesn't he need the consent of council for decisions of this magnitude?"

"Maybe, but he's offering me a promotion, so what would council have to question?"

"What about the take it or leave it clause?"

Tom sipped from his beer, "I really don't feel up to a protracted battle with *Little Napoleon*. Hell, maybe it would be best if I just retired. I've heard they need greeters up at Wal-Mart." Tom had another thought, "Wait a minute, the more I think about it, maybe being chief wouldn't be so bad."

"Come on, Tom. How long do you think you'd be able to stand that desk job?"

"I know, but sometimes all this fighting for what's right seems like a losing proposition. Sometimes it's a waste of time."

"Amen, brother. I know exactly what you mean, how about another?"

"Sure and while you're in there, grab Bella some treats. That'll give her something else to chew on."

They carried on and talked into the evening, managing to drink the last of the beer. John stood. "All the beer's gone. I guess that means I'll be goin' home."

"Yeah, you sorry ass, drink and run. I know the type."

They stood and faced one another and exchanged a rare man hug.

"See you in the morning, Tom."

"Yeah, be careful out there. Be on the lookout for the police. You've been drinking."

Tom watched as John backed out of the drive and waved goodbye before he closed the gate. He and Bella went inside. It was time for bed. He noticed the microwave clock as he entered the kitchen. Hell, it's after ten. Where'd the day go? Darlene wasn't home. She hadn't called. She must be too busy. His day of R&R hadn't been terribly beneficial.

He stood and took measure of himself while he brushed his teeth. Dark circles were beneath his eyes. Maybe he needed some of Darlene's makeup. That should help with freshening him up in the morning. It seemed to work wonders for her. He climbed into bed just before eleven. As he drifted into sleep, he hoped Darlene and *friends* were having a good time.

• • •

Tom knocked on the Mayor's door bright and early the following morning. He turned the knob and walked in, and cut straight to the chase. "Mr. Mayor, I accept your most gracious promotion. And, I'm looking forward to my duties as the new chief."

The Mayor was busy mopping up the remains of some brown gravy onto a biscuit. He was just about to swallow a mouthful and nearly choked. Finally, Bud recovered, coughing as he said, "Good, Tom. Good for you."

"Thanks," Tom quickly exited, closing the door behind him. He was anxious to get settled into his new office.

Alone again, Bud leaned back in his comfy leather chair to think. What had happened to his well laid plan? What went wrong? What's Padgett up to? Is this some kind of trick? He felt positive that Padgett would have wanted to resign. Why the sudden change?

Bud needed another plan. He was confident that he could force Padgett into early retirement. He just had to find some additional type of motivation, something that would push more of Tom's buttons. Bud scrunched up his pudgy face in rapt concentration. A wide smile spread, stretching his flabby lips. He had an idea, an absolutely great idea.

Tom sat idle in his new office and looked around at four empty walls. So, this is what it's like to be chief. It surely didn't feel exhilarating. He laughed when he recalled the Mayor's shocked expression, especially as the gravy dripped from his chin.

He thought back to when he started with the department; all those years ago back when he was a cadet. That seemed so long ago. He remembered making his first arrest. He remembered how nervous he had been. Tom hadn't felt that kind of adrenalin rush in years. He seriously doubted that he would ever feel it in this assignment. He missed the excitement of real police work. Can I really do this job?

• • •

Darlene felt the time spent with Candy had been productive. Before going out with her friends for girls' night, she and Candy had gone to Sterling Lanes for some 'private' divorce strategizing. Candy had a very successful track record of screwing over ex-husbands; screwing them over in divorce proceedings, that is. So far, Candy had gone through three husbands, and had managed to take every one of them to the cleaners. She had just turned forty. To date, her average marriage lasted just under four years. Darlene was enthralled as she listened to Candy lay the ground work for an advantageous split. She gave Darlene the name and number of a high-powered divorce lawyer in Lexington.

Darlene was seven years younger than Tom. She had always dreamed of seeing the world. That, however, was something Tom showed little interest in. She felt that with her looks and charm, she could still corral most of the single men in Mt. Sterling. Yes, exactly what she had done to Tom. She could get the married ones, too, if she put her mind to it.

She still possessed a youthful appearance, although her eyes were now deeply wrinkled from years of exposure to cigarette smoke. Wrinkled eyes or not, she wasn't quitting. Smoking wasn't only a habit; it was a way of life. Darlene had barely worked a day in her life. That lifestyle allowed her to stay fit and tan year-round. Besides, Tom hadn't married her for her cooking anyway.

She reminisced about giving birth to Andrew twenty-four years ago. Now that was some hard work; and on top of that, living in that ratty old farmhouse, so far from everything. It was absolute torture; no friends nearby, no one to talk to. Tom would often remind her, it's only three miles to town. What's the problem? She hated it when he said that, insinuating that she was some kind of spoiled brat.

After Andy finally went away to college, Darlene unleashed her move to-the-city plan. She knew she could break Tom's spirit easily enough, especially if she started whining. But, now even with a place in town, it still wasn't enough. She needed her freedom. Darlene needed to spread her wings and hopefully a couple of other things as well. For this, she needed a new man; someone for sexual satisfaction, and who also shared her aspirations for travelling.

•   •   •

When Tom returned home after his first day as chief, Darlene's car was parked in the drive. Well, look at that, will wonders never cease? He entered the house and walked down the hall to change clothes.

Darlene yelled from the kitchen, "I heard you got yourself a promotion?"

He paused a moment and wondered how she knew about it. "Yeah," he yelled back at her, "you heard right."

He wished she was going to have another girls' night out, but he'd heard somewhere that lightning never strikes the same place twice. He was full of idioms tonight. Was this some sort of sign?

Luckily he'd picked up some more beer. It could easily turn into a long night. He grabbed a beer and headed to the back yard. If Darlene cared to have a civil conversation, she knew where to find him.

As Tom sat petting Bella, he thought about Darlene. What had happened to the girl he'd met and fallen so madly in love with? He knew right now she had her ass parked at the kitchen table, where she smoked one cigarette after another. She knew better than smoking in the house. It was obvious she was looking for a confrontation. He had enough confrontations for one week. She could do whatever she damn well pleased. I'm not going to rise to her baiting tonight, no chance. She isn't going to ruin my night. He continued petting Bella while enjoying his beer, as Darlene defiantly stared at him through the kitchen window.

CHAPTER 3

The Mayor felt that he'd been a patient man. He had waited nearly two weeks. He'd allowed Padgett to get settled in. Bud thought about the best way to deliver his latest message to Padgett. Maybe he'd use the friendly stop by-the-office to chat technique. Then, he realized that maybe the subtle approach was still the best. All indications were that Tom was doing well. That really pissed him off. Why can't that SOB just crash and burn? It almost seemed like the bastard enjoyed being chief.

During the staff meeting, Bud appeared more than a little preoccupied. It seemed like he had big issues that weighed heavily on him. As the meeting ended, a smile slowly emerged, working its way across his flabby lips. "Tom, come down to my office. I've got a special assignment for you."

Tom was conscious of the harmony which existed in nearly everything he'd done lately. He figured a reality check was long overdue. Things had been good both at home and the office. Maybe it was time for the shit to hit the fan. That morning, Darlene asked Tom to meet her at Applebee's for dinner. And now, the Mayor wanted to have a little fatherly chat. It almost felt conspiratorial. He laughed to himself, trying to imagine the Mayor and Darlene together. It just seemed ironic that they were both using the same playbook.

•   •   •

Stamper was adjusting well in the role of Captain and only required Tom's occasional expertise. That was good because he knew that Tom, the new chief, had his own learning curve to deal with. Things on John's watch were going smoothly. Crime was in check, no major catastrophes. He was well aware of some of the new procedural guidelines that Tom was trying to implement. They should help do away with some of the mountains of paperwork that all members of the department had to deal with. Tom had invited him over to a party. It was the start of Tom's two-week vacation. Stamper was looking forward to it. It should be a good time.

Tom was at the Mayor's door. This was getting far too familiar.

After he knocked the Mayor yelled, "Come in." No wining and dining today. No coffee or donuts, strictly business. The Mayor wore a sad expression on his face, "Tom I'm afraid I've got some bad news."

"What's that, Mayor?"

"I know you had your vacation scheduled, but I'm afraid you'll need to cancel it. There's a state audit due at the end of the month, which must be completed. Unfortunately, Chief Bryant was delinquent with his audits to state. Not only was he behind on the weekly paperwork, he was negligent on the quarterly reports as well."

Tom was at the station a few minutes later. He wasn't upset about the sudden change to his vacation plans. He didn't have anything grandiose planned, anyway. An interesting thought crossed his mind. Why is Bud even aware of my upcoming vacation? The Mayor was up to his old tricks again, actively trying to get under his skin. Maybe there's something to the knowledge that Bud and Darlene suddenly share, about me? Tom understood that two more years under Bud's thumb would present some real challenges. He cleared his desk of some of his daily paperwork. He was going to give the audit backlog a look.

●　　●　　●

Darlene was already seated at a table in the bar when Tom arrived. Although there were plenty of open tables in the dining room, she obviously needed drinks to be readily available. That was fine by him. He took a seat facing her. No hi, how you doing, or affectionate peck on the cheek non-sense. Darlene just stared across at him like he was some sort of adversary. He stared back at her. He wondered, how long has it been since I've even seen her naked? That thought helped him validate what their relationship had become. He motioned for a drink. "Could I have a Fat Tire please, a grande?"

"Darlene would you like to order dinner, or is there something you need to get off your chest?" He figured that the way his day had been; why not face whatever issue was lurking straight-on?

She seemed to be having a difficult time focusing. Finally she got her thoughts together and blurted out, "Tom, I want a divorce."

"Alright then, I guess that means were not eating dinner." He motioned for the bartender, "Could we get another couple of drinks, please?" Tom smiled at Darlene. He actually felt relieved.

●   ●   ●

It had been a week since Tom had tendered his resignation. Interestingly enough, it had also been a week since he'd agreed with the terms of the divorce. Good things come in twos? Maybe they really do, he smiled. He sat in the back yard with his faithful companion, Bella. She was busy licking and scratching, as Tom pecked away on his laptop. He was granted temporary permission to stay in the house on Swiss Stone Rd. He never had cared much for the house; even though it was in the 'Pines on Main'. Darlene used to boast about living there to people around town.

Darlene had done extremely well in the divorce. All that crying she did worked in her favor. That junk about being a captive woman with no opportunities available to her, made Tom sick. Raising a child, slaving away for twenty-five years; she played the system like a drum. Well, good for her, and good riddance. She was awarded the house, the car, and last but certainly not least, half of Tom's pension. Darlene was extremely pleased with the settlement. Why wouldn't she be? Now she could actively search for that new life she'd been dreaming about for so long.

Tom was bitterly resigned to the fact he had to give Darlene half his pension. He never recalled seeing Darlene once at an arrest, a domestic dispute, a traffic accident or a robbery. And now she earns half of my retirement? Hell of a pill to swallow, but that's the way the system works. He wondered if she'd still be able to sustain her lifestyle. He was amused thinking about her skin paling because the tanning bed visits might become too expensive. Well, he couldn't worry about her. He had problems of his own. He needed to find a place to live. He smiled slightly. He got a couple of things. Darlene had to pay him half the equity that was in the house, and naturally, he got Bella.

He chuckled, just thinking about his retirement party. It was a pretty wild party, especially for a bunch of old guys. Yeah there was lots of food, plenty of beer, and cops talking about the old days. Darlene stayed with friends, so the house was his for one last night. The neighbors had called the police, which did little good, because most of them were already there. The Mayor wasn't invited, but his ears had to have been burning that night somewhere in Mt. Sterling. After hours of partying, many of the guys called it a night. Tom couldn't blame them. He knew that most of them probably had to work the next day, but not him.

The only negative thing that came out of the party was the unfortunate opening up of the 'old wound'. And now as Tom sat alone, he just couldn't stop thinking about it. He thought about the day, years ago, when he and his partner, Cole Bishop, had been radioed to respond to a robbery in progress. Thinking back, he still couldn't remember the gas station's name. All he remembered was the robbery call to a gas station near I-64. He somehow blocked much of that night from memory. If only he could block it all and remember nothing.

However, he did remember Cole's reaction like it was yesterday. They arrived on the scene. Cole rolled out of the cruiser and approached the station. It was text-book; not a single mistake made. Cole had no clue that a maniacal nut was lying in wait. As they both cautiously approached, several shots rang out. Tom saw Cole go down, and he instinctively knew where the shots originated. He spun and emptied his revolver in that direction. He really didn't remember firing all those shots. After the shootout, as everyone began calling it, Tom was subjected to numerous examinations. Most were aimed at trying to determine whether or not he had acted improperly. He was put on paid leave while the crime was thoroughly investigated.

He wrestled with his thoughts again. How can shooting a crazed drugged- up lunatic, who had just murdered your partner of ten years, not be justified? Tom spent months with psychiatrists and psychologists using psychobabble on him to determine if he was fit for duty. He had a hard time dealing with all the scrutiny, especially when the criminals had attorneys that aggressively protected their rights. He felt very alone. The investigation made him feel like a criminal. What about Cole's rights?

After what seemed like an eternity, he was re-instated to the force. He had been off for over six months. His return to the department wasn't as warm as he had hoped. Fellow officers were standoffish. *Damn it!* I did the right thing.

He recalled the psych sessions; there was one doctor that seemed to really have it in for him. Dr. Sharma, of all the shrinks that had spent time analyzing him, he was the only one who felt that Tom potentially had MPD. Multiple Personality Disorder patients suffered from more than one personality. Tom immediately realized that Sharma's suggestion posed a threat to his continued employment on the force. So, it came down to this, either Tom winning the psychobabble game, or Sharma winning it. If the doctor won, it would effectively end Tom's career. Tom didn't plan on letting that happen.

Dr. Sharma became Tom's primary analyst. He was the only shrink he saw. Tom knew the deck was stacked against him. He paid extremely close attention as the doctor questioned him. The doctor tried to force him to remember events that his other self might have performed. The sessions were difficult, but Tom managed to maintain his focus, especially when he visited the doctor. In the end, the doctor gave up, and signed off on Tom's evaluation. He hadn't been able to prove his MPD diagnosis. He had passed the psycho hurdle. Tom realized that the doctor had only been trying to do his job, but thought his suspicions were absurd.

When Tom was finally given the green light to go out on patrol again, he partnered up with John Stamper. Tom initially wondered if Stamper viewed him as a partner or a questionable cop. The assignment, for Stamper, was definitely a tough one, because Tom continued to have issues in his own head. At first, Stamper was distant, slowly he came around. Tom was the senior officer, but senior officers with baggage could still be a problem. But, John was patient and understanding, and that probably contributed greatly in Tom's recovery. He and John became an effective team, but it was a long time coming.

Tom couldn't stop thinking of all the shortcomings in his life. His son, Andy, had proven difficult. He assumed Andy felt the same way about him. Darlene had coddled the boy all through Andy's childhood. As a matter of fact, the way Tom saw it, she still did. Granted, much of the time Andy was growing up, Tom had been busy. He had missed much of his son's childhood and he regretted it. But, there was nothing he could do about that now. Whenever he couldn't make it to a school event, Darlene would say negative things, "Your father doesn't have time for you." All the negative reinforcement from his mother helped turn Andy against him. Tom believed this contributed to Andy becoming a mama's boy.

When Andy visited, it was usually for a very short stay; especially true if Tom was home. Andy always managed to free up more time when his mother was home alone. He graduated from UK and still lived in a rental apartment in Lexington. Tom wondered why Andy rarely made an effort to visit. The drive from Lexington was only forty minutes. But Darlene would always defend their son; she always said how busy Andy was. Tom realized that once the divorce was finalized, he would rarely, if ever, see him. Add Andy to Darlene's list of divorce winnings.

Tom broke from his daydream and returned to his property search. He was running out of time. He had to give up his car when he'd left the force and Darlene had been awarded their family car. So, Tom had to find wheels. He needed transportation. He was fortunate enough to find a used five-year old, four-wheel drive Ford F-150. The truck was in great shape and would be just the vehicle for a place in the country. His property priorities were simple; land, woods, and privacy. He never wanted to live in a city again. He focused his search on Nicholas County. There were plenty of wooded tracts, and from what he could tell, they seemed really reasonable.

Tom found a real estate broker on-line with many listings in Nicholas County. Mattox Real Estate handled real estate sales as well as auctions. Tom spoke to an agent, Bill Myers, and arranged to look at some property the next morning. Bill had several parcels to show him. Tom indicated that he thought close proximity to the Licking River would be a plus. So, that was where they started to search, driving east, west, north and south; never straying far from the river. Bill loved customers like Tom because Tom wasn't picky. Tom quickly decided on a parcel off of Abners Mill Rd. It seemed to meet all his criteria.

Land, woods, privacy, everything Tom had been looking for. As an added bonus, it even had an old trailer that was part of the deal. The land was rough to rolling, unfortunately it was also briar covered. The trees weren't great, mostly cedar and honey locust. The trailer sat a quarter mile off the road. It was partially hidden behind an old overgrown hedge row. It had ten acres with a trailer for only $25,000 that seemed cheap to Tom. He offered $22,000 cash. He also asked for immediate occupancy. The offer was accepted ten minutes later. Maybe he should have offered less? He couldn't worry about that now. He and Bella had a new home.

Tom walked around the exterior as he studied the trailer. It had both front and rear handicap accessible ramps. Why would anybody relegated to a wheel chair live way back in here? He did a more thorough look around inside. He realized that it'd probably been a year or more since it'd been occupied. He would worry about cleaning the place once he got all his things from Mt. Sterling. Out back, the property adjoined a large wooded tract. He wasn't sure, but the woods looked extensive. He and Bella would definitely take advantage of that. Tom knew that the woods were privately owned, but that shouldn't present any problems for him and Bella.

The following morning

Tom handed Darlene the house keys after he finished loading all his possessions. As he was packing the few things he owned, she stood watch over him like a hawk. What'd she think he planned on doing? Steal some remembrance of her? He didn't think so. The truck was packed; good thing it was a crew cab. There was just enough room for Bella to stretch out. Darlene was quite glad to see him leave. He and Bella were also glad to see her go. He watched in the rearview mirror as Mt. Sterling disappeared. It was July 23rd and time for a new chapter in his life. He thought about the trailer. He hoped that it didn't need too much work.

CHAPTER 4

The first time Tom visited the trailer, the electricity had been turned on, but not the water, but it was now. Not too bad, there seemed to be only a few problems. All the leaks and drips around the place weren't really any big deal. Nothing he wouldn't be able to handle. He unloaded all his stuff right on the living room floor. He could put things away later. AT&T was coming to hook up DSL tomorrow and then he'd be able to use his laptop.

He unfolded a lawn chair, sat under a tree and drank a beer. Ah, I'm a free man. Bella ran around smelling and chasing anything that moved. No fenced in yard, she was in dog heaven. Tom smiled as he watched her move from place to place, scoping out her new home.

He hoped the wireless worked well. He wanted to be aware of things going on around the country. He had no need for television. His laptop should satisfy his needs. He looked at the trailer as he sipped his beer. He figured it might take two or three days to make the place livable. After that, he and Bella would go out and explore.

He thought about Carlisle. It was the only town of any size in Nicholas County. Yes, once he was settled and more comfortable, he needed to go check it out. That would give him a better feel for the area. Maybe he'd get to know some of the locals.

Tom was satisfied with his new situation. Bella laid breathing heavily at his feet. She had been chasing deer, squirrels, and chipmunks. She'd even tried to catch some birds and was worn out. He laughed at Bella believing she'd catch a bird. I need to get her a tick collar, he thought, as he bent over and pulled another tick from her neck.

He got himself another beer and grabbed his 870. The old Remington twelve-gauge needed a good cleaning. When he finished, he took it back inside and hung it over the bed. Tom though it looked natural hanging there. He remembered painful lessons he'd learned as a policemen. It's always good to be prepared, bad things can happen even when you're off duty.

When he was younger he'd been an avid hunter, but work, marriage, children, and whatever else got in the way. Things change. Maybe he'd take it up again. As he sipped his beer, fond memories of his hunting days entered his mind. He had a long time hunting buddy named Joe Puckett. Puckett was a big guy, most of his bulk around the middle. Tom was half a foot taller than Joe, who was only five six, but Joe outweighed Tom by 125 lbs. He was one great hunting partner though, especially during bow season. Tom laughed at the memory; looking at big burley Joe nobody would ever have guessed that Joe was scared of the dark. As a result, whenever they went hunting together, they used a proven hunting technique. Tom would enter the woods first, while it was still dark. When the sun came up, Joe would wander in and head in Tom's direction. Tom could barely contain himself as he watched Joe come crashing into the woods. Joe would scare every animal within a thousand yards, some of them toward Tom. Tom scored a lot of deer, especially with Joe's help.

But, during gun season, watch out. Joe was a hell of a shot with a slug gun. Tom remembered one time when Joe handed him a hedge apple and said, "Throw this as high as you can." As it came back down, Joe blasted it with a slug. What a great shot! Another time when they walked through the field to one of their afternoon hunting spots, Joe quickly raised his shotgun and fired at a group of trees at least a hundred yards away.

"What in the hell are you shooting at?" They both stared at the group of trees.

"That tree was walking," Joe said. Sure enough, when they got to the spot, a ten point buck lay less than thirty yards from the tree.

Joe was excited and very proud of that deer. Whenever they hunted, they always rode together. Joe drove that day, but unfortunately for him, he didn't own a truck. They had to load that big buck into the trunk of his car. Luckily, the Chrysler had a huge trunk. It was a great big buck. Joe needed to show off his trophy. They drove around to all the check stations and places hunters might be hanging out. They drove around a lot. As they pulled in, Joe would pop the trunk and everyone would stare at the buck and congratulate him. Joe was so excited, that is, until he got home. Then, he tried to remove his bloated prize. Rigor mortis had set in, making it impossible to pry the buck out. The antlers and hind legs were jammed up inside the trunk.

All the reminiscing about Joe and hunting made Tom anxious to get back into the woods. When he was younger and actively hunting, he was quite accomplished, especially bow hunting. Most hunters might get a deer during gun season, but Tom always filled his tags during bow season. He preferred bow hunting, because it was more of a challenge. He could get in and move around the woods and make very little noise. He could successfully sneak up on game, unlike Joe. Maybe he could get out into the woods for a couple of hours tomorrow, after the phone company came and he'd made some progress on the trailer. He was sure Bella would love it.

• • •

The Next Morning

Tom's cell rang, "Padgett."

"Hey, old man," John teased.

"Hey John, I wasn't expecting to hear from you so soon. What's happening in the Mount?"

"Not much, I was calling to check and see how things are down in the holler?"

"Bella and I are good. We're contemplating a little romp through the woods. How's the new Captain? Are you getting along with *Little Napoleon*?"

"I'm trying to keep a low profile and stay out of his way," John joked. "It has been busy in the Mount since you left. Hey, could I possibly interest you in coming back?"

"That's great that things are going well, and no, I'm not interested."

"Tom, you'll never guess what I'm up to. I've taken up acting."

"Acting, since when did you ever have interest in acting?"

"Oh, since the Mayor appointed me acting chief, you sorry ass," John grumbled.

"Acting chief; good for you John, I hope you enjoy sitting on your ass."

"That's not remotely funny. I guess I should thank you for the promotion, or possibly Darlene."

"Darlene, what's she got to do with anything?"

"Rumor has it that Darlene has been dating the Mayor."

"But, isn't old lard ass married?"

"Yeah, but it seems that Bud's wife kicked his ass out."

"John, can you imagine that, two of the vainest people in Mt. Sterling, a couple?"

It was good to catch up on the Montgomery County gossip. But, Tom had promised Bella a hike in the woods. After he hung up, he looked at Bella. "Bella, you want to go for a walk?" That got her tail thumping.

The woods were quite wooly behind the trailer. Thankfully, the fences were nothing to worry about. It was easy to locate open gaps that Bella could walk over or through. After a short distance, the woods opened up considerably. There were many more deciduous trees; elm, oak, poplar, hickory, sycamore, walnut and maple, and greater variety than on his plot, with only honey locust, a few shag bark hickories and a bunch of cedars.

The further they walked into the woods, the more boundary fencing they encountered. There were lots of rotted posts lying around along the way, most with rusted barbed wire stapled to them. Many of the posts were cedar, which happened to be terrible fence posts. Cedar was really only good for firewood.

Tom changed course. He needed to stay acclimated with where they were. Walking south, they came to an old road. He wasn't sure if it was a county road that was no longer used or an old logging trail. Looking more closely, he noticed ATV tracks. Maybe it was being used by hunters. Some of the tracks appeared fresh. He knew there were currently no open seasons. Maybe they were from people playing around on their ATVs. Tom had purchased a topography map for Kentucky. He was curious to see if this road was on it.

He usually carried a short lead for Bella, just in case they spooked up some game. It had been a while since Bella had been in woods and she might easily ignore Tom, especially if she got caught up in a good chase. He commanded, "Here girl." She obeyed and Tom rewarded her with a good chest scratch. Suddenly her head turned and ears perked. Tom also heard the engine noise. It sounded like an ATV. "Bella, let's get off this trail," he said as he attached her lead. They both stepped back from the trail, and stood hidden in some nearby cedars. He whispered, "Be quiet Bella, no barking." She understood many commands. She was well trained.

Moments passed before the ATV crawled around the bend close to where they stood. Tom first thought the rider might be a hunter looking for a spot to put up a tree stand. But then, his intuition from years of policing and hunting made him think otherwise. The guy riding the four-wheeler was looking back and forth rapidly. When Tom noticed his wild expression, Tom was confident that he wasn't interested in hunting. This character had an agenda. Tom was convinced it wasn't hunting game.

He glanced in their direction but didn't notice Tom and Bella. Tom realized that the guy was far less focused than he thought he was. Jack Estep was more out of it than usual, while he made his way to his lab. As the machine disappeared deeper into the woods, Tom turned to Bella, "That's enough excitement for one afternoon, girl. Let's head to the house."

●　　●　　●

The Following Morning

Tom woke with a start. His pulse raced. He'd had another dream. In it he had been in the woods. It was dark out, somehow he could see clearly. There was a cabin burning, or was it a shed? There was a body near the fire. His head pounded. He walked to the kitchen and swallowed three aspirins. Tom didn't understand the dream, but who understood dreams?

He cranked the air conditioner to high. It slowly rattled its way up to speed. The window unit was 8,000 BTU, but unfortunately, it seemed to be on its last leg. That was most likely why they'd left it. Hopefully, it would keep Bella cool when he was gone. She had plenty of water. She even had an emergency pan, under the pipe that was the dripping in the kitchen.

Tom was going to Carlisle this morning. Even though it was early, he could tell it was going to be a scorcher. He studied the topo while he sipped his coffee. He noticed the old county road they'd found yesterday. So, it had been a county road and was now abandoned. Bella got up and padded to the bedroom to lie nearer the AC. Tom smiled. She's a smart girl.

He planned on taking different routes to and from Carlisle today, to better familiarize himself with the area. He waited for a break in traffic before he turned southwest on Route 68 toward Lexington. As he drove, he noticed Blue Licks State Park. He remembered reading about it years ago, something about Daniel Boone. He wasn't terribly interested in history. He liked things that were real, things he could actually touch and see. To the left, he noticed a trailhead. Bella would definitely like that. A sign read *Thanks for Visiting Robertson County*

As Tom drove along, he noticed several mobile homes that had yards covered with junk. He thought about his own trailer. It wasn't the greatest, but the yard was clean. One place in particular had acres of junk; cars, trucks, farm equipment, miscellaneous old metal. What a mess. Tom slowed down while looking at all the junk and noticed a young girl. She might have been twelve or thirteen years old and she was climbing around in the enclosed cab of some rusty junk tractor. He worried about her accidentally disengaging the transmission, which might allow the tractor to roll. She could get hurt. After a closer look, Tom realized that the tractor wasn't going anywhere, not anytime soon. Its tires were buried rim deep in the soil.

Padgett turned left on Route 1455 which bordered a nice golf course, probably a nine-hole. He then passed a lake on his left. He'd seen it on the topo. It was named Lake Carnico. The lake had a small sand beach. He and Bella both loved to swim. He wondered if dogs were allowed in. The road dead-ended at Highway 32. Turning left would eventually lead to Flemingsburg, and right led to Carlisle. He turned right. He pulled into a parking spot adjacent to the courthouse. Tom had no plans today, just a little information gathering.

He walked to the front of the courthouse and admired the set-up. Carlisle had an old fashioned square, with the courthouse in the middle as the dominant feature, and parking on all four sides. He noticed a lot of interesting old buildings, but many were vacant and desperately in need of renovation. He glanced up to the courthouse tower and admired the unusual neon American flag. He'd like to learn more about it.

There was a public library across the street. He'd see about getting a card. Once inside the library, an overly helpful librarian overwhelmed him with details about getting a card. How hard can this be? He hadn't been in the woods that long had he? Tom found books about the area and also picked up some flyers that were lying on the counter. He wanted to educate himself about the local lore. After checking out, he piled the books in the F150.

He made his way to the courthouse. Just inside the main entrance on the right was the sheriff's office. He wanted to introduce himself.

"No," the clerk told him, "the sheriff's out, somewhere in the county."

"When's a good time to catch him? Where does he usually eat lunch?"

"The sheriff usually eats lunch at Garrett's, almost every day of the week."

Tom told her that he wanted to eat wherever the locals would be hanging out. He was new to the area, and was hoping to meet people.

"Oh, then you should try the East End. It's always busy, and you'll meet some of the local characters there. Listen, you just stay on the main drag out of town past the funeral home. It'll be on your left. You can't miss is."

Tom thanked her. He noticed the time on the lobby clock, it was nearly noon.

As he drove through town, he saw groups of people just standing around on the corners. They're probably unemployed or waiting for their government check, he thought. Maybe they're waiting for delivery of some black market prescription drugs. Seeing this made him sad, no, it made him angry.

He remembered one of the last things he'd done in Mt. Sterling, shopping with Darlene. He waited in the car at Wal-Mart, while she was inside. He hated shopping; he really hated shopping with Darlene. He usually parked on the fringe of the parking lot and watched, that way he could see her come out of the store. Then, he would simply circle around and pick her up.

While he waited he saw two young girls work the parking area. Initially, they carried an empty gas can around with them. They waited for people to get out of their cars. Then, they'd cry their tales of woe. This seemed to be effective, as many of the men opened their wallets. They obviously felt sorry for them. The girl toting the can was dressed in shorts, flip-flops and had a very drawn face. Her helper appeared to be pregnant. The pair then made another pass through the lot. They returned, *sans* gas can, and continued to work the crowd, and still got paid. Tom shook his head. Sometimes, people need to question their own generosity. When the cons were finished, they each pumped their fists in the air. They must have had a good score. Tom felt this was extremely aggravating.

Tom pulled into the parking lot at the East End. He noticed it was both a gas station and diner. He wondered, as he looked at all the cars, doesn't anyone cook anymore? Stepping inside, he sat at the only table available. Someone politely asked if he planned to eat, then directed him to the counter where he needed to place his order. Tom decided on the special, whatever that might be. As he waited for his food, he could hear only the women talking. They were all chatting about who said this or who did that, typical gossip nonsense. There were also men inside the place. But, being men, they were much more interested in eating than gossiping.

One woman in particular was holding sway. Her husband listened intently while he chewed. Tom wondered about her. She might be a good source of information. He watched her swing her arms around in the air as she tried to get her point across. Most of the people seemed to know her. Some of them even seemed genuinely interested in her spiel. Was there a local election coming up? Tom wasn't sure but this woman might just get his vote. She sure appeared compelling. Even though he couldn't hear a lot of what she said, he mused, that might just be the secret for being a good politician.

After lunch, he bought a couple of newspapers before heading to his truck. Carlisle had two local papers, the *Carlisle Courier* and the *Mercury*. He would take them home and look them over. Maybe he would get a subscription, but, if he went to town every week he could just pick them up.

It had been a productive day. He had found the East End. And he also learned that the police and sheriff preferred eating at Garrett's. Tom planned to eat at Garrett's at least once a week. That would help him keep abreast of local law enforcement happenings, and get to know some of the boys. But he needed to get home to check on Bella, just in case the AC had died.

Padgett followed Route 32 northeast toward Flemingsburg. He noticed on the topo that Abners Mill dead ended at Route 32. So, he'd need to make a left on it up ahead. As is the case with many rural roads in Kentucky, turning from a main route onto a small country road can be challenging. Sometimes it's nearly impossible. That's because there's usually some lunatic right on your ass that's going 65 mph and constantly trying to pass you. This was just Tom's luck. The maniac was also smoking and texting. Tom muttered to himself, multi-tasking bastard. He turned left as the impatient idiot blew his horn and roared around him, driving on the shoulder of the road before flying out of sight.

It'd be very easy to miss the turn onto Abners Mill. It was poorly marked. Tom slowly rolled along as he checked out the area. He noticed a bar to his left, pulled off the road onto the shoulder, and studied the place. Gyp Joint, Gyp Joint? What kind of name is that? This will positively be an interesting place. He'd need to come back. The good news about the Gyp Joint was the proximity to his trailer, probably no more than four or five miles.

Back on the road, Tom began the ascent into the neighboring hills. The terrain was rough with steeply wooded hills on either side. He spotted a couple of worn out looking trailers perched haphazardly on ledges to his left. These trailers made his appear grand. With garbage all around, maybe this was where the phrase *trailer trash* came from. Looking in the rearview mirror, he wondered how long those trailers had been clinging to that cliff. It's probably just a matter of time before they break free and tumble down the hillside, before finally coming to rest on the banks of the Licking River.

He passed a church further up the hill, which was also perched on the left side of the road, just prior to a railroad crossing. Tom shook his head; don't they put churches in some strange places? The church was situated in an equally precarious setting. It couldn't have been more than five feet from the tracks. If many trains passed that way, the vibration would surely cause the church to crash down the hillside to join up with the trailers. The tracks crossed the road at a severe angle. There were no lights, only the crossing signs. Trains that followed these tracks obviously crawled along in order to keep from meeting misfortune.

Five minutes later Tom was home. He pulled into the drive, and then walked to the road to check his mail. What a bunch of junk mail. How did anyone know he was even living out here in the middle of nowhere? He wasn't surprised to find Bella still asleep exactly where he'd left her, lying in the air-conditioned bedroom. She didn't even lift her head when he entered the room. Well, Tom had always known she wasn't much of a watch dog. Aggressive little yippy dogs cause Bella to roll over in submission, allowing them clear access to her throat. He was surprisingly tired from the Carlisle adventure. A nap might feel pretty good.

CHAPTER 5

Wilson knew he was a small fish in a big pond, but that didn't change things one bit. He was the sheriff. Even though the county only had 7,000 residents, they were under his watch. He checked his profile in the mirror, sucking in his gut while he puffed out his chest. He slowly spun, standing on his tip toes. He thought he looked good. He knew he looked good. Slowly buttoning his shirt, he readied himself for another day of law enforcement. He remembered all the political games he'd been forced to play to win election. Most people running for political office embellished their ads, but not Bill Wilson. Actually, he downplayed many of his accomplishments, keeping all pertinent information short and to the point. Yeah, he was young, but that didn't mean he was inexperienced. Then again, maybe it did. But, he planned to master the job quickly and do it well.

Pulling himself up to his full six-foot-one, he grinned as he looked at himself. Leaning closer to the mirror, he inspected his face and picked some of the morning's breakfast from his teeth. Yes sir, he looked and felt good. It was going to be a great day. He strapped on his holster and pulled it tight. He stared at his reflection then quickly drew his weapon. Wilson loved theatrics. He rehearsed an exchange. Boy, oh boy Sheriff, if I didn't know you as well as I do, I'd be scared shitless. Yeah boy, you just remember that. Wilson looked approvingly at his reflection in the mirror as he holstered his weapon. Thirty-two years old and already sheriff; not many people could make that claim. If he could make a name for himself in the county, who knows? Maybe bigger and better things were just around the corner.

●　　●　　●

Lisa loved to ride on the old abandoned county road, especially since it was so close to home. She climbed on her sorrel pony, Miss Annie, and followed the neighbor's lane which led directly to the old road. Today, she was preoccupied. She thought about school. It was going to start in a few weeks. As most kids her age, she lamented, where had the summer gone? She'd be happy to see her friends, except for the boys. She didn't have time for them. Besides, she was only twelve. Riding horses, now that she had time for. She slowly rode Annie over the section of trail where she'd seen the Polaris ATV hidden on two previous occasions. There it was. It seemed as if the thicket was enveloping it.

Lisa rode Miss Annie harder and faster from the woods. She was suddenly much more anxious to get home. Lisa told her mother about the abandoned ATV in the woods. Her mom Rita, simply replied, "So?" What Lisa had failed to mention was the fact that she'd seen the ATV hidden in the woods on three separate occasions. And, this was during the past week. Rita reluctantly agreed to follow her daughter into the woods. She hoped to catch a glimpse of the mysterious ATV. After she followed Lisa up the trail, she was quite surprised. The Polaris that was covered with briars was very similar to her own.

Rita, a little less confident now, asked her daughter, "Are you sure it's been here the last three times you've ridden up here?" Rita pulled out her cell and dialed the sheriff's number.

"Nicholas County Sheriff," the clerk yawned.

"Hello there. This might be nothing, there's an ATV that might be abandoned in the woods over here off of Abners Mill Road. I know there are a lot of ATVs in the woods, but this one hasn't moved in at least a week."

"I'll let the sheriff know, ma'am. Just leave me your name and number and someone will get back with you."

Rita left her information. She agreed to show the sheriff or deputy where the ATV was located.

Wilson never liked going by his first name, Bill. He felt it sounded much too plain. He felt he was anything but plain. However Wilson, that had a much more distinguished sound. He was okay with being called Sheriff, but Wilson, that felt more respectful to him in some way. He was at Garrett's drinking coffee and chewing the fat, when his deputy wandered in. He really hated being interrupted.

"Sheriff, dispatch just got a call from out in the county."

"Yes, a call from out in the county. A call about what," Wilson grunted?

"Some woman phoned in, somethin' about an ATV in the woods, over by Abners Mill."

Wilson put his cup on the table and thought for a moment about what his deputy had just said.

"Deputy Leland, let me get this straight. Some woman called and reported an ATV in the woods?"

"Yes, Sheriff, that's what she said."

"Deputy, there's all kinds of ATVs in Nicholas County. As a matter of fact, they might even outnumber cars. What does this woman expect us to do about this ATV parked in the woods?"

"Sheriff, I believe she wants to show us where it's located. She believes something might have happened to the owner."

Wilson was just about to let the subject drop, but then reconsidered. "Ok, Leland, now we might be getting someplace. Do you have an address?"

Wilson and his deputy drove out to Rita's. After they arrived, Rita agreed to take them up to the spot where the ATV was hidden. Wilson rode one of Rita's ATVs. As he rode, he thought about the Sheriff Department's budget, and wondered if he could somehow get one of these machines. It would be good for policing, and it would also be a lot of fun.

After reaching the scene, Wilson had Leland record the VIN number from the mystery Polaris. Today, they weren't prepared for a search. Besides that, nobody had reported an incident other than this lady Rita. Wilson had Leland take photos of the machine from various angles. Leland got tangled in the briars, but managed to free himself without breaking the camera. "We'll see if we get anything on the VIN number," Wilson said to nobody in particular.

Wilson felt this little venture had been a waste of time. He knew that finding any information on the ATV would be difficult, especially if it hadn't been reported stolen. While his deputy drove, Wilson thought out loud, "Why would someone steal an ATV, then hide it in the woods? It just doesn't make sense."

"I don't follow what you mean, Sheriff?"

"Leland, it's obvious that someone hid that ATV in the thicket. Most likely it was the owner. So, maybe the owner had something to hide."

"What would someone be hiding in the woods, miles from nowhere?"

Wilson ignored the deputy, "Maybe we should concentrate our efforts on finding the owner."

That afternoon

Wilson began organizing a search party. His plan was to start the search first thing in the morning. For his search team, he requested men who owned ATVs or had access to them. The plan was to double up on the ATVs into the woods, dismount there, and then canvas the area on foot.

The next morning

They parked at Rita's, with all the trucks and trailers in the yard, it looked like Rita was throwing some sort of hunting party. When the search team reached the Polaris, there were ten men strong. From that point, they would spread out and do a sweep in all directions. Hopefully, they'd find what they were looking for.

Minutes after the search began, Wilson received a call on his radio.

"Yes, Leland, what's up?"

"We've located a body. It's a few hundred yards north of where the machine had been hidden."

"Leland, don't touch anything. Just preserve the area. Close it off with crime scene tape. I'll be right there." After his radio communication with Leland, Wilson was very excited. "Okay, men, we've located what we were looking for. Now just follow me." He was preoccupied, already thinking about the article that would appear in the newspaper, as he rapidly made his way through the thicket.

Wilson was fired up when he arrived where the body laid. However, he was totally unprepared for the grotesque deformed figure that lay before him. Wilson almost lost both his macho attitude and breakfast when he saw it. The body had obviously been lying in the sun for a quite some time. It seemed that all kinds of wildlife had been feeding on it.

He wondered whether or not he should bow out. He wasn't sure he was up to the task. Maybe he could let the state boys handle it? But, he sure would like the media exposure. As Wilson looked around, it was obvious to him what had happened. Did he even need to bother with the coroner? The main thing that needed to be done was identification of the body. He'd better call Keith Poole in Carlisle and run his thoughts by him.

•　　•　　•

Keith Poole had been busier than normal this summer. But, this was the nature of death. It just happened when it happened. As a Funeral Director/Coroner, you had to react. When duty called, you had to respond. He wasn't complaining. The money sure was good. He had just gotten off the phone with the sheriff. Wilson had unfortunately heaped more onto his plate than Keith was hoping for. He gave Wilson explicit instructions about what to do. He should receive the deceased's remains from Wilson later that afternoon.

His elected position had turned out to be everything he'd hoped for. However, running two funeral homes plus all the duties entrusted to the Coroner's office, was beginning to wear on him. But, vacations didn't seem to be an option for a funeral director, especially now that he'd become coroner.

Wilson had guessed right, right about what needed to be done, anyway. However, he was totally ignorant about the requirements pertaining to hazardous material cleanup. He hated to admit it, but it'd been the right thing to do, calling the coroner for additional expertise. However, as he looked at the remains of the meth lab that was beginning to be overgrown with weeds; he wondered if this was just another waste of taxpayer dollars. That wasn't his problem. All he had to do was cordon off the site and let the so-called experts do the rest. He looked in the direction of the rotting corpse wondering who it was.

The following morning

Keith phoned the Aftermath team. They would dispatch a cleanup crew that should arrive shortly after noon. Even though there were just remnants of the lab, as Wilson had mentioned, it would still require extensive cleaning. Even the ashes were toxic and needed to be removed.

Keith contacted the forensic lab in Frankfort and informed them that he would be sending over samples from the deceased's tests. He would also require help with dental verification. They had the manpower and experts to handle this. After Keith had done his portion of what was required with the deceased, he could put the body in cold storage until proper identification could be determined.

•   •   •

Tom woke from another fitful sleep and tried to clear his head. He hadn't had intense nightmares in quite a while. Now he'd had two in recent days. The dream he'd just woken from disturbed him. The face of the guy on the ATV that he and Bella had hidden from days ago filled his head. Funny how dreams worked, but this one was particularly vivid. What was going on? Did he need to seek help?

He walked to the kitchen and warmed some coffee in the microwave. He picked up the paper that he hadn't read, even though he'd bought it days ago. He paused and thought about his nightmare, and then he re-read the article about the body which had been discovered in the woods. It'd been found a couple of miles from his trailer. The article stated that the man had supposedly blown himself up in some kind of meth lab accident. It also stated that the Coroner, Keith Poole, was working on the identification. The article in the *Courier* was quite short. Maybe the sheriff would be willing to shine some additional light on the subject.

The sheriff and city police usually ate lunch at Garrett's. Tom usually ate lunch there on Wednesdays. He generally sat at a table near the officers. He listened to their conversations, hoping to learn more about on-going investigations in the area. Tom liked to stay in touch. Maybe this stemmed from his law enforcement past.

He had been coming to Garrett's for a few weeks now and seemed to have been accepted. When he first introduced himself around Carlisle, he told everyone that he was a retired policeman from Mt. Sterling. He never mentioned his previous position. It shouldn't matter anyway. He didn't want his past to ever become a conversation starter. He just wanted to be treated like one of the guys. Just new in town, simple as that. It didn't really matter that he'd been chief. It didn't matter that he'd been pushed into early retirement. He was just an old retired cop now. He just happened to be curious about how things were done around Nicholas County.

Today, as Tom suspected, the topic of conversation centered on the recent death of the man he'd dreamt about. Keith Poole had identified the body. His name was Jack Estep. It seemed the police all harbored similar feelings for the guy. It was rumored that he had sold meth both in Carlisle and out in the county. They all suspected him, but he'd never been caught. They all assumed that Estep was the one who'd sold meth to a high school student that had overdosed and died. That happened earlier in the year and the case had never been solved. The overriding consensus was that Estep had met with an unfortunate death, but they were still glad to see him gone. Tom listened as the banter continued. This was interesting. One less drug pushing hood living in the county was definitely a plus.

Tom thought of the dream he had this morning. Something about it was familiar. Not just the guys face. Not the ATV, but the cabin, the one that had blown up. It was almost like he had information that they didn't. He felt he knew more than the police did. They should have caught the guy. Why hadn't they? Was he becoming some type of weird psychic?

Wilson paused for a moment, as if mulling something over. "Hey Padgett, don't you live off Abners Mill?"

At first he didn't hear him, but then Tom snapped from his thoughts, and managed a blank expression, "Yeah. I do Wilson. Why do you ask?"

"Oh, just curious, you wouldn't by chance know the deceased would you?"

"I've only lived in Nicholas County a few weeks. What makes you think I know the man?"

This seemed to satisfy Wilson for the moment, but now he stared at Tom. "It just seems a little odd how close your trailer is to the crime scene. Kind of a coincidence, don't you think?"

Tom looked directly at him and Wilson quickly turned away. What's Wilson up to? He decided that Wilson shared some of the same attributes that the Mayor of Mt. Sterling did. Not the Napoleon Complex, but he definitely seemed to have similar issues.

Tom had been thinking that he needed a night out. Tonight might be the perfect night for it. He didn't like Wilson's accusatory attitude. A beer or two should help him forget about it. He recalled the face of the man on the ATV, and wondered was that Jack Estep?

He'd go home, take a short nap, and then take a vigorous hike in the woods. He knew Bella would really enjoy that. Now that Jack Estep was gone, there will be fewer people in the woods, good for when he and Bella took their walks. Tom thought he might as well give the Gyp Joint a try after dinner tonight. He hated leaving Bella in the trailer long, but if the AC was cranking away, she didn't seem to mind.

CHAPTER 6

Becky Atkins was forty-one, married, albeit far from happily, and currently unemployed. She had been laid off from a major pharmaceutical company; she had been jobless for nearly two years. The odds were against her getting that job back. Her unemployment had ended months ago and her cash reserves had begun to dwindle. So, she picked herself up, and started her own spirited entrepreneurial campaign, doing what she did best. The Pill Mill, Oxycontin express. She'd heard that country boys knew how to survive, so did this country girl. Her friend, Zane, was always eager to help with the driving. They could easily shoot down to Florida and still make it back the next day.

She had been married for thirteen years. They had been long years, too. You could say that their best years were well behind them. Her husband, Adam, seemed to have lost all interest in her. And, after she'd lost her job, it seemed to have gotten even worse. That was fine with her. Adam hadn't done much for her for some time anyway. He even seemed to blame her for the difficulties she was having finding work. This had caused them to drift even farther apart. She kept her side job secret from him. Hell, he wouldn't understand it, anyway. Actually, she was starting to enjoy their limited time together. It seemed to be a lot less stressful.

The house they shared was a modest three bedroom brick. It was located off Route 32, ten miles outside of Flemingsburg. They had it custom built when they had first gotten married. That seemed like an eternity ago to her now. She recalled how she used to love working in the flower beds, but now those beds were neglected and weed covered. Whatever made her think something as mundane as working with flowers was relaxing? Becky now realized what relaxation really was, as she felt the effects of the Oxycontin. She thought that making money while being under the influence of the drugs was an added bonus. It was something that she'd never experienced while working for *Big Pharma*.

Becky realized that Adam was probably having an affair, but she was actually kind of okay with that. Tonight she was going out. She planned to have some fun of her own. She'd been faithful for the majority of their marriage. Just a few slipups here and there, but who hadn't?

There was a guy she'd met at the Brown Hotel in Louisville; now he was a good time. She realized that there really had been several perks to selling pharmaceuticals, especially all the free samples you had available to give to clients. Becky and her new man had met at the hotel's bar, and talked over drinks. They went to his room, and shared a sample drug. The rest of her memory was sketchy, other than the king sized bed, everything else was quite fuzzy. It must have been great.

Then there was a guy in Paducah over at the Comfort Inn; *whoa now*. He was a real gentleman, too. He even paid for beer. Once again the pills came in very handy. They could surely be ice breakers. What a man. And who could forget that hunk from Evansville, Indiana? Those were really fun times.

Yes, technically speaking Becky had had an affair or two, but spread those indiscretions out over thirteen years and it's like nothing at all. She calculated to herself that if you had four or five one night stands over thirteen years, that's only like once every thousand nights. That's nothing. So once again, Becky managed to convince herself that she'd been faithful after all.

●　　●　　●

Tom woke from his nap energized. It seemed Bella was also pumped, as her tail swung wildly slapping him repeatedly across the face. "Alright, Bella, I'm getting up." Boy, she could be damned persistent at times. He threw on a shirt and a pair of hiking boots before he stepped outside. It was hot and humid, but it should be shouldn't it? It was August. After they entered the woods, it cooled down a little. Bella bounded off and treed a squirrel, which now mocked her from overhead. He watched as Bella intently stared at the squirrel, challenging it to come down and play. "Come on girl, let's go."

Tom was becoming quite familiar with these woods and was now actively checking for deer sign. It wouldn't be long before the deer hunters would be wandering the woods looking for a place to put up a stand. He noticed a decent game trail heading off to his left. There had been some showers overnight, so the trails were quite pronounced. There were some fairly large tracks. He might need to get that hunting license. He paused a moment as he heard an engine start, but soon realized it was only a chain saw somewhere off to the south. Firewood, it'd be nice to have a wood stove, but that might not be a good idea in his little trailer. It'd probably go up like a tinderbox.

There were far fewer ATV tracks now. Tom figured the guy, what was his name? Jack Estep? He must have been the wood's most frequent visitor. He and Bella found themselves at the scene of the explosion. As Wilson had indicated, it wasn't far from his trailer. Tom glanced around the area and was surprised with the familiarity of the place. As he looked around, he had a strange sensation. It was almost as if he'd been here before. He'd never been here, had he? He brushed the thought aside.

There was no sign of the lab remaining, just the footprint of where the shed had been, and some charred trees nearby. It was an isolated spot, a very secluded spot. The fact that he just stumbled upon it troubled him. He scratched his head. He was confused. Why was he here? Bella found a small creek and lay down. "Ok Bella, I can tell you're hot. Let's go home."

As she entered the trailer, Bella headed straight to the only air conditioned room in the house. Obviously, she was ready for her nap.

•　　•　　•

Wilson went back in his office after lunch at Garrett's. He thought about Padgett. There was something about the guy that just didn't add up, something he just couldn't figure out. Why would a cop from the city come here to retire in Nicholas County? Maybe it was the peace and tranquility or maybe there was something else. Why was he so curious about what happened in the county anyway? He was supposed to be retired, wasn't he? Something about him just didn't make sense. He needed to do some checking to see what he could find out about Padgett. The clerk stepped in and told him that he had a call.

"This is Wilson. Ok, I'll be right out."

"It seems there's some more mystery marijuana growing in some corn rows over off Stoney Creek," he told the clerk.

Wilson didn't have a secretary. The clerk, that had other miscellaneous county responsibilities, had to answer Wilson's phone. Another budget cut. Marijuana was growing everywhere, but what amazed Wilson, was that nobody seemed to know who planted any of it. Imagine that?

He turned right off of Route 68 onto Stoney Creek and followed the road to the small corn field. While he talked with the man who called in about the weed, he couldn't help notice how small this corn field was. Why would someone even bother trying to hide marijuana in this little patch? Word must have gotten out that Wilson was actively cracking down on growers, because now all kinds of calls came in to the station. He snipped the few plants off and loaded them in the back of his truck. He knew the answer but he still had to ask, "You don't have any idea how this stuff got here, do you?"

"No, no idea at all," the man replied.

It was just another waste of time and taxpayers' money. He had bigger crimes to deal with. He couldn't allow himself to become known as the marijuana cop. But, since he was in this part of the county, maybe he'd drive down Abners Mill, on his way back to town. As he slowly drove by the trailer, he could see Padgett's truck was in the drive. He muttered, "Padgett, I've got my eye on you."

• • •

Becky was looking forward to a few cold ones later that afternoon. But unfortunately, this meant heading over to Nicholas

County. Fleming was a dry county, so if you wanted to enjoy a drink in a bar, you needed to go elsewhere. Wet, dry, moist counties; this always made her crazy. It was absolutely silly how the liquor laws of Kentucky worked. The Gyp Joint was just seven miles or so from her house, which was no problem. She hadn't spent much time in Nicholas County lately. Not since the football game last fall when that high school girl had bought some pills from her. How could she have known how much the girl had been drinking? It didn't matter anyway. Becky hadn't forced the girl to mix her poisons.

At halftime, the girl approached her. She'd somehow learned that Becky sold Oxy. At first, Becky was apprehensive. She thought that it might be a setup, but then figured she was over-reacting and went with the flow. It was a sale, which would net her some much needed cash. The stadium in Carlisle had been fertile ground for selling hillbilly heroin, at least until that night. She remembered hearing about the accident a few days later. The girl had tried to drive home after drinking and doing the pills. No telling how she administered the things, whole, crushed or intravenously. Regardless, she didn't make it home. She wrecked her car a couple of miles outside of town, out on Moorefield Road.

Lucky for the girl, she had survived. But unluckily for her, she was now a paraplegic. Becky felt bad about what had happened to the girl, but not badly enough to stop selling pills. What was that girl's name? It was something like Marian or Miranda. She just couldn't remember what she'd read in the paper.

Becky still planned on getting back into the Carlisle scene, hopefully this fall. Surely the pressure would be off. The money to be made selling Oxy in Nicholas County was as good as Fleming, even though Nicholas County's population was much smaller. At this point, Becky didn't care where she sold her pills. Her own dependency seemed to increase daily.

•   •   •

Tom showered and slipped into a short sleeved oxford shirt and jeans. It felt odd to be dressing up, not that this was dressing up. It was casual in the country. Casual, that was fine by him. Thirty years of wearing uniforms had made him really appreciate relaxed attire. Tom gave himself a look in the broken bathroom mirror. It returned his reflection with a distorted view. Seeing his face that way, split in two, was interesting. One of these days, he needed to replace that mirror. Half-pleased with what he saw, he was ready to go out and meet some of the locals.

Bella watched Tom anxiously. She realized that he was going out, and began to get depressed. "I won't be gone long, girl. You stay here and guard the place." Bella dropped her chin to the floor with a thud an obvious expression of her displeasure.

As he attempted to pull out of the drive, a car careened around the bend toward him. Luckily, the driver managed to slow down, which enabled Tom to back out of his way. Damn nut. Why do they need to drive so fast on this one and a half lane track? Maybe I should have a culvert installed, that way I can get out of the driveway faster.

• • •

After Wilson arrived back in town, he continued to stew about Padgett, especially after he'd seen where he lived. Why does he live way out there anyway? The bastard appears to be fairly intelligent, so why's he living in that little broken down trailer? He looked through his rolodex and found the number he was looking for. After connecting, he was immediately put on hold. Damn it. He hated being put on hold.

After nearly a minute a voice returned and said, "Sorry for the delay, Mt. Sterling Police Department."

"Yes, ma'am, this is Sheriff Wilson, over in Nicholas County. The reason I'm calling is I'm trying to verify some information about a former officer in your department. Could you patch me through to someone who might be of assistance?"

"Yes, Sir, hold please."

"Yes, Sheriff Wilson, this is Chief Stamper. How can I be of assistance?"

"Chief Stamper, the reason I'm calling is to learn more about a former officer that worked in your department, Tom Padgett?"

John waited a beat before responding. "Sheriff, you're referring to Chief Padgett, is that correct?"

Wilson was intrigued now. Why didn't Padgett mention that he'd been chief?

"Chief Stamper, Mr. Padgett has led us in Carlisle to believe he was simply a retired policeman. Do you happen to know any reason why?"

"No, Sheriff I don't. I suggest you direct your questions to Mr. Padgett. I'm sure he'll give you an honest answer. Sheriff, if there's nothing more, I've got a department to run." After Stamper finished talking with Wilson, he decided to give Tom a call.

Tom recognized the caller, "Hey John, this is the second time you've called. It's only been a couple of weeks. Do you miss me?"

"Yeah I do, Tom, but that's not why I'm calling. I just had an interesting call from Sheriff Wilson. I assume you know him?"

"Yes, I know him. What's he up to?"

"Well, he seems quite interested in you, and was especially curious why you didn't reveal that you'd been chief in Mt. Sterling?"

"What the hell does that matter?"

"It doesn't matter to me, Tom. But, now he believes you're hiding something, so watch your back."

"Yeah, I guess you're right. Thanks for the heads up. You know, I just wanted to keep a low profile."

"I can understand that. Are you doing ok?"

"Things are good. I'm on my way to a little place, called the Gyp Joint. It should be exciting. The roads hilly, hope I don't lose signal."

"The Gyp Joint, you really do live way out in the country don't you?"

"But it's so peaceful out here. How's Kathy doing now that she's the chief's wife?"

"She's fine. Things are still pretty much the same around here. Oh, I did happen to see Darlene and the Mayor out on the town the other night. They made quite the pair."

"Yeah right, when you see them again, be sure to give the mayor a kiss for me."

●　　●　　●

Becky looked through her closet for the second or third time. She knew that the Gyp Joint wasn't fancy. She removed several things, and then dug through numerous drawers. Finally, she found exactly what she wanted. That would be good, a pair of jeans with flats, and the sheer top she liked so well, the one she wore when she was on the hunt.

After she got out of the shower, she looked at herself in the full length mirror. She still looked pretty good. She smiled before she wrapped the towel around herself. While she applied her makeup, she scrutinized her face more closely and was more than a little pleased with what she saw. She looked no more than thirty. How could she possibly be forty-one? There wasn't a hint of gray in her sandy brown hair.

She was going to drive her Mustang tonight. The car was Jet black with vanity plates that read 'HOTBABE'. The license plates guaranteed her plenty of looks. She usually left it parked in the garage and elected to drive her old beater. The same one that she used for pill runs, but not tonight. She was feeling fantastic. She probably needed to sell the Mustang, but it was the only thing that remained from better times. She needed at least one memory of the good old days. She knew that Adam might be around tonight, but she wasn't worried about him at all. Maybe she would run into him at the Gyp Joint. Maybe he'd even be with another woman. That'd be all right, too.

• • •

Wilson contemplated reasons why Padgett would say that he was simply a retired policeman, when he'd actually been the chief. If Wilson had been a retired chief, he would have shouted it out. Why did Padgett hang around Garrett's whenever the police were eating lunch there? Why did he care so much about what was happening around Nicholas County and Carlisle? Why did he live down around Abners Mill, near where Estep's sorry ass was killed? What was he really up to? How was he going to get Padgett to talk openly about himself? Maybe he needed a new tactic, one that would enable him to get closer to him.

Wilson thought about Padgett's desire to learn about things going on in the county. So, why not give him the chance? Wilson's deputy was going on vacation next week. Maybe Padgett would be willing to stand in and help him out. He'd ask Padgett to help cover during his deputy's absence. Padgett would probably jump at the opportunity, especially being able to pick the sheriff's brain. And, he could do likewise. He could dig into Padgett's past. Wilson smiled at the thought. He knew how to be manipulative sometimes in order to get things he wanted. And, he wanted Padgett; he wanted him on a stick. He'd give Padgett a call in the morning to see if he was game.

CHAPTER 7

Nick Mitchell lived alone in Flemingsburg. He had lived there for the last eleven years. After his wife Barbara died, he pulled up stakes and moved away from Lincoln County. He would soon turn sixty and after twenty-four years of marriage and eleven years a widower, he was finally getting comfortable with his bachelor lifestyle. Nick especially liked the part of being a bachelor that allowed him to keep a messy house. He missed the companionship of a woman, but lately he was beginning to prefer the company of men. He didn't feel like he was gay or anything like that. At least that's what he continued trying to convince himself of.

The house Nick lived in was just north of town on Maysville Road. It was a practical two bedroom ranch, which was easy to take care of. That was great for him because less housework meant more free time to do the things he liked. Nick could have gotten by with even a smaller home. Basically, he only used four rooms. He worked on a second cup of coffee and wondered. When was the last time that he'd entertained anyway? Not that he suddenly had some urge to entertain. Now that he was thinking about it, he realized that he hadn't entertained at all since his wife had died.

He was having difficulty with that thought. Could it really have been eleven or twelve years since he'd had visitors, anyone at all? Although he partied on his lonesome well enough, he was amazed how much of a recluse he had become. He still enjoyed going out, though. That's what he planned on doing this evening. The Gyp Joint might not be hopping on a Wednesday night, but he suddenly felt the need just to be around some people. And besides that, he hadn't been to the Gyp since - when was it, last Friday night? You never know, maybe some new blood would wander in.

Nick had gained a lot of weight after his wife died. Nick believed taking care of his health was more trouble than it was worth. On his last medical check-up, he'd measured in at five-ten and two-hundred-forty-five pounds. He was sure all the beer he drank didn't help matters. The doctor continually warned him about the negative impacts of alcohol consumption, but he didn't care. Wait a minute; he remembered being five-eleven last year. Was he shrinking? Gaining weight and shrinking, what's a guy supposed to do about that? No, he wasn't about to give up beer. Maybe he should start watching what he ate. Go on a diet, now that seemed reasonable, as long as he could drink more and eat less.

• • •

Tom pulled into the lot at the Gyp Joint. He parked his truck alongside four or five others. They were all pick-ups; imagine that, the vehicle of choice around these parts. Inside, he was greeted by the bartender and received nods from the other men sitting at the bar. Yeah, this was exactly what he'd expected, fifteen or so barstools, a couple of rarely used tables and two bar size coin-op pool tables. Perfect.

He ordered a Budweiser. He paid and then sat at the far end of the bar. From that vantage point with his back against the wall, he could keep an eye on what was happening around him. It took less than ten minutes to drive here from the house, which was good. The road was a little dicey at points, but he had no plans of getting inebriated, not tonight anyway.

The door opened and a man of average height and fairly heavy set wandered in. People at the bar nodded recognition.

The bartender greeted him, "Evening Nick, Bud Light?"

The man nodded, pulled up a stool and sat next to Tom. He took a sip of his beer before he turned to face Tom and introduced himself, "Nick Mitchell."

"Nice to meet you, Nick, I'm Tom Padgett."

For the moment they silently enjoyed their beer.

Nick again turned to face Tom. "I haven't seen you around before. You live near here?"

"Yeah, I live up the road a-ways. I just moved in a month or so ago."

They touched cans and Nick said, "Welcome to the neighborhood."

Tom studied Nick as he slowly sipped his beer. For some strange reason, he already liked the guy. "What about you, Nick, you live nearby?"

"Uh huh, I live over in Flemingsburg. It's about ten miles."

"Fleming County, that's a dry county isn't it?"

"Yeah, doesn't that just suck?"

Tom laughed at the comment. Nick seemed to be quite the character.

Nick continued, "I was married for twenty-four years, then my wife died. I lived in Lincoln County all that time, which also happened to be a dry county. So my wife dies and what'd I do? I move to another dry county. Isn't that just stupid?"

Tom clapped Nick on the back. "Let me buy you another beer."

Nick listened as Tom talked about himself. "So, you were a cop for thirty years? Why move to Nicholas County, way out here in the middle of God's country?"

"It's a long boring story. Just thinking about it makes me thirsty, how 'bout another?"

Nick told Tom that he had been an accountant and still occasionally dabbled with tax returns.

"So, I'm an old cop, and you're an old bean counter. Now there's a pair." Tom watched as a group of Mexicans came in to buy beer and cigarettes. Most Hispanic men working the tobacco farms in that part of the state spoke little, if any English. But, they knew how to communicate their wants and needs to Steve, the bartender, 12 *cervezas*.

The door opened and a nice looking young woman wandered in. Actually, she was quite good looking. Both Nick and Tom followed her reflection in the mirror behind the bar. She made her way to the only remaining stool, which was next to Nick.

Nick whistled to himself, Glory! Look at the trophy that just landed next to me.

Tom nearly choked on his drink as the woman turned to ask, "Do either of you gentlemen have a light?"

Nick was visibly shaken. He replied, "I don't smoke, do you Tom?"

Before Tom could say no, Steve was at the lady's elbow, carrying her drink and a lighter.

Tom shook his head at Nick's next line, "My name's Nick. And what, may I ask, brings a pretty young thing like you out tonight?"

Becky looked at Nick and thought that he was cute, cute in a fatherly kind of way, that is. But Tom, he was intriguing. She hadn't seen either of them at the Gyp before, which wasn't surprising. She really didn't get down here that often. "I'm Becky, and to answer your question,   I was going crazy sitting around the house. I just needed to get out."

"I can relate to that, I know exactly what you mean," Nick managed.

"So, what is it that you and your friend do?" she asked

Tom was happy to let Nick exercise his charm with the lady.

"Oh not much, I'm and old accountant and Tom's an old cop. Retired, that is."

Becky leaned on the bar. She moved closer to Nick so she could speak more easily in Tom's direction. She inquired, "So what was it like being a cop?"

Tom really didn't want to talk about the past. He already wanted the questioning to end. "Well, it had its ups and downs, to put it bluntly. I retired kind of in a downward spiral, not necessarily on the best of terms."

Nick asked, "You didn't get fired did you?"

"No, nothing like that, let's just say I'm not the cop I used to be."

Becky was now even more intrigued, "You mean, like you aren't a straight arrow anymore?"

"You could say that," Tom replied. He thought to himself, yeah, you could, definitely say that.

The three of them talked for another hour. They really hit it off and seemed to enjoy each other's company. Becky mentioned that she might return on Friday night, when she could stay longer. Both Tom and Nick thought that coming back for a friendly rendezvous on Friday might be fun. She stood, said goodbye, then made her way to the door. Tom and Nick both tracked her movements, along with every other man sitting at the bar.

After she left, Nick turned and whistled out loud, "If I was twenty years younger."

"Twenty years ago, hopefully, you would've been more imaginative with your pick up lines."

CHAPTER 8

Thursday morning

Wilson was busy going through some old cases. He was preparing them for next week's volunteer, Padgett. Wilson had phoned Padgett first thing that morning. He listened intently as Padgett eagerly agreed. Sure he'd help out while the deputy was on vacation.

Wilson flipped through the pages of an unsolved drug-related file. Miranda Johnson had been a senior in Nicholas County High School last fall, when she had wrecked her car and nearly lost her life. Excessive amounts of both alcohol and drugs had been found in her system. She was now confined to a wheelchair. Maybe after nine months some of the things she couldn't remember about that autumn night would have come back to her.

He re-read the file and noted that Miranda had recalled buying Oxy the night of her accident. Wilson had all the information on the desk in front of him. The only thing of significance that jumped out at him was that the seller was a woman. Miranda claimed to have drunk several beers before deciding to do the pills. She did the pills mostly because of friends' urgings. She had first crushed the pills and then swallowed them with beer. That was what her friends had recommended, saying it gave the best high. *The voice of experience,* Wilson thought to himself. Maybe Padgett could accompany him when he visited the girl for questioning. That would enable Padgett to put some of his many years of interrogation expertise to use.

•　　•　　•

Tom had been surfing the internet and enjoying his coffee when Wilson called. It seemed Wilson wanted his help next week. Wasn't this the same guy that had just quizzed Stamper about his work history in Mt. Sterling? This is interesting, what's Wilson up to? What is he looking for? Tom wasn't too concerned. It'd be an interesting change from his day to day. Plus, it'd be nice to learn more about how the sheriff did things. He might even be able to teach the guy a thing or two. He had no clue what Wilson had planned for him, but perhaps after spending some time together, they might get better acquainted.

Tom had a pretty good idea about the sheriff's methods. He knew there might be a hidden agenda. But, the more he thought about his temporary assignment, the more he liked it. It should be a good opportunity to gain a better understanding of the goings-on in the county. He worried about being stuck in an office. Then again, maybe he'd be riding shotgun with Wilson? Well, he would find out soon enough. 8am Monday morning to be exact. He laughed to himself, thinking about working in law enforcement for the week. He might have to give Stamper a call and tell him that he was back in the saddle.

•　　•　　•

Nick reluctantly stared at the bloodshot eyes looking back at him. An idiom came to mind, *you're as young as you feel*. What silly idiot had come up with that one? He thought that last night had been fantastic. He had met Tom, had really enjoyed talking with him, and wow, then there was Becky. That wasn't too bad either. Maybe he should start pumping iron, try working out again. *It's never too late*. He wondered if the same imbecile had come up with both of those goofy expressions. Exercise, now that might be a good idea. He'd have to give it some serious consideration. Yes, some serious thought, someday.

•　　•　　•

Becky had gotten an early start. She had business to attend to just outside of Flemingsburg. Her stash of pills seemed lower than she remembered. She didn't recall increasing her intake that dramatically. But, then again, maybe she had. She figured what she had to do was bump up her prices slightly. She'd raise them just enough to cover for her own increased use. Not too much though. Drug pricing can be a tricky game. If she raised her prices too much, she might lose some customers to heroin, as it becomes the cheaper alternative. She'd work that out. She was looking forward to finding out more about Tom. That might just turn into something.

• • •

Tom was anticipating good times and conversation this evening. Both something Nick would provide. He chuckled to himself thinking about some of the things Nick would say. Nick was hilarious. He ventured a thought about Becky. She may or may not show tonight. If she didn't, that would be disappointing. He felt she might be interested in him. But, he wasn't about to lose any sleep over it. Hell, she was young enough to be his daughter, nothing wrong with that.

• • •

Friday afternoon finally arrived

Nick found himself anxious to get to the Gyp. He really couldn't believe he felt this way. He was feeling almost giddy. He was behaving like some lovesick teenager. He was confused about who he most wanted to see. Was it Tom or Becky? He was fine with having male friends. But, his attraction to both Tom and Becky made him further question his own sexuality. Maybe he was entering a stage in his life where companionship was the determining factor. It didn't really matter, male or female. It was obvious that Tom was more interested in Becky than he was in him. That was only natural, he thought.

• • •

Becky finished her business early. She needed to talk with her drug *compadre*, Zane, and soon. They would need to make a Florida run at the beginning of the week, at the latest. That would definitely make him happy. A few pills and a little cash usually kept him quiet. She had done some checking around with some of the local drug depots, or pain clinics. They couldn't compete with the connections she'd developed down south in Broward County. There had been quite a bit of added pressure lately. Fortunately, her suppliers had managed to steer clear of trouble.

●   ●   ●

Wilson smiled with satisfaction as he kicked his feet up onto the desk. Another successful week put behind him. Padgett was scheduled to be his temporary underling. He was actually looking forward to Monday. Tonight though, he might just pull out that bottle of *Jim Beam Black* and celebrate. He just needed to be careful. He didn't want to get carried away and end up doing something that he'd regret. Being a recovering alcoholic wasn't easy. But, he was keeping himself in check. At least he had been lately, anyhow. That bourbon was so damn smooth. He was salivating. He was salivating just thinking about it.

●   ●   ●

Tom arrived at the Gyp about half past five. He wasn't surprised to find Nick already there, knocking back a Bud Light.

"Hey Nick, how are you doing?"

"I'm fantastic, Tom. Just look at me."

"Did you start pumping iron?"

"I thought about it. What is it, my abs or biceps?"

Tom took a pull from the cold Bud. Man, it sure tasted good. This afternoon was hot. Tom could see Nick was on a roll, openly engaging everyone in the bar.

Tom leaned against the wall and took in the room. He was content to observe for the moment. A few of the men that sat at the bar had been here Wednesday night. There were also a few that Tom didn't recognize. Becky wasn't here yet, but it was still early. Nick came back, out of breath from all the stories he'd been telling.

"Hey Nick, you seem quite excited tonight. What's the occasion?"

Nick beamed, "It's my birthday. Number sixty."

"Congratulations Nick, hey Steve, how 'bout getting the birthday boy another beer?"

"Yeah, this morning when I woke up, I was worried about being sixty and all that. But you know what? I don't feel any different than I did yesterday."

"Well, Thank God for that. Cheers."

● ● ●

Becky left the house around six-thirty. She hadn't seen Adam in a couple of days, but she knew that he was still around. It's just that their paths hadn't crossed. Her car purred as she pulled out of her driveway onto Route 32.

She'd confirmed that she was using more Oxy than she used to. She'd watch herself and not let things get out of hand. She thought about her relationship with Adam. If they could stay married, and share the house without running into each other, that would be great. He could do his thing and she could do hers. Perfect.

● ● ●

Wilson sat in a recliner and listened to *The Bull, Better Country 98.1*, as he sipped his first drink. He didn't listen to a whole lot of music. But when he was drinking whiskey, the music that sounded best was country. Man, oh man. The whiskey just filled that void deep inside him. He'd been good, damn good. It'd been a month or more since he'd even thought about having a drink. He held the glass up in front of his eyes. He was mesmerized with the clarity of it. Yes, he could control himself. All he needed to do was take it slow. That's right Wilson, slow and steady.

● ● ●

Nick wanted to know, "Tom do you think Becky's going to make it tonight?"

"I'm not sure. Did you tell her it was your birthday?"

"No, do you think that would have made any difference?"

"Maybe, if you'd told her, she might have bought you a present."

"What kind of present would she give to an old man like me?"

"Knock off the nonsense about being old. I'm just a few years behind you. You're making me feel old."

"Maybe she'll feel sorry for me and give me a gift anyway. Something old, something new, something borrowed something blue."

"What in God's name are you going on about, Nick?"

"Oh I don't know, maybe I'm being overly nostalgic."

"Ok, Nick, forget about the memory lane stuff. Hey Steve, could the birthday boy and I have a couple?"

"Tom, I was wondering, you can tell me it's none of my business, but why'd you leave the force?"

"I haven't told anyone about this, so keep it to yourself, ok?"

"Mum's the word, Tom. If I should die before I wake, I pray to God my soul to take."

"Stop it, what's up with you tonight?"

"I don't know, but why'd you leave?"

"Let me give you the short version. I was given a promotion to chief, which all but guaranteed I'd quit."

Nick pondered this. "Now you're even talking in riddles."

"No listen, the Mayor gave me a promotion to chief, which had an attached take it or leave it clause. He knew I couldn't stand being chained to a desk, so it was a sure thing that I'd quit."

"Wow, is that even legal?"

"It doesn't matter now, its history, end of story."

"Tom, I think that is just crap, being forced to take a job you don't want."

"I agree, but look at the bright side, we're sitting here celebrating your birthday, and if I'd still been working we might never have met."

"I can't argue with that. Cheers."

●　　●　　●

Wilson first glanced at the clock then looked at the whiskey bottle sitting on the end table. It was only eight o'clock, still early yet. He pulled the karaoke machine out of the closet and plugged it in. He couldn't even remember the last time he'd sung. He sat back down, leaned back in the chair, and sipped whiskey while he flipped through the karaoke CDs. He was definitely loosening up. As he stood to connect the microphone, he only wore his hat, socks and underwear. He stretched and considered which song he wanted to try.

He felt energized as he sang, "Hotel California." Actually, Wilson felt he sounded just like Don Henley. He had put on his boots and pulled out his acoustic guitar. Doing that air guitar thing, he was on a roll. He was even taking it easy on the Jim Beam, with nearly half a bottle left. Maybe he had the whole drinking issue solved, especially if tonight's singing was an indicator. He took a big swig as he looked for his next song. He'd almost forgotten how much fun singing was. Alright, this was great, Glen Campbell's, "Lineman for the County." He knew he could absolutely nail this one.

●　　●　　●

Becky parked the Mustang away from all the pick-up trucks that filled the Gyp Joint parking lot. Her car was pristine and she preferred to keep it that way. She climbed from the car and walked toward the door. Suddenly, she tripped in her wedge pumps. Damned gravel, she muttered under her breath. There was a truck load of Hispanic guys nearby that stared at her as she recovered. Luckily, they didn't say anything, content to drink their beer while they sat on their tailgates. Becky, get a grip, let's not stumble as we make our entry.

Luckily, Becky made it inside without tripping. She noticed that Tom and Nick were already there. Nick appeared highly animated, but so was she.

Nick noticed her and slurred, "C'mon over here darling. You can have my seat."

Before Nick could move, Tom got up. "Here Becky, take my seat. I'll go find another stool."

"What, may I ask, brings a pretty young thing like you out tonight?" Nick slurred.

"Nick, that's the same line you used on me two nights ago. Maybe I should help you with your material."

Tom returned with a barstool in hand. He told Becky that Nick had been celebrating his birthday.

"Yeah, I can tell he's been celebrating something."

Nick stared blankly at them. He was suddenly totally incoherent.

"Steve, I think Nick's finished." Steve nodded in agreement.

"Well Becky, it's just the two of us now. For lack of a better term, Nick seems to have 'shot his wad'."

They both looked over as Nick laid his head on the bar. He was in no condition to drive. Tom reached over and grabbed his keys.

"I guess I'll take him home with me."

"You're not leaving are you?"

"Oh no, I'm just going to help Nick out to my truck, before he falls off this stool. Maybe he can sleep it off. I'll be right back."

Tom partly led, partly carried Nick through the door, and over to his truck and deposited him in the back seat. "Nick, just lay back and go to sleep. I'll just be a few more minutes."

"Yeaaah, alright," was all Nick mumbled.

Becky was in Tom's seat when he returned. She looked good tonight. They had a couple more drinks and shared some small talk.

"So, does this mean that you're not taking me home tonight?"

Tom hadn't expected this level of forwardness. But, actually, he kind of liked it. He hadn't been in the hunt for twenty-five years. Wow, things must have dramatically changed since he'd even thought about women, other than Darlene.

"I would love to have you visit my humble abode. Keep in mind, it isn't much, but at least it's clean. Maybe you could leave your car here, and I'll give you a ride back later?"

"No Tom, I'll drive. There's no reason for you to come all the way back here."

Tom called out, "Hey Steve is it ok if Nick leaves his car here till morning?"

"Not a problem."

Leaving the Gyp, Tom walked Becky to her car. "That's one fine car. Are you sure you don't want to leave it here? Some of these roads are pretty rough, and my driveway's pretty bad, too."

"It'll be fine Tom, I'll just follow you."

Tom drove slowly as he started out. Becky stuck to him like glue, even pushing him at times. He thought she obviously wasn't as worried about something happening to her car as he'd been. He could hear Nick mumbling in his sleep, between snores. Hell of a night this was turning out to be. He'd have to throw all the boxes off the guest bed to make room for Nick.

They slowly rolled over the ditch and into the drive; the mobile home was clearly illuminated. There was a dusk-to-dawn pole light mounted near the trailer. It probably scared all the would-be robbers to death. Even if the light failed, the bad guys would still have to deal with Bella. As he and Becky got out of their vehicles, Tom found he was slightly embarrassed at his meager existence. Tom led Becky up to the house, saying that she could entertain Bella, while he cleared the stuff off the bed for Nick.

As Becky climbed the steps, she tripped again. This time she spilled the contents of her purse. Together she and Tom quickly scooped everything up. Tom was apprehensive as he opened the door. Bella was very excited to see them. There was another person to play with. Bella was wild, jumping up on Becky.

"Down, Bella, go outside and use the bathroom," Tom directed as he opened the door.

Becky shared the same concern and asked where the bathroom was.

"It's down the hall on the left." Becky, would you like a beer? Unfortunately I don't have the greatest selection here."

"Yes, a beer would be great."

Tom quickly piled the boxes on the guest room floor, revealing a small bed.

They sat on the sofa and sipped their beer. Meanwhile, Bella struggled to be part of the encounter. She always wanted to be involved. Bella was very protective of Tom. Especially around other women, it seemed.

When Tom went to grab a second beer, Becky asked, "What about Nick?"

"Oh yeah, Nick. I nearly forgot about him," he flashed a mischievous grin. "I guess I'll go get him out of the truck."

Becky petted Bella as Tom struggled to drag Nick up the steps and down the hall, before dropping him onto the bed.

"Boy, you talk about dead weight. Nick is really heavy."

Tom was thirsty after hauling Nick's bulk into the trailer and drank a huge gulp of beer before plopping down next to Becky. For once, Tom was at a loss at what to say, as he glanced at the woman that was mere inches to his left. Becky didn't appear to have the same issue. She leaned over and kissed him aggressively on the mouth. *That was nice,* he thought. He knew what to do next, but didn't exactly know how to broach the subject. Becky solved his dilemma.

"Tom, you do have a bedroom in this place, don't you?" She stood, reached for his hand and said, "Come on, I believe it's this way."

She pulled him down the hallway. They both laughed as they passed the guest bedroom where Nick snored loudly. Becky spun Tom around and pushed him backwards onto the bed. He laid there like an inexperienced teenager and waited as she preformed for him.

As she slowly began to remove articles of clothing, he asked, "What about Nick?"

"If he wakes up, he can join us. You're not afraid of a little ménage à trois are you?"

"If your twin was here that'd be great, but with Nick, I don't think so."

He'd never been entertained like this, in all the years he'd been married to Darlene. As long as his heart didn't fail him, he could get used to this. Becky was naked. She stood at the foot of the bed and watched as Tom fumbled as he tried to pull his pants off. He was so caught up in the show that he'd forgotten to take off his shoes. That was no problem. Becky strolled over and kneeled next to the bed and expertly removed them for him.

•　　•　　•

Tom woke around six. He was absolutely shattered. Boy, Becky had turned him every way but loose last night. He remembered finally submitting to sleep at around 3am. He wasn't as young as he used to be. She had more moves in her repertoire than he remembered from his younger days and an energy level that didn't falter, either.

He dragged himself to the bathroom and looked into his broken mirror. Mirror, mirror on the wall, who's the most worn out old man of all? As he walked to the kitchen, he noticed a note on the counter. *Had a great time, see you at the Gyp next Friday, 'B'.* Hell, it might take that long just to recover.

Bella and Tom relaxed in the front yard. He was already on his third cup of coffee. He was beginning to worry about Nick. But, then he heard a small crash inside and realized that Nick finally must have woken up. Moments later, the screen door opened as Nick slowly poked his head out into the daylight. Tom knew Nick had no idea where he was.

"Morning, Nick. How's our *post* birthday boy this morning?"

Nick grunted.

"There's coffee in the kitchen. Get yourself some, and then come outside for some fresh air."

Nick appeared after a few minutes and held his coffee shakily in both hands. He sighed, "So this is where you live?"

"Yes, this is home sweet home. Not much, but it serves me well."

"Thanks for taking care of me, Tom. Did I do anything stupid?"

"No, you were well behaved. At least I think you were. I haven't heard any complaints out of Bella that you were untoward. How about if I whip us up some breakfast? I'm sure you're just as hungry as I am."

"You don't have to bother."

"It's no bother at all. Besides, you need to keep up your strength."

After they finished eating, Tom drove Nick back to the Gyp.

"Are you going to come out to the Gyp this week?" Nick asked.

"Yeah, I'll be around, probably on Friday night. It seems to be a hopping place on Fridays."

Nick didn't look good. "Are you sure you're alright?"

"Yeah, I'm fine, nothing that three or four nights sleep won't fix."

When Tom returned to the trailer, he let Bella out. She immediately went under the steps and dragged something out in her mouth. Tom wrestled the bottle from her and read the label, Oxycontin 50 tablets 60mg.

• • •

Becky woke early on Saturday and immediately grabbed her purse. As she rummaged through her bag, she was at a loss as to where her other bottle of pills had gone. She vaguely recalled taking one or two before leaving for the Gyp Joint last night. Maybe they were in her car. She noticed that Adam still wasn't home. She wrapped a cotton robe around her and walked up the hallway before she stepped out into the garage. Her Mustang was parked crookedly in the middle of the two-bay garage, but didn't appear damaged. No pills in the car and none in the house. Where'd they go?

• • •

Tom wondered why Becky would be carrying such a big bottle of Oxycontin in her purse. Sadly, he realized he might already know the answer. What an absolute shame. That helped explain some of her physical prowess. Was she also selling drugs to make ends meet? From talking with Becky, he learned that she had been unemployed for some time. Hopefully, they were for her habit only, and that she wasn't supplying other people. He wouldn't mention anything about the pills when he saw her later in the week. Maybe she'd fess up and tell him about her addiction.

CHAPTER 9

Both Nicholas County Middle and Nicholas County High Schools were abuzz Monday morning. Nicholas County had become famous when a resident of the county had uploaded a video onto YouTube. It had gone viral. Conversations centered on the fact that the sheriff had posted the video anonymously over the weekend. Supposedly, he sang a song called "Lawman for the County," the karaoke version. It was originally done years ago by some character none of them had ever heard of named Glen Campbell. The video was a bit grainy, but the suspicions seemed correct. Someone blew the video up large enough to clearly identify Bill Wilson.

The video was currently the most heavily viewed on YouTube. It had just over four million views in the last 24 hours. It was fantastic, sweeping the school like wildfire. Even the teachers were checking the video out on their I Phones, droids or whatever smart device they had. No work was getting done in school and it was already the start of third period.

It was a classic video. The mystery man wore only his sheriff hat, mirror sunglasses, underwear and knee high socks under fancy cowboy boots. Adding to the excitement of the video was the acoustic guitar he swung around, clearly exposing his gun in its holster, which repeatedly slapped against his bare thigh.

●　　●　　●

Wilson woke early Monday morning. At least he thought it was Monday. He felt like absolute shit. Where had the weekend gone? He wandered into the living room and found empty pizza boxes, empty food containers, garbage strewn everywhere. He also found two empty Jim Beam bottles lying on the floor. His video

85

equipment was out, the karaoke was out, and even his guitar was out. What's going on, had he thrown a wild party? His phone rang. He didn't want to answer, but he did reluctantly. "Wilson."

Over the line he could hear many people laughing in the background. Finally, a young boy's voice rang out, "Hey, Sheriff. Nice video, nice outfit, too."

The caller hung up. What the hell was that about? Wilson was starting to have a really bad feeling about things. He looked around the living room and desperately tried to put the pieces together. The last thing he recalled was that Padgett was helping him today. His head pounded, his stomach was a mess, and he seriously needed coffee. His phone rang again.

He snatched it up, "Wilson."

"Sheriff, I love the way you shake your hips."

The caller hung up. Damn it, what is going on? He put coffee on and headed for the shower. What were his hat and gun doing in the bathroom? Maybe he didn't want to know. As he showered, he heard his phone ring once again. Maybe he should just turn the damned thing off.

● ● ●

Tom was anxious to get going. He had already walked Bella, showered and had breakfast. He had just finished his third cup of coffee. It wasn't even seven yet. He wasn't meeting Wilson until eight, so he tried to locate some local news on his laptop to kill some time. He wasn't sure why he was so excited. Was it because he hadn't been doing much lately? Or was it the possibility of finding out why Wilson took such issue with him? He hoped Bella would be okay in the trailer for nine hours. Maybe he needed to build her an outdoor run.

Tom arrived at the courthouse fifteen minutes early and plopped down on a bench in the lobby. At exactly eight, the County Clerk unlocked the Sheriff's office to begin her day. She immediately got busy with a vehicle inspection or something. Tom pulled up a chair and waited. She returned from the vehicle inspection as the phone rang.

"No, the sheriff isn't in just now. No, I don't know anything about a video." Again the phone rang, "No, the sheriff isn't in. What video are you talking about?" The clerk was already stressed out. She'd only been in the office ten minutes.

Five minutes later Wilson dragged in. He looked really bad. He mumbled something in Tom's direction before going into his office.

• • •

Jimmy Fugate was seven days into a thirty day sentence at the Mason County Detention Center. He wasn't happy about being there, simply because of a fight between him and his wife. She was his wife, wasn't she? And, what happened between a man and his wife was their business, not the Court's. So what if he hit or slapped her. He was a man and that was part of a man's nature, part of a man's right. One thing that being in jail had given Jimmy, that was plenty of time to think.

He was glad when his wife Woozy finally showed up for visitation. They had been married seven years, but he wasn't one bit happy with the fact that she waited seven long days before coming for her first visit. Seven days he waited in that damn cell, while she was out doing whatever, having a good old time, messing around on him. But, Jimmy was all cordial to Woozy while the guards stood nearby. He said things like, "I miss you, baby. I'll never treat you bad again, baby. I need you baby."

She cried and said "I miss you too, Jimmy."

After her short visit, he began to stew again. Why'd it take her so damn long to come visit? Why'd she only stay for ten minutes? She should have stayed longer. As soon as he got out of here, he would teach her a thing or two about wifely obligations and respect. He'd even been in here on his forty-sixth birthday. No cake, no card. That really pissed him off.

•　　•　　•

Woozy Mae was forty-four and beginning to feel that her second marriage was nearly at an end. She looked at her face in the mirror and noticed that the bruising was finally leaving from where Jimmy had hit her. Luckily, she had dark hair, which she managed to brush over the spot, keeping it mostly hidden. She convinced herself that Jimmy was probably justified with what he had done. After all, she had smiled at that guy after she'd served him a drink that night.

A man that expresses no jealousy probably doesn't love you. Her first husband did the same thing. He beat her often, claiming she deserved it. Some of the girls that worked at other bars around Maysville confessed that they'd been beaten by their men, also. So, she wasn't alone. But, she was the only one whose man happened to be in jail.

She remembered the night that her first husband, Mike, had died. He was all hyped up on drugs and alcohol. He was also furious at her for some mysterious reason. He said he was going to give her what she deserved, but first he needed to get some more beer. As she sat in the house, she was terrified as she waited for his return. She wondered should she go hide at her friend's. Then she reconsidered because that would only make him angrier. So she waited. Maybe she could smack him with a ball bat or something when he walked through the door. No, that wouldn't work. His reactions were still pretty good. Even drunk and stoned, he'd probably grab the bat, turn it around and use it on her. Woozy remembered hearing distant sirens that night, not realizing until later, that her husband would never make it home again.

•　　•　　•

Jimmy was thinking about his childhood. Hell, he didn't have anything else to do while he was locked up in Maysville jail. His dad had been one hard ass. He beat his mother constantly. But, nothing ever happened to him. He never got hauled off to jail. That was obviously a different time. Yeah, things were simpler then. Apparently, things were better then.

His dad always saved some leftover strength after beating his mother to work on Jimmy. Man, the guy could really hit. His Mother never told him where his dad had gone. One day, he just never came around again. That was something like thirty years ago. Things were good for a time after that. At least his mother seemed happier.

Then it happened. His mom supposedly fell in love again. In love with Jake, that worthless bastard. Jake blew in like a bad storm. He seemed to especially hate Jimmy. The feeling was mutual, because Jimmy hated him, too.

After a short time, his mother and Jake married. Jimmy was twelve at the time. His mother had a nice little house in Maysville and that scrounge just moved in. Jake was all nice for a few weeks before he changed and started getting violent. He'd start in on Jimmy for some crazy reason. When Jimmy's mom would tell Jake to quit, he'd turn on her. If Jimmy had been bigger, he would have killed Jake, but it wasn't meant to be. Jimmy moved out when he was seventeen, and as soon as he turned eighteen, he enlisted.

●　　●　　●

Tom noticed that Wilson was having a difficult time concentrating this morning, so he was content to wait. After he'd meditated for about ten minutes, Wilson seemed to grab hold of a plan. He pulled a file from the cabinet behind him and laid it on his desk.

"Padgett, today I need you to help me interview a crime victim. It's from an unsolved case."

"I'm not a policeman anymore. So how can I help you interview anyone?"

"Don't you worry about the details? I'll handle that. I'll initiate the questioning, and you just jump in when you believe you've got something to contribute."

"Can I ask why you think I'm going to be useful to your investigation?"

"Let's just say I'd like to see how an old pro, handles himself," he smiled. Wilson continued, "Here's the deal. There's a girl from the high school that was severely injured in a car wreck last fall. It seems she bought some Oxy from a dealer while she was at a football game. It's been nine months since the accident, so I'd like to see if her recollection has improved any."

"Can I have a look at the file?" Tom quickly skimmed through the file before commenting, "She's no longer a minor, so her parents won't need to be present."

"Good point. See, I knew you could be of assistance."

Tom knew Wilson had an ulterior motive, but he would play along for a while.

•　　•　　•

Becky and Zane made great time. They arrived in Florida early Monday morning. She used her pharmaceutical experience in order to gain certain favors, such as circumventing long lines and not needing to prove she was in pain, in order to get drugs. It helped immensely that she offered occasional sex to some of the doctors. That helped them look the other way about certain procedures. Still, it'd taken longer than normal to fill all her requirements. Becky realized that she needed to fine tune her restocking capabilities.

•　　•　　•

Woozy was called in early at O'Rourke's Pub. She tended bar and had been for several years. It wasn't great money, but every once in a while, the tips still surprised her. Sometimes one of the regulars would give her ass a friendly squeeze as she walked by. She kindly reminded them to knock it off or she'd give them a good kick between the legs. That would usually get her some cheers, "Yeah, you tell that ass hole, Woozy."

When business was slow, she cleaned the bar and listened while patrons cried about the difficulties of life. "Hey Billy, listen, everybody's got it rough, ok? It's not just you." Woozy advised.

Woozy still looked good, that is, if she wasn't sporting a black eye or two. Her bottom wasn't what it'd once been, but it still didn't deter the bums from grabbing it. She hated that her black hair had streaks of gray in it. It was probably because of her daughter Charlene.

Charlene had just turned eighteen and drove Woozy absolutely nuts. Maybe with a little luck, she'd move out soon. Charlene *knew everything* and she reminded Woozy about it constantly. She could visualize her daughter rapidly texting away to all her so-called friends. Woozy didn't know why, but for some unknown reason, Jimmy left Charlene alone.

• • •

Wilson and Tom were going to visit Miranda Johnson. She still lived at home, but today her parents were both working. Miranda was happy that someone was coming to visit, even if it was only the sheriff. She laughed to herself as she thought about the video of Wilson that she'd watched earlier that morning.

Wilson was just about to climb into his truck as one of the city cops yelled over at him, "Hey, Wilson, that was a hell of a good video. You know, it's approaching five million views."

Wilson ignored him as he climbed into the truck. Tom was curious about the video, but he wasn't about to stress Wilson out anymore than he already was.

Miranda's parents had a three bedroom ranch on the northeast side of Carlisle. The sheriff drove in silence after the city cop had aggravated him. Wilson thought about the supposed video. He had to find out what it was. When they arrived at her house, Miranda was already waiting at the door, sitting in her electric wheelchair. They entered and followed her as she silently rolled to the living room.

Wilson began, "Miranda, this is Tom Padgett. He's helping me out on your case, so he might have a question or two. Is that alright with you?"

"Sure, Sheriff Wilson, it's not like I've got anything else to do."

Wilson continued, "Miranda, I know it's been quite a while since you had the accident. And, I also know that you've already been questioned about it. We're just making sure no stones have been left unturned, ok?"

"Fine, Sheriff. My social calendar is completely open."

"The last time anyone spoke to you about this was October of last year. Miranda, that night you'd been drinking beer and then you were persuaded to try some pills, right? So, has anything about that night come back to you over the past few months?"

"If you want to say I was persuaded, Sheriff, that's fine. I think I acted of my own free will."

"Ok, Miranda, has anything rattled your memory, at all?"

"No, Sheriff, nothing at all."

Tom listened as Wilson struggled to make headway with the young lady. When Tom finally spoke, he spoke softly, "Miranda was the person selling the drugs a woman?"

"Yes, but you guys should already know that."

"Ok, but what do you remember about her, was she pretty?"

"Yes, I believe she was."

"Miranda would you say she was young or old?"

"She was older, but not real old, probably like thirty or something."

"If you saw a photo of her, could you identify her?"

"Oh, I don't know about that. I was kind of messed up."

"Can you remember the color of her hair?"

"I believe it was either brown or blonde. It was one or the other."

"Miranda, how tall do you think she was?"

"Actually, we were around the same height, which used to be five-seven," she grimaced.

Tom thanked Miranda before heading to the truck. Wilson handed her his card and said to call if anything else came up.

Miranda had been dying to ask, "Sheriff Wilson, how long did you work on that video? It was great."

Wilson jumped in the truck in a huff and told Tom he was going to drop him at the station. He had to run home, he had some things he needed to attend to. That was fine by Tom. Maybe he would run down to the East End to have lunch. When Tom got to the East End, it was packed, standing room only. There was only one item on the gossip agenda, and that was Sheriff Wilson's video.

Wilson finally managed to not only find, but delete his YouTube video. He now painfully realized why his weekend had been such a blur. He knew that there were probably plenty of copies still floating around out there, but hopefully this would put an end to most of the hysteria. What in the hell had he been thinking? Maybe he should take the rest of the day off. No, he needed to be out and about and put this silly episode behind him. Plus, he had Padgett to deal with. When he returned to the courthouse, he found Padgett in the lobby talking with a group of people. They were all laughing loudly, probably about that damned video.

● ● ●

Becky drove north on I-75. There were plenty of cops and many of them had cars pulled over. She wondered if search procedures in Kentucky had changed. She knew as long as she stayed in her lane, watched her speed and obeyed the law, they wouldn't bother her. Besides, even if she did get pulled over, the police would need to have a reason to search her car. Zane snored softly. He had driven most of the trip, so she took it the rest of the way. Becky believed she might be able to make it approximately a month on the stash she picked up. She hoped so, anyway.

•   •   •

Tom's phone rang just as he and Wilson were wrapping things up.

He stepped out into the lobby, "Padgett."

"Boy oh boy, don't you sound official," Nick laughed.

"What's up Nick? Have you recovered from your birthday overload?"

"Yeah, I'm feeling fit as a fiddle. I was wondering if you'd like to try a new bar tonight."

"Sure. I just need to stop by the trailer and look in on Bella. What are you thinking?"

"There's a place in downtown Maysville called O'Rourke's that has a decent happy hour and the pizza's not bad either."

"I'll tell you what; I'll meet you there around six or six-thirty?"

"Fine by me Tom, I'll probably be there in about twenty minutes. By six, I'll be all warmed up."

Tom entered the pub and found Nick doing what he'd promised, getting warmed up, as he clung to the bar. Nick didn't appear as animated as he'd been the previous Friday night, but he was quickly getting there.

"Hey Nick, how you doing?"

"Great, Tom. Hey, Woozy, this is my friend Tom."

Woozy was tending bar. She nodded, "It's nice to meet you, Tom. What are you having?"

"I'll have a Budweiser." Tom looked around the place as he enjoyed his beer. It was nicer than the Gyp Joint, but it took forty-five minutes to get here. It took less than ten to get to the Gyp, so he definitely wouldn't be coming here often. Woozy was serving the people at the bar. She also filled waitresses' drink orders. She was busy.

As Woozy worked the other end of the bar, Nick whispered to Tom, "Woozy's husband is locked up in Maysville jail for spousal abuse."

Tom listened before replying, "I hate hearing things like that. Does he get out anytime soon?"

"I believe she said he gets released in two weeks."

"Well, I know all about the effectiveness of rehabilitation, especially for abusive husbands. It's something like zero percent." Tom sipped his beer, while he watched Woozy deal with customers. "You know, Nick, just watching her interaction with other people, I can guarantee you she did nothing wrong. Besides, nothing a woman does should ever lead to abuse. It's generally some engrained issue with the man, usually a learned thing from childhood. Who knows, maybe genetics even play a part."

Tom glanced around the room and noticed that there was a mixed bag of people in the place with almost as many women as men. About half the people probably had some sort of white collar job. The remainder might have worked construction, or worked in the local limestone mine, or maybe even at one of the power plants. It made Tom feel good when he saw people of diverse backgrounds hanging out enjoying one another's company. Nick returned from a nearby table where he had been rambling on about something.

"Hey, Tom, why don't we order a pizza? I'm starved." Nick called, "Woozy, could we get a pizza, with everything on it, everything except anchovies? Tom, is that alright with you?"

"That sounds great by me."

Woozy interjected, "We don't have anchovies."

"All right, Woozy, a pizza with everything then." Nick grinned.

When the pizza arrived, they devoured it, and then decided to call it a night. Tom had his temporary job and he needed some sleep.

"Tom, do you think you might be able to come up to Maysville every once in a while? You know, for some more variety?"

"Yeah, why not, this seems like a fun place."

Tom was home by nine. He relaxed as Bella ran around and barked at all the noises in the woods. She was always excited to see him, especially when they sat outside at night and it wasn't hot. Tom didn't blame her. He wasn't too crazy about hot days, either. He wondered what Wilson would have in store for him in the morning. He was quite curious about the video he'd heard so much about, but didn't have the energy to search the internet for it. He woke around midnight and found himself still lying in the lawn chair. Bella was asleep at his feet, "Let's go to bed, girl."

• • •

Becky needed to get some fast cash. Her plan was to hit some of the local colleges. She could shoot down to Morehead quickly, and from there she would head over to Lexington. She hoped to spend less than three hours on the road. She had texted several of her regulars at Morehead, UK and Transylvania. She should be able to generate a good deal of cash. She hated driving so far in order to do business, but this would help her overcome this bad patch. Hopefully, by Wednesday or Thursday, she could once again be doing business as usual in her two to three county territory.

• • •

Wilson was in an unusually unaggressive mood toward Tom. He must still be feeling the effects of the weekend, Tom surmised. This morning, they were going to gather up some marijuana plants that just happened to be growing wild in some nearby corn rows. He and Wilson even shared a laugh or two about the fact that marijuana was growing wild all over the county. Lately, the Kentucky State

Police were getting more involved. They utilized a helicopter, which enabled them to fly overhead and spot plants from the air. The Marijuana Eradication Task Force supposedly flew over the entire state searching for plants. It did this under the authority of the Cannabis Suppression Branch of the KSP.

Wilson was starting to wonder whether he'd been wrong about Padgett. He didn't seem like such a bad guy. Maybe he should try and utilize Tom's knowledge and take advantage of his years of experience while they worked together the remainder of the week.

"Tom," he said, "maybe I was wrong about you. I had some preconceived ideas that may not have been merited. Will you accept my apology?" he asked.

"Sure Wilson. Maybe I had some wrong ideas about you, too, so why don't we let bygones be bygones."

The day went smoothly. Tom felt pretty good at the end of the day as he turned off Abners Mill into his drive.

•   •   •

The remainder of the week, Tom rode shotgun with Wilson. He looked forward to a night at the Gyp. Nick wasn't going to come this week. He had phoned and said something had come up. So, it would be just him and Becky.

He sat in the front yard and drank a beer. He was contemplating what he should do about the bottle of Oxy he'd found last week after Becky had left. Originally, he was going to say nothing, but that wouldn't solve anything. Maybe he would just have it sitting on the table in case Becky came by this evening. It might be interesting to see her reaction.

He thought about Miranda Johnson, and realized her life would never be normal. Sure, she shared some of the blame. But, would she have wrecked her car if she had only drunk beer? She might have, but then again, maybe not.

At the Gyp, Tom had finished his first beer when Becky arrived. He pulled out a stool so she could sit down and keep from falling in those shoes she insisted on wearing. After they talked for awhile, Tom suggested going back to his place. Maybe he'd throw something on the grill. This was a fantastic idea, as far as Becky was concerned. She was quite anxious to leave the Gyp. She said that one of the guys sitting at the bar seemed to be eyeing her. That was giving her the creeps.

Tom realized Becky hadn't driven her Mustang as he saw her approach an old Honda. He climbed into his Ford and felt gravel strike it as Becky accelerated out of the parking lot. Obviously, she was ready to get out of there. He was apprehensive about what awaited him at home. Becky had quite a wild look in her eyes. And, she obviously wasn't feeling much pain. Her car was nowhere to be seen as he cautiously rounded turns.

Tom found her lounging in a lawn chair. "What took you so long? Aren't you familiar with these parts?"

Becky seemed a lot less interested in drinking or eating once inside the trailer. She began undressing as she moved down the hall.

Tom told Bella, "Sorry girl. You need to entertain yourself for a few minutes." Bella longingly looked at the screen door as Tom closed it. When he entered the bedroom, he found Becky stretched out and lying naked on the bed.

"Why hello," he smiled and with fumbling fingers, tried to remove his clothing. He hoped that he was up for the challenge, recalling their previous marathon session. He felt much more confident tonight. He had gotten beyond his initial shyness. Why did he need to be shy? She was young and wild. He was not so young, and not so wild. What's the problem?

She surely was flexible. Tom wished he was the same. He watched her body arch and move beneath him like an advanced yoga instructor. He was happy with his performance; at least he had kept pace for about twenty minutes. But, after thirty or forty minutes of ultra, high intensity cardiovascular activity, Tom was spent, not Becky.

She propped herself up on an elbow. "I'm starving. Tom, would it be ok if I took a shower?"

Maybe he needed some of that Viagra, especially if Becky continued to visit. "Sure. There's a towel on the shelf over the toilet. I'll be right outside."

He threw his clothes on, grabbed a beer, and started for the door, noticing the pill bottle on the table. He wondered what Becky's reaction would be. He waited outside while he petted Bella and sipped his beer. He heard the shower stop and the bathroom door open. The walls were paper thin. At last, Becky stepped out into the yard. She seemed a lot less energized.

"Hey, would you like a beer?"

"Sure, that'd be great."

Tom handed her a beer. "What would you like to eat, hamburgers or chicken breasts?"

"Oh, I don't know. I'm not really that hungry, now."

"I thought you were starving."

"I was hungry, but I guess I must have lost my appetite." They studied one another for a moment before Becky spoke. "I see you found that bottle of pills? What do you think of me now?"

"That depends on what you do with the pills. Are they for you, or are they for sale?"

"What? You mean, you think I sell pills?" She sounded hurt.

"I don't know what to think. That's one hell of a big bottle of Oxy, especially for carrying around in your purse."

"Tom, I think I'd better be going. I can't believe you think such things about me."

"Look, Becky. I'm not suggesting anything. You tell me. Why do you have all those pills?"

"This isn't going anywhere. I'm going home."

"Are you alright to drive?"

"Of course I'm alright. Why wouldn't I be?"

Tom watched Becky snatch up her purse and fidget for her keys. Then she tromped off to her car.

"Becky, be careful."

"Yeah, like you give a shit about me being careful." She slammed her door and threw a slew of gravel Tom's way as she fishtailed out the drive. After she cleared the ditch, she floored her car and headed back toward the Gyp. Tom stood and watched as her tail lights rapidly faded. He hoped she'd make it home okay.

• • •

Becky was furious that Tom would assume such things about her. It didn't matter if they were true or not. It was the sense of betrayal she felt. Becky knew that she was far from perfect, but who was he even to suggest such a thing. She was driving too fast. Her rear tire dropped over the lip of the road when she rounded a turn. She corrected, accelerating out of the mistake. She continued accelerating as she crested the hill a mile or so from the Gyp. Again, Becky questioned, what made him think he could judge her? Wrapped in her thoughts, she forgot the poorly marked rail crossing ahead. Seconds later, her car wildly bounced over the tracks.

• • •

Tom slowly walked into the kitchen and grabbed another beer. He noticed that the bottle of pills was gone. He figured that the brief relationship he and Becky had shared might also be gone. Maybe he should have flushed the damn things and been done with it. Tom scratched Bella's stomach as he looked at the stars. Becky surely had gotten worked up. Had he really been that hard on her? He hoped she hadn't taken any pills before she left.

He recalled some of the arguments he and Darlene had over the years. He remembered how mad it would make Darlene when she realized that he was right and she was wrong. Becky behaved the exact same way. But, he knew that drugs probably played a part in it.

•   •   •

The car's wheels barely touched pavement as Becky tried to fight for control of her car. There was nothing to stop the car as it went airborne over the shoulder of the road before it crashed back to earth farther down into the woods. The car rolled twice, then broadsided a stand of trees, breaking them all off at the base.

Becky's thoughts raced as she tried to remember whether she had fastened her seatbelt. Somehow, the car continued moving. It gathered speed again and rolled toward the Licking River. Finally, her car slammed into a tree, which stopped it cold. The old Sycamore had survived over a hundred years and wasn't about to give ground to a Honda.

•   •   •

Wilson received the call around ten o'clock. Thank God he hadn't been working on another video. He arrived on the scene at the same time the life squad did. After they had all climbed down the hillside and had gotten to the car, they found an injured female. The paramedics were confident they would be able to extract the woman and safely transport her to Nicholas County Hospital.

As the EMTs worked to stabilize the woman, Wilson examined the mangled car with his light. He noted a strong presence of alcohol on the victim's breath. He also found a large bottle of Oxycontin lying on the passenger's side floor. He put the bottle into a zip lock bag. As she was lifted into the ambulance, Becky woke and realized what had happened.

CHAPTER 10

Albert Rankin couldn't believe what he'd just read in the *Courier*. The obituary contained a bio about his high school buddy, Jack Estep. He was stunned. After reading it, he finally put two and two together. First, there was an article about the unidentified victim of a meth lab accident. That had occurred over off of Abners Mill Road, a couple weeks back. Now this, Estep's death, he was just twenty-seven.

So, old Jack had made a fatal mistake. He remembered a conversation he had with Jack a few years back. It was about how stupid it was to have a meth lab in your house. Jack told him that he had a foolproof way of making meth. And, he could do it without getting caught. Albert sat and contemplated, remembering his high school days with Jack.

They had been kind of close in high school. Neither one of them was a jock. Sometimes they hung out together and looked for things to do. Yeah, back then, it was pretty easy to get into trouble, but they both managed to steer clear of it. Sure, there were occasional run-ins with the cops, but that was just part of growing up in Carlisle.

Albert's mother was nothing like Jack's mom. She didn't care what he did after high school. As far as Albert's mom was concerned, he should quit school and start bringing home some money. He recalled how envious he felt around Jack when his mom was drunk and she started to hound him about bettering himself. Jack hated that. Albert loved it. Secretly, he wished she'd been his mom.

Albert thought of the different paths they'd taken after graduating. He remembered how Jack rubbed it in about going to engineering school at the University of Kentucky. On a scholarship even. Albert's grades weren't as good as Jack's. But, he still landed a good job at Fed Ex in Lexington. Too bad the job only lasted for six months. Who would have thought that his truck would have gotten rear-ended by a Home Depot truck?

He remembered that awful December day clearly. He was stopped on the side of the road. He had called dispatch to verify some directions. It was a cold day with blowing snow, so he pulled his van far off the road, onto the shoulder. Obviously, he hadn't pulled over far enough. The big Home Depot truck slid toward him. It wasn't the driver's fault. He may have been speeding, but the patch of ice was what kept him from stopping.

●　　　●　　　●

Becky was very lucky. At least, that's what the doctor had told her. She had a fractured collarbone, two broken ribs, internal bleeding and facial lacerations, requiring twenty-five stitches. Somehow, the number of injuries didn't make her feel all that lucky. The doctor also indicated that the injuries could all be treated with medication and prolonged bed rest.

How was she supposed to take care of business if she was stuck in bed? Well, they said that she required medication, so where the hell was it? She definitely needed some meds. She pressed the call button. A nurse came in and asked her what she needed.

"I need some pain medication because the dosage you've given me doesn't appear to be working."

"The doctor will be in to see you shortly. He'll review your chart and determine what, if any, additional medication you'll need."

"Listen, honey, I take stronger medication if I have a headache than what you're giving me through this damned IV."

"I'm sorry, ma'am. The doctor will be with you soon."

Becky lay back and felt her ribs throb harder due to her increased agitation. She needed to get out of here. Where was her purse? She rang the nurses' station.

The duty nurse returned. She was clearly getting aggravated.

"Can I help you, ma'am?"

"I need my purse. Do you know where it is?"

"Yes, it's in the bag at the foot of the bed."

"Well, can you hand it to me? I sure as hell can't reach it myself."

●　　●　　●

Wilson was off duty, but he needed to stop by the hospital. He wanted to clarify a thing or two about the accident that happened over on Abners Mill Road. Wilson hummed to himself while he walked to the nurses' station.

"Is Mrs. Adkins receiving visitors?"

Two nurses momentarily stared at him before they both broke into a fit of hysterical laughter.

They spoke in unison, "Sheriff that was one great video you put on."

Wilson was angry. He was not remotely amused. "Could one of you ladies kindly give me her room number?"

"It's 107, but I don't believe you'll find her in a very good mood."

"Young lady, I'll be the judge of that."

Becky had gone through her purse twice. She couldn't find her medicine. What could have happened to it? Just then, she heard a rap on the doorframe. She looked over and saw the sheriff standing in the door.

"Mrs. Adkins, would it be alright if I came in?"

"I guess so. The door seems to be open anyway."

Becky continued to rummage through her purse while the sheriff watched.

"Is there anything I might be able to help you find, Mrs. Adkins?"

"I don't think so, Sheriff, not unless you happen to have my meds?"

"As a matter of fact, I do have your meds. I took them as evidence last night when you had that unfortunate accident."

Becky couldn't believe what she had just heard the sheriff say. "You took my medication? Isn't that like against the law?"

"Normally maybe, but under the circumstances it was very lawful."

Becky threw her purse aside and wondered what he wanted with her. Wilson stood at the foot of the bed, and held his hat in his hand, as Becky glared at him. This was turning into a battle of wits.

Finally, Becky gave in. "What can I help you with, Sheriff? As if you couldn't tell, I'm not in the greatest shape at the moment."

"Becky, is it ok if I call you Becky?"

"You can call me whatever you like, as long as it gets you out of here and lets me get some rest."

●　　●　　●

Tom had enjoyed his breakfast. He and Bella were working it off by taking a long hike in the woods, covering several miles. He wondered how Becky felt today and was curious if she was still mad at him. "Don't go running off too far, Bella. It's bow season. I don't want someone mistaking you for a deer."

The heat of the summer finally appeared to be easing. Bella ran around with more energy than she had in months. Today, they were hiking along the abandoned county road close to where the meth lab explosion occurred. He saw several tree stands this morning. However, none of them were currently being used.

•   •   •

Wilson was getting ready with his first question, when the doctor walked in. He looked intently at Wilson. "Sheriff, I believe it might be best if the patient is allowed to rest. She's had a traumatic experience."

"I'd like to question the patient about the accident. This is a police matter."

"I understand that, Sheriff, but I'm also trying to access her overall condition in order to determine when she can go home."

Wilson didn't like being told what to do. "Doc, do you think she'll be released today?"

"That's a possibility, but most likely it will be tomorrow. Now, if you'll excuse us, Sheriff."

Wilson angrily left the room. Where'd that doctor come from anyway? And why do so many of them seem to be foreigners?

•   •   •

After the accident, it was determined that Albert had damaged discs that would require surgery. In hindsight, he regrettably realized that he would have been better off if he hadn't gone under the knife. But, the doctor had told him that the success rate was greater than ninety percent. Well, Albert had never been very lucky.

At first, his mother was frightened for him. She worried that he wouldn't be able to work anymore. Now, seven years later he was on disability for life. He was making a thousand dollars a month, doing nothing. Albert remembered how happy his mother was as she thought about that thousand dollars coming into their general fund. Yeah, he'd share that money with his mama that is until he got back on his feet. He moved back home with his mom. He worked at trying to walk again, meanwhile his good for nothing mom did nothing.

Even as he lay on his back trying to recuperate, his mom would bitch about how he'd never be able to earn enough money to live on. She got some money somewhere. He didn't know where and he didn't really care. As soon as he could move about without too much pain, he'd be out of there. She wouldn't see him or his money again.

When finally strong enough, he did move. He found an old trailer to live in on Cassidy Creek Road, bordering the Clay Wildlife Management Area. He knew additional ways to supplement his income, and he wasn't about to go down the way Estep had. Albert shared Estep's feeling about having a meth lab in your home, that it was a bad idea to cook meth in the place you lived.

After Albert moved into his trailer, he went to look for an old abandoned farm house. Albert was fortunate. He located a neglected house just a mile inside Robertson County. It was perfectly situated, a half mile down an overgrown gravel lane.

The house hadn't been visited once by anyone in the two years since he'd set up shop. Initially, he complained to himself about the daily drive. It took thirty minutes each way. But, as business increased, it proved more than worth it. Even though he cooked and sold it, Albert didn't take methamphetamines. Marijuana was his choice of medication. He had plenty of suppliers of pot from either Cassidy Creek Road or Mexico Road. Being a neighbor, they gave him a friendly discount.

• • •

Becky was appreciative for the doctor's intervention, "Thank you Doc. Can you prescribe stronger pain medication for me?"

"Mrs. Adkins, we have the blood work and tox screen that was performed on you. I realize you might need medicine for your possible addiction, but I will only be addressing the injuries sustained."

"But what about the pain, can't you help with that?"

"Look, I know the level of anxiety you're under is difficult, but we are not a detoxification unit. Also, the medication you are being given for internal bleeding could possibly be compromised if mixed with unknown toxins."

After the doctor left, Becky closed her eyes and once again tried to sleep. *Bastard, who the hell is he to tell me what I need, or what my body can take?* She was exhausted, but sleep wouldn't come. She ached and was perspiring. She felt sick to her stomach. *What had they given her?* She wasn't sure whether or not she had fallen asleep.

Again, there was a knock on the door and the Doctor entered. "Mrs. Adkins, I've reviewed all your charts and I'm releasing you this afternoon. Maybe you can call and make arrangements for someone to pick you up?"

At least the sheriff hadn't taken her phone. She looked at the screen before dialing Adam.

●   ●   ●

Tom decided that he'd take up bow hunting again. The season had just gotten underway. It sure would feel nice to spend some time alone in the woods. His recent hikes with Bella had rekindled the desire he felt he'd nearly lost. He looked at some archery equipment online and was surprised at how much it had changed over the years. The equipment was quite pricy, too. He was amazed that you could easily spend five-hundred dollars, and that was only for the bow. Then, there were all the other accessories that were needed; such as sights, arrows, a tree stand, camo clothing, etc. Whatever happened to the $150 bow kits? They included everything.

Years ago, when he was a younger man, Tom owned a PSE compound bow. He always had good luck with it. So, he looked at various websites to see what they offered. He read all about the specifications, such as let off and fps of the new bows and was amazed. He last remembered let off of something like 30% being significant, now that was as high as 80%. And the velocity of the arrows; some of them were 350 fps. Man that was zipping. He liked to shop on-line, but he really needed to see the new bows in person.

He decided to drive down to Lexington and check out some of the sporting goods stores.

•   •   •

Becky was finally home resting, no thanks to Adam. He hadn't answered or returned her call. She left him a message about her accident. She told him she needed a ride home, but obviously he didn't care. Maybe those thoughts, about them being able to just co-exist in the same house, weren't as realistic as she'd originally thought. Luckily, Zane still had wheels. And for twenty bucks and a couple of pills, he agreed to help her out.

"That's what friends are for, right?" he said as he stuffed the twenty dollars in his shirt pocket.

At least he was patient enough to watch her hobble into the house. Zane sat in his car and watched through the rearview mirror.

Becky lay on the sofa in the living room. From there, it was easier for her to get up and go to the bathroom. Her bed was too high off the floor. She had visions of falling from the bed and reinjuring herself. She was trying to temper her own home medication. She didn't want to go overboard, while home convalescing. She could move about very slowly, but it was difficult. She had a sling for her fractured shoulder, along with the aspirin, or whatever weak-ass pain medication the doctor prescribed for her. If everything went according to plan, she should be good as new in about six weeks. She'd just have to take her chances with the internal bleeding. Her own medication was much more effective than the stuff she'd been prescribed. What's the worst that could happen, anyway? At least the sheriff shouldn't come poking his nose around, especially here in Fleming County.

•   •   •

Tom got all the equipment he needed to start hunting. Now, all he needed was some practice. He felt he was getting as impulsive as an old woman. That morning, the hunting thought initially intrigued him and by afternoon, he had purchased everything he needed. He got a PSE bow and some Easton carbon arrows. He also bought some field tips for practicing, along with some Phantom 125 grain 4 blade broad heads. While he was in Dick's Sporting Goods, Tom examined some of the new-fangled mechanized broad heads. He thought about all the associated problems those tips could cause if conditions weren't absolutely perfect. He couldn't find the broad heads he'd used years ago, the Razorback Five. He couldn't imagine how, but maybe the manufacturer had gone out of business.

He finished setting up the target, just north of his trailer. Bella was curious about the odd contraption he was messing with as he prepared to practice. Tom finished putting the field tips on and planned to get the feel of the bow, shooting at thirty paces. Bella watched as he pulled back on the bow and let the first arrow fly. Two inches left of bulls-eye. Not bad, especially considering he hadn't shot in thirty years. Even though the bow was quiet, Bella was still leery of it. He finished his first round. He'd grouped six arrows in a four inch pattern. Not bad for an old guy. Maybe this high tech bow would actually help him become a better shot?

CHAPTER 11

Monday morning

Wilson rolled up Route 32 toward Flemingsburg. His destination was Becky Adkins' house. He smiled to himself and wondered whether or not she'd be happy to see him. Probably not, but he had a job to do. Just because she had an accident and had gotten herself all messed up, didn't change the fact that she'd committed a crime. He shook his head. People actually felt that way. Just because they got hurt while all drunk or doped up, they felt that somehow they deserved to be felt sorry for. No, the law didn't operate that way, and he was paying a house call to remind Mrs. Adkins of that fact.

• • •

Becky felt a little better, probably the result of her self-medicating, but that was okay. The pill regimen she put herself on was lower than her normal dose. She wasn't having any withdrawal problems, so maybe the other medication the doctor prescribed contained something she was used to? She was going to take it easy for a few more days before she went back to work. She had clients that depended on her and she depended on them. It was a complimentary situation. She lifted her head slightly.

Did someone just pull in the drive? Surely Adam wasn't home finally coming to check on her. She struggled to get to her feet, being careful not to wrench her shoulder. Then she began her slow shuffle to the door.

• • •

Wearing a lightweight camouflage coverall and a little face paint, Tom was well hidden. He didn't really expect to see much today. This was more of an exploratory mission. He hadn't done any serious scouting in these woods. The morning was cool, so why not give it a try? His bow only weighed five or six pounds, even with four arrows in the quiver. He remembered his first compound bow, a very old four-wheel Jensen. It had to have weighed twelve or thirteen pounds. He stopped moving and watched because he had just spooked a couple of deer. Well, it didn't matter. He was just doing a trial run, anyway.

●　　●　　●

Before she even reached the door, Becky could see the sheriff's hat that he held in his hands. Ever the gentleman, she muttered to herself. When she finally got to the door, she spoke through the glass, "Yes, Sheriff? Is there something I can help you with?"

"Why good morning, Becky, how are you feeling this morning?"

"What do you want Sheriff?"

"I would just like to ask you a few questions. Would it be alright if I came in?"

Becky really didn't feel up to entertaining the sheriff. But, she knew he probably wouldn't leave until he got what he came for. She unlatched the door and began the slow trek back to the relative comfort of the couch.

Wilson entered and waited for Becky to get comfortably back on the couch, before he leaned back in the recliner.

"This is a nice place. Is your husband around?"

"No, Sheriff. My husband's not here. Did you come all the way out here to talk about my house and my husband?"

"Neither. I was just trying to make conversation."

Becky didn't like Wilson's way of making conversation. She glowered at him.

"Mrs. Adkins, in case you've forgotten, there's the little matter that involves you over in Nicholas County. As of yet, it hasn't been resolved."

"Oh Sheriff, I'd almost forgotten about that, how silly of me."

Wilson frowned at the snide remark, "Well, let me refresh your memory."

●   ●   ●

Tom enjoyed a relaxing morning until his phone rang. After he finished the call, he wasn't as happy as he'd been. It seemed there was one final document that was either improperly signed, or wasn't signed in his divorce decree. Apparently, the document needed to be addressed. This meant that he had to go to Mt. Sterling. He would unfortunately have to stop by the courthouse and face Darlene. Then, they could both sign it and be legally divorced. Well, he guessed he'd better get his ass over to the courthouse before something tragic happened to him. In that case, Darlene would become heir to all his worldly goods. It had been quite a while since he'd seen Darlene. He wasn't exactly looking forward to seeing her now, but apparently, it had to be done.

"Come on, Bella. Let's go for a ride in the truck." At least someone should be happy with this adventure. He should look at the bright side. Maybe he, Darlene and the Mayor could go out to lunch. Bella hung her head out the window as they drove through the countryside. She really enjoyed looking at cows, from a distance that is.

Darlene stood in the courthouse with her stoic expression that he remembered so well. Man, it was great to get the final paperwork straightened out. He was out of there fast, really fast. Not a word was spoken, just like old times.

●   ●   ●

Albert sold his drugs mainly in the county, where he felt the most secure. He occasionally ventured into Carlisle, but he was wary of the police presence there. However, he was getting more comfortable working in town. He felt the way he did deliveries made it difficult to connect anything to him.

One of his most effective methods of communication was texting his clients. Albert made a point to text moments before the drop. Even if the police had a way of tracking his phone, they would be hard pressed to catch him. He usually parked his car in a remote location. From there, he would send the text. Then he could walk around town and take care of his business in a matter of minutes.

•　　•　　•

"Becky what were you doing last Friday night before you wrecked your car?" Wilson asked.

"I was coming home from the Gyp Joint."

"Excuse me, but you were coming from the opposite direction when your car went crashing into the woods. How's it possible that you were leaving the Gyp Joint?"

"Ok, I'd been visiting a friend. I was on my way home and must have fallen asleep."

"Do you mind telling me who this friend might be?"

"Yes I do. What's my friend got to do with anything?"

"Becky, you do your share of pills and alcohol, don't you?"

"No more than I can handle."

"So, do you think there's a chance that this friend could have spiked your drink?"

"Why would he do that?"

Wilson smiled at Becky as he asked, "So, do you mind telling me who *he* might be? Wouldn't it be nice to wipe the slate clean and put the blame elsewhere?"

"What are you talking about, put the blame elsewhere? How can that happen?"

"Becky, I'm the Sheriff and I have a lot of influence in what happens in the county. I also know that many of the Gyp's clients live on Abners Mill. Does the name Tom Padgett mean anything to you?"

Becky felt positive her reaction betrayed her. She was in dangerous waters now, and should she really trust Wilson? "Yes, I know him."

"Were you with him Friday night?"

• • •

Tom left Mt. Sterling. He hoped this would be the last visit for a while. With a little luck, maybe this would be the last time he'd have to see Darlene. The thought quickly faded. He realized this would never happen. They had a child together, and children eventually got married and had children of their own. A grandchild, how would old Darlene handle that? It would positively cramp her style. He laughed about her selfishness and wondered how she'd get out of the obligation when Andy asked her to babysit for a weekend. Tom was confident that Andy would not be bringing any *would-be-wife* to visit him. Even if Andy did get married and had children, Tom was sure that he wouldn't be asked to have anything to do with the child.

Bella was stretched out and slept on the rear floorboard. She loved road trips. Some of the old trailers out there made his look luxurious. He turned north on Upper Lick Road after passing through Moorefield. After about three miles, Tom turned left and traveled northwest on Cassidy Creek Road which bordered the Clay Wildlife Management Area.

He had applied for a special quota hunt at Clay. He heard it was supposed to be a good hunting area. Tom followed Cassidy Creek until it dead ended at Route 32. He was a couple of miles from the Gyp Joint. He glanced at the clock, 11:30. Why not? Bella wouldn't mind if he only stopped for a couple.

•   •   •

Wilson thought about how to proceed. He had to get this story right. "So, you went into Padgett's trailer? And the pills were right there on the table?"

"Yes. Then, we sat outside and he went into the house a few times to get us beer. I guess he could have crushed some and then put it in my beer."

"So how long were you there that night?"

"Oh I'm not sure, probably two hours."

Wilson was getting excited, "So, when you left, did you take the pills? Or did Padgett drop them in your purse?"

"He must have put them there. I would never carry around that many pills."

Wilson thought to himself. So, he planted the evidence. "Becky you're a user, aren't you?"

"Yes, I've already told you that."

"But, you also told me that you're not an abuser. So, Padgett was getting back at you for some reason. What do you think that might be?"

"Well, he could have been upset because I told him I didn't want to see him anymore."

"So, you had been having a relationship?"

"Yes, but it was only for a short time, because he started getting too serious."

"So Padgett was feeling jilted. Does that sound about right?"

"I guess so. He did seem rather upset when I left that night."

Wilson got up and paced. "So, let me think about this. Jilted lover sets up girlfriend to get revenge. Does that sound about right?"

"Yeah, Sheriff, but what's going to happen to me? And, what's going to happen to him?"

"Oh, if this plays out right, Padgett should be the only one that suffers."

●　　●　　●

Tom made sure to open the back windows so Bella had some fresh air, before he went inside the Gyp.

Steve gave him a surprised look as he pulled up a stool and sat down. "Budweiser Tom?"

"Yeah, thanks Steve."

After a moment, Steve asked, "What'd you think about the wreck on Abners Mill Friday night?"

"What wreck? I didn't hear anything about a wreck."

"Yeah that lady, the one you left with on Friday night, wrecked her car up by the railroad tracks."

"Becky? Is she alright?"

"Think so. It sounds like she got sort of banged up, but nothing life threatening."

Tom recalled that she was awfully loaded. If they did blood work, she could be in big trouble.

He drank slowly from his beer and remembered how angry Becky was when she left his house. Man, she could reverse her moods in a heartbeat. Lucky for her, at least she hadn't killed herself. Tom was sure the drugs combined with the alcohol had contributed to her state of mind. She had totally flipped. Maybe she did need to be on drugs, but not Oxycontin. He believed that Becky might be suffering from depression. He wasn't a doctor, but he had seen Becky swing from wild to mild and back again in no time. He was glad that she was alright, and hopefully the trouble she now found herself in would help her get her life straight.

Tom climbed back into his truck which woke Bella, "Let's go home, girl."

He thought it might be a nice afternoon to scope out the woods, to see if there were some good hunting sites close to home. He liked the looks of the Clay WMA. Maybe he'd go over there tomorrow to find out about hunting. Tom knew that there were special hunts, but what if a person just wanted to hunt during the regular seasons? Were there any restrictions? He checked his laptop and found no restrictions on bow hunting at Clay, except for when the quota hunt was taking place. "Come on, Bella. Let's go see what we can scare up in the woods." Bella suddenly started breathing like she'd just run a mile. She always did that when she got excited.

•   •   •

Wilson was in his office. He pondered what his approach should be regarding Padgett. It'd be best to get him away from his house in order to question him. Wilson wondered if Padgett would be willing to cooperate. He really needed Padgett's cooperation because some of the accusations seemed a little thin. He wondered if Becky could be a reliable witness. But, if Becky wanted to save her ass, she needed to help him help her. He decided to give Padgett a call to see if he'd agree to come into town for some questioning.

•   •   •

Tom answered on the second ring, and wished that he hadn't. What's with Wilson, he thought they had finally buried the hatchet? But no, here he comes again, wanting him to come into town for some questioning. Tom was really getting tired of Wilson. What's wrong with the guy? He wasn't sure why, but he volunteered to go into Carlisle for a few questions, tomorrow. A few questions about what, he could only surmise. But, some of them would concern Becky. He was almost sure of that. Yeah, good old Wilson, he wouldn't divulge anything about the upcoming interrogation. He obviously didn't want Padgett to be able to fabricate some defense strategy. Tom wasn't going to lose any sleep worrying about whatever Wilson was up to. He pulled a beer from the fridge and stared distractedly into the nearby woods.

• • •

The following morning

Wilson was up early. He was feeling great. Hell, he might even work out. When he'd first taken the job as sheriff, he was quite a bit more active. Maybe after Padgett had been taken care of, he could get back to the business of being sheriff. He bought a bow flex machine last year, but used it only once or twice. It'd been gathering dust ever since. He hated the damned machine and seriously doubted that there were unlimited exercises you could perform with it. The only thing Wilson got out of the thing was sore muscles and a aching back. But, he was going to work up a good sweat today. Could he make Padgett do the same?

• • •

Tom took a hike early, making sure to keep Bella in check so she didn't run off and end up getting shot. He was preoccupied about the so-called meeting with Wilson. It seemed that all sorts of people were finding issue with him lately. Maybe he needed a change of lifestyle or something. Hell, he didn't remember being this controversial, even when he was busting hoods on the streets of Mt. Sterling. The Mayor, Darlene, Wilson, and now Becky; they all got totally agitated just being in his presence. What was he doing wrong? Maybe he needed to start going to church or something. Maybe *the man* upstairs could help explain some things to him?

• • •

Wilson worked out for about fifteen minutes and was already sweating profusely. Based on what he saw reflected in the mirror next to the Bow Flex, it was no wonder. It looked like he'd gained ten pounds since he'd made that video. Well, at least this morning he was disciplined enough to complete his workout. As he tightened his belt, he winced and noticed he had gained another notch on it. He went to the kitchen, grabbed a cup of coffee and stepped out on the back porch. It was peaceful out here this morning. Hopefully his neighbor, the old lady that had made so much fun of his video, was still asleep.

• • •

After his hike, Tom enjoyed his morning coffee. It would have been even better if he hadn't agreed to meet Wilson. But, he was just going to take everything in stride, not let Wilson try and get under his skin.

Bella was lying on her back and scratched her way across the yard. It seemed that her never ending allergies were kicking up again. He better take her to the vet before she drove herself and him absolutely crazy. Those damned allergy shots worked like clockwork. Thirty days, and boom she'd need another one. He needed to ask the vet if there was some kind of new and improved, multi-month, time-released allergy formula available.

Tom entered the courthouse and noticed Wilson chatting with someone in the lobby. He just pulled up a chair and waited. Wilson strolled past and entered his office. No good morning, Tom. Not even a morning, Padgett. Okay, so Wilson seemed to have another hair up his ass and was going to be all business. Tom followed him into the office.

Wilson held up a hand to stop him. "Padgett, we're going where we can carry on a conversation in private."

Where might that be in Carlisle, the East End? Tom followed in Wilson's wake as he waltzed out the door and crossed the street, "Where are we going, Wilson?"

"Padgett, the Chief has agreed to let me use their interrogation room."

Tom shook his head, "Interrogation room. Ok, Wilson. I'll play along with your game."

Tom couldn't help notice that Wilson not only carried a notebook, but also a file folder. He wondered if *mister efficiency* happened to have a pen or pencil. Wilson walked down the hallway like he was some sort of cracker-jack lawyer with his obviously handicapped client in tow. After they entered the room, Wilson motioned for Tom to take a seat.

Tom reluctantly complied before asking, "Mr. Sheriff, Sir, could you gets me a glass a water, fore you turn on the hot lights?"

Wilson ignored the jab, content to position his paperwork for whatever he had cooked up in his devious mind.

●　　●　　●

Becky had been home for a few days. Adam hadn't come to the house once, as far as she could tell. Where in the world did that lowlife go? Where was he now when she needed him most? She got up and hobbled down the hallway to their bedroom. She opened Adam's closet and was shocked to find it was empty. Why would he do that to me? Leave with no explanation. It just isn't right. Did he have another woman that he was living with? Was he going to file for a divorce? Becky hated the silent treatment more than anything else, and she always had. All Adam had to do when they argued was clam up and it would nearly drive her berserk.

●　　●　　●

Tom watched patiently as Wilson ambled about the room, trying to get his thoughts together. Suddenly, something must have clicked in his mind and he appeared ready for the charade to begin.

"Padgett, I have a few questions to ask you. Are you okay with this?"

"I'm here aren't I? I really have much better things to be doing."

Wilson let out a breath, "Alright then, let's get started. Where were you on Friday?"

"Any particular Friday, or do you want me to pick one?"

"Last Friday, damn it!"

"Ok, Sheriff. Do you have a time in mind? That might be pertinent to this question."

"Friday afternoon and evening. Does that help clarify things for you?"

"Yes it does. I was at home. Then I went to the bar."

"What bar would that be, Padgett?"

"Well since, there aren't that many bars around, I generally go to one that's close. So, on that particular evening, I chose the Gyp Joint."

"So you're admitting that you were at the Gyp Joint?"

"Yeah, is there a law against that, Wilson?

Wilson scribbled on his pad as Tom watched. "And who did you meet at the Gyp Joint?"

"Oh, you're testing me Wilson? Let's see, there was Steve, John, I believe that's his name, and then there was Mike."

"What lady did you meet at the Gyp Joint?"

"Well, there was only one lady there, but I didn't technically meet her. We'd met previously."

Wilson started to get red in the face, "Was the lady Becky Adkins?"

"Yes it was, Sheriff. Does that mean I can go now?"

Wilson scribbled again with his face two inches from the paper as he gripped the pencil like it was a hammer. "So, you were at the Gyp Joint and you met Becky Adkins while you were there?"

"Yes. I hope this allows you to tie up that loose end that seems to be unraveling."

"I'm not finished yet Padgett. What did you do that evening?"

"We each had a couple of beers and talked about how our week had been, you know, things like that."

Wilson glared at him, so Tom asked, "Anything else, Sheriff?"

"Obviously, I'm not making myself clear. Padgett, did you take Becky Adkins home with you last Friday night?"

"No, I did not."

Wilson gripped his pencil in his fist as he tried to write legibly. Looking up from his notepad Wilson verified, "So, you're saying you didn't take Mrs. Adkins home with you?"

"That's right, Sheriff, she drove herself."

The pencil in Wilson's hand snapped. Again he glared at Tom. "So, Mrs. Adkins was at your home last Friday night?"

"Yes, she was."

Wilson grabbed another writing instrument. He now held a pen in his paw. At least the pen appeared more substantial. When he finished writing, he again glanced at Tom before asking, "What did you and Mrs. Adkins do on Friday night?"

•　　•　　•

Becky was beginning to get nervous, especially since she seemed to be scheming with Wilson. He was quite the cagey character. Why would he want to help her anyway? It just didn't make sense. Granted, Tom deserved to be punished after the distrust he had shown her, but what were the real chances of him getting in trouble? Someone was going to go down, so better Tom than her. Maybe she should just get in her car and drive. Pack up her clothes, lock the house and get out of town. She could start fresh someplace else, especially now with Wilson on her case. The only problem, was she well enough to drive? She looked around the house and tried to figure out what she'd need to take if she really planned on disappearing.

She was happy that the hospital had telephoned. Her stitches needed to come out, the next day. It had totally slipped her mind. She was told that if the stitches stayed in too long, then more scarring was possible and it could leave a zigzag-like trail. Becky told the woman on the phone that she couldn't get to a clinic because she couldn't drive. The woman told Becky that she would contact a home health provider in the area and see if she could get one to come to her home. "Thank you." Becky felt relieved.

She wasn't ready to drive yet. She looked at her reflection in the mirror, wondering if she could remove the stitches. She quickly determined there was no way to do that. Trying to do such delicate work while watching your own reflection, would be nearly impossible.

Becky thought about Adam and felt not only hurt, but disappointed that he hadn't even checked up on her. Well, his clothes were gone. That was a pretty strong indication of how he felt. Tom also seemed to have forgotten her. Men, they were all the same. All they ever thought about were themselves. But, she couldn't worry about that now. She needed to plan. She had big changes to make before her house of cards came crashing down. She wasn't confident that Wilson would be able to catch Tom in his snare of deceit. She suddenly decided she should ponder those troubles later, now that her dose of self-prescribed medication was beginning to take hold. She'd just sit back for a moment and appreciate the rush.

CHAPTER 12

Albert should probably be grateful, but never the less, he felt stressed. He had more business than he could handle. He realized that some of the new users that sought him out were former Estep clients. Estep had been out of business for two to three months, and his former clients were scrambling to find replacement drugs. There were plenty of people cooking meth around the county, but some of the formulations were questionable. Some of the dealers just weren't reputable. As far as he could tell, he had had only one client die over the years that he'd been selling meth. That client had been twenty-years old and had overdosed a couple of years ago. He thought about the death and remembered. You can't take this shit personally. At least that's what he'd always heard.

The product he delivered was cleaner than the majority of the junk being pushed out there. Yeah, he incorporated some bad ingredients in the process, but he steered clear of some of the really nasty stuff. Sure, he had to use some harsh materials to try to mask the ephedrine, in order to make it harder to detect. But, things like battery acid and drain cleaners were used sparingly. He smiled, thinking about the humaneness of that gesture. Albert used more friendly products, such as bleach, paint thinner and lye. He laughed thinking about the greenness of it all, his so-called healthier process. Yes, all the various mixes and concoctions accomplished the same thing, and that was to get the user to a place they wanted to be.

● ● ●

Woozy was already dreading that day, the day that Jimmy would be released and once again control her life. The two times that she'd visited him over the past three and a half weeks seemed reasonable to her. Jimmy needed to understand her point of view. He had beaten her pretty badly, so why did he deserve to have frequent visits? Each time she visited, he had been on his best behavior. He would tell her how much he loved her, or how much he missed her. She wasn't stupid. She should probably cut her losses and get away from Jimmy. But in some strange twisted way, she still needed him, needed Jimmy in her life. She pictured him smiling and saying he loved her. She couldn't recall the last time he'd actually shown her or told her that, except since he'd been in jail.

She tried to talk with some of her co-workers about how Jimmy treated her and that she'd done what she did in order to survive. They weren't even remotely sympathetic. It seemed they even thought she got what she deserved. It made her wonder how much abuse was a woman supposed to take? She still wrestled with the fact that she was responsible for Jimmy being in jail. None of the other women she knew would even have considered subjecting their abusive husbands or boyfriends to such hardship. She worried that Jimmy might find support for what he had done, while he was in jail. All he needed was some additional empowerment. That would be the straw that might finally break her back.

• • •

After Woozy left, Jimmy was led back to his cell for some more damned *wait time*. So, it'd taken his wife three and a half weeks to show up for her second visit. What was the point of coming to see him at all? He told her he was sorry. What else was he supposed to do? Maybe she was being coached by some of that crowd she worked with. Well, he'll fix that in another week. So, his wife was obviously doing okay without him around. Was she having an affair or something while he was rotting in this cage? Maybe she's gotten all independent and thinks she doesn't need him around anymore. Jimmy wasn't sure, but something was cooking in that head of hers.

He was tired of acting like he was really sorry, because he wasn't. That was just his dog and pony show for those stinking guards. Yeah, he missed Woozy, but after a night or two, he'd be all caught up with his sexual needs. Then he could begin the lessons. *Respect* that was lesson number one and *a woman needs to know her place* was lesson two. Jimmy hadn't gotten beyond lesson two, but he still had a few more days in this hellhole to get it figured out. He liked having her around, that is at least for sex, meals, and running errands, but beyond that she was more of a nuisance than anything. But there was one thing that Jimmy was absolutely sure about, if Woozy tried having him locked up again, he'd kill her.

• • •

Tom was frustrated with Wilson. He started to feel that volunteering for this meeting was going in the wrong direction. "Wilson, what does what I do with my free time, have to do with any of these questions?"

"That's what I'm hoping to find out, Padgett."

"I'll tell you what I'm going to do, I'll play along a bit longer, but, if I start feeling threatened, I'm out of here."

"I'm not threatening you, Padgett. I'm just trying to verify certain facts. So, back to my question, what were you and Becky doing at your place on Friday night?"

"Ok Wilson. But you're rapidly approaching my saturation point." Tom seriously considered saying something about Wilson's love life, but realized that wouldn't help matters. "Becky came over to my place to have drinks and maybe grill out."

"Did you do that, that is, have drinks and grill out?"

"No, it didn't work out exactly as planned. Before we grilled out, Becky decided to leave."

Wilson seemed to ponder this, "So, she just got up and said I'm leaving now, and that was the end of the evening?"

"Yes basically. Do you doubt what I'm telling you?"

"Yes. It just seems unlikely that anyone would even consider driving over to your trailer on that winding treacherous little road, just to have a couple drinks."

"What in the hell are you alluding to, Wilson?"

"What I mean is there obviously needed to be a better reason than that, for her to make that trip."

"What is it? What is it you need to hear? Okay, sex. She came over because she wanted to have sex. She desperately needed to have wild sex. Are you happy now?"

"Not quite, Padgett. So you had sex, and drinks. What else happened?"

"Nothing else happened, damn it."

"Don't get all testy, Padgett. What are you trying to hide?"

"Wilson, are you getting some kind of weird sexual pleasure from prying into the intimacies of my sex life?"

Now it was Wilson's turn to get angry as he considered his next line of attack. "Drugs, what drugs did you do that night?"

"Drugs, what are you talking about Wilson? I don't do drugs, unless you're grouping beer in the mix."

"No, not beer, I'm talking about the Oxycontin she got that night."

Tom had about enough of Wilson. He pounded his fists on the table. He stood and pushed in the chair. "Wilson, if you want to accuse me of something, you had better have some proof. As far as getting me to chat with you again, that's highly unlikely."

"I'm not finished with you, Padgett."

"But I'm finished with you, and unless you have some compelling reason for me to stay, I'm going."

"Let me tell you something, Padgett. I'm working on that. You haven't heard the last from me."

Tom left the Carlisle Police station and made his way home. He had no intention of staying there, though. He found Nick's phone number on his contacts list. Nick answered after several rings.

"Hey, Tom, long time no see."

"Hey, Nick, are you thirsty, or will you be thirsty in an hour or so?"

"You know, that sounds like a good idea. Want to come up to Maysville?"

"That's my plan. See you around eleven."

● ● ●

Nick wasn't expecting that call out of the blue, but it put him in a good mood. Now he had something to do, besides sitting home all alone in Flemingsburg. He turned the noisy vacuum back on and finished his monthly lap around the house. Did he have time to do that week-old pile of dishes? Why not? It would make him feel better about himself. Nick hummed as he finished. He would jump in the shower and feel like a new man. He wondered what Becky had been doing. He wondered if she and Tom were still seeing one another. He'd better hurry. He had one other stop to make before heading to O'Rourke's.

● ● ●

Woozy unconsciously applied her eyeliner and thought about Jimmy. In a way, she was looking forward to his homecoming, but, in more ways she wasn't. Sure they would have wild animalistic sex when he walked through the door, then it would be the same old, same old. He would complain about the way she dressed, the way she talked, the way she cooked, and the way she walked. She just couldn't please him. But, she knew better than to stick up for herself because that would really make him angry, especially if she questioned his authority. She was scheduled at O'Rourke's today at eleven, her only weekday shift. At least she would be preoccupied and not constantly thinking about Jimmy. She realized she had just a few more days, then no more freedom.

Woozy was wiping down the bar as Tom entered. She asked if he wanted a Budweiser. He nodded. She had a good memory. It was early and obviously slow this morning, so Tom asked her how things had been going for her.

"Well, I can't complain. Tending bar isn't an easy way to make a living. It seems to get tougher every day."

"I hear that, Woozy."

"So what about you, what do you do?"

"I'm a retired cop, so I try not to do too much."

"Cop, huh? Were you a good cop or a bad cop?"

"That usually depended on the scene. Anyway, now I'm just an old cop."

"Honey, you don't look so old to me." They laughed as Woozy grabbed him another Budweiser. Tom turned as he heard the door open.

Nick walked in the door. He was all smiles.

"Well, look what the dog drug in."

"You'll never guess where I've been."

"Nick, I have absolutely no idea."

"I've been at Wal-mart. I'm going to be a greeter."

Tom toasted Nick after Woozy handed him his beer. "I would have never guessed you were even interested in being a greeter. Do they let you greet if you're drunk?"

"Funny, Tom. I just needed something to do. You know, a couple days a week."

"Well, congratulations. Hey Woozy, Nick's going to be a Wal-mart greeter. Isn't that great?"

They all laughed as more people began to enter the bar for lunch.

"A bean counting greeter, that's interesting. Maybe you can hand out business cards as you greet people?"

Nick laughed, "I don't think so. That could be viewed as a conflict of interest." Nick jumped up and walked over to a nearby table. Some people he recognized had just sat down.

Woozy wiped the bar in front of Tom. "Woozy, I understand your husband's in jail?"

She stopped what she'd been doing, "Yes, so what about it?"

Tom looked her in the eye, "Let me tell you this, Woozy. You don't have to tolerate abuse, never."

Woozy seemed to relax and nearly broke down, "It's hard though. He gets out in just a few days, and I'm afraid."

"It'll be ok, Woozy. Trust me, it'll be ok."

For some reason, Woozy felt more confident hearing those words from Tom, a man she hardly knew. "Thank you."

Nick returned all smiles after boasting to friends about landing his greeter job.

•   •   •

Becky had quite the buzz going on, but she needed to concentrate. What were her chances of getting off the drug charges scot free? Would Tom really fall into Wilson's trap? Would he be that easy to entrap? Somehow she didn't think so. She tried to rationalize what had happened. She replayed Friday night's events over in her mind. *She went over to his place. They had had sex. Then she took a shower. Tom probably laced her drink while she was showering. Then he got mad at her because she wanted to go home. He wanted to cook something on the grill. Tom must have put the pills in her purse before she left his place. In her drugged condition, she fell asleep and crashed her car.*

Becky felt her story was at least plausible. Tom was a retired cop, but maybe he did have something to hide. She still worried about parts of the story. If anyone did a thorough investigation, would it hold up? She needed to be prepared, ready to flee. She had her car title and some clothes. All she needed were some toiletries and cosmetics. She could easily move across the border into Tennessee and set up shop there. Her shoulder was feeling better, but her ribs were still tender. Her left eye was black and swollen closed. She would look suspicious, wherever she went. Fortunately, the home health nurse had come and removed her stitches. She padded to the garage and opened the Mustang's door. Pain coursed through her body as she attempted to sit behind the wheel, even in her drugged state. She wouldn't be driving anywhere soon.

• • •

Tom was lost in thought when Nick returned and sat back down. Eventually he looked over at Nick and asked, "Did you hear about Becky?"

"No, I didn't hear anything. What about her?"

Tom took a moment before replying, "Friday night, she came back to my place. Then she had an accident on her way home."

"You're shitting me. Is she alright?"

"Yes, from what I've been told. She seems to be doing okay."

Nick ordered more beer before speaking, "So, how did you find out about the accident?"

"I stopped in the Gyp the other day and Steve told me about it. When Becky left my place the other night she was pretty messed up."

"Tom, you can't blame yourself for that. She's a grown woman."

"Oh, I know that Nick. But I seem to be having a hard time convincing the Nicholas County Sheriff of that."

"Wait a minute, how come the sheriff is involved with this?"

132

"Because when Becky wrecked her car, she was under the influence of both alcohol and drugs. She was also in possession of a controlled substance."

"I don't mean to sound heartless Tom, but she's a big girl. She's responsible for her own actions, isn't she?"

"Yeah normally, but in this instance it seems Sheriff Wilson wants to hang the blame elsewhere."

"What the hell, on you? Why would he want to do that?"

"I wish I knew the answer to that. Wilson's been dogging me since I moved into the county."

They both took sips of their beer and thought about the gravity of the situation.

"Tom, what can you do about Wilson?"

"That's a great question. I'm not sure. He's like that itch that just won't go away."

•　　•　　•

The next morning

Bella was extremely excited when Tom mentioned a walk in the woods. He actually had to be careful using the word *walk* even in a sentence around Bella. Because the word *walk* piqued her interest more than any other word. But today was beautiful, and he was ready for a long, satisfying hike. There didn't appear to be many bow hunters frequenting the area. He realized that during gun season, this would surely change. Just inside the woods, two deer bounded off. Tom watched as Bella excitedly gave chase before he called her, "Bella, Come."

She pranced toward him, holding her head high. She was proud of her deer chasing accomplishment. "Good girl, Bella."

Tom paused and looked around as the sunlight broke through the trees. It was so peaceful this morning. He listened to all the noises that surrounded him. This was why he lived in this isolated region. This was what was really important. Bella was onto something, and she was momentarily acting like a champion blood hound on a scent. He smiled as she smelled everything there was to smell. "Come on girl, let's go."

A few hundred yards further, a group of turkeys started to run, and so did Bella. She chased them till they were forced to take flight, crashing through the branches to escape the pest. Bella stopped and watched the big birds clear the trees before running back toward Tom. Once again she'd proven her worth, "Good girl, Bella."

After an hour or more, both he and Bella were tired, "Let's go home, girl." She led the way, taking a game trail as Tom walked the abandoned road. Suddenly, a cubby of quail burst out near Bella. It surprised her. No hero antics this time. Tom laughed, "Where's my prancing girl?"

● ● ●

Albert had been cooking for hours and he needed some fresh air. The vapors from cooking meth were potent. Meth production was anything but a neat process. There could be anywhere from five to seven pounds of chemical waste created in order to make one pound of meth. Marijuana was a much easier product to deal with. But, he didn't have the land or the inclination for farming, even in the recreational sense. Standing outside he coughed up some of the remnants of his evening cook. The air was clean outside the run down house, although when the wind shifted, you could smell the batch cooking that was for sure. Luckily, his lab was hundreds of feet from the road.

He was pleased with himself, pleased that he'd never been busted. Even if the cops did visit this place, they wouldn't find much. He stored everything that he produced elsewhere. And, he always cleaned up after a cooking session. Yeah, he was neat, nothing like most meth makers. If the cops tested the area looking for chemicals, they'd surely find traces of it. But so what, all kinds of people had meth labs around here. What was it they said? A meth lab was a hazardous waste site? And besides that he didn't own the place, he was just borrowing it. But he was tired with the commute. Albert decided to pack up and move operations into his trailer. He felt confident he could set up shop, and the police would never suspect it.

●   ●   ●

After Wilson hung up the phone, he was angry. Not just angry for what he'd been told, but also for the apparent lack of cooperation within the law enforcement community. He had sent the bottle of Oxycontin off to the lab with hopes of getting prints from it. Having those prints would have hopefully shown Padgett's involvement. But no, the smart aleck college boy didn't want to do the extra work, even though it would help Wilson catch a criminal. The lab tech had even gone as far as telling him that lifting fingerprints from prescription bottles was nearly impossible. Nearly impossible, did that mean the same thing as impossible? One thing was obvious to Wilson. The guy didn't want to be bothered. Maybe he should just take this matter higher up the ladder. But Wilson reconsidered. That might shine some unwanted light his way.

Wilson needed a break. What he really needed was for Padgett to make a mistake. He knew Padgett was one cool customer. He seemed to always maintain his control. Wilson needed to rattle him somehow, but how? Maybe if he let him learn some of the incriminating evidence he held against him. That might unhinge him. Maybe if Tom knew that Becky was going to testify against him that would change things. This was a tricky scenario and Wilson didn't want to show Padgett his hand. Yeah, if Padgett knew that Becky was out to save herself at all costs, that might shake him up. He had to think. He definitely needed an ironclad plan. Wilson felt Becky was the key. Maybe he needed to spend a little more time with her, in order to help Becky get her story down pat.

CHAPTER 13

Jimmy inhaled a long deep breath, smelling the Ohio River for the first time in twenty-eight days. Normally, he wasn't anxious to smell the river, but after four weeks inside, it smelled good. The *prisoner daycare* was less than a half mile from the river. Boy, it felt great to be out. His cell phone battery was nearly dead so he ended the call quickly. He didn't really expect the prison to keep his phone charged, but it might have been nice. A friend was picking him up. He probably wouldn't mind dropping by the liquor store. Jimmy needed a drink. Yeah, Woozy was going to be surprised to see him when she got home from work. He was looking forward to seeing her expression when she walked in the house, especially since they released him two days early. Maybe he'd even be lucky enough to catch her cheating on him. Wouldn't that be something?

Jimmy sat on the porch swing and sipped from the fifth of Jack. Boy, he'd almost forgotten how good whiskey tasted. Woozy wouldn't get home 'till about midnight. Maybe he'd just wander down to the bar and surprise her. He had to think about this, surprise her at the bar, or surprise her here at home? He was having fun just toying with the idea.

He tilted his head and took a long swallow, feeling the burn all the way to his gut. Boy, he sure did miss his whiskey. He was going to let Woozy know how much he missed it, too. Yeah, whiskey was just one of the things she'd deprived him of. Jimmy took another sip and remembered something he had nearly forgotten, the lesson plan he had in store for his wife. He'd only come up with two lessons, but as he sat there enjoying the Jack, he could surely come up with more.

●   ●   ●

Woozy was unenthusiastic and for good reason. Jimmy had made his triumphant entrance three nights ago and things were returning to normal, normal in the abusive sense that is. The night when she entered the house, she was surprised to find Jimmy half-drunk sitting on the couch in the dark living room. She turned on the light and there he sat smiling at her, as if he was saying, "'Honey, I'm home."

That night she was exhausted. It had been a rough night, but that didn't matter to Jimmy. He was going to get his rocks off, regardless if she wanted to partake or not. The following morning wasn't any better, as he complained about the eggs she made him, they were too damned runny. She wanted to flip the plate up into his greasy face.

Woozy found that she was actually anxious to go to work. That would give her more time away from Jimmy. She wished he would find a job, but that seemed unlikely. Jimmy had never held a job for more than a few weeks. He just couldn't get along with anyone. But, getting fired or whatever was never his fault.

Friday night

Woozy was scheduled six until closing. She should make some decent tips tonight. She hoped that Jimmy didn't come in looking for trouble. He just couldn't seem to get happy. The guy was forever angry. She wished she could understand why. Was it something she'd done? She thought about it while she obliviously served a couple of drinks. The door opened and Woozy heard familiar voices. Tom and Nick walked into O'Rourke's.

• • •

Wilson found Becky still couch-bound when he arrived that afternoon. She was more agreeable than the last time he'd visited, but not much. Her eyes were glazed over, so he hoped this wouldn't prove a waste of time. She unlatched the door and allowed him to enter. Wilson felt that this was a step in the right direction. He asked how she was feeling, and she started to get upset.

"Come on, Wilson. Get on with whatever it is you want."

Wilson smiled, but decided not to provoke her, "Becky, I thought we needed to go over some of the particulars from the night of your accident. You know, to make sure we're on the same page."

"I'm comfortable about what happened that night, why the additional training?"

"We just need to make sure that no mistakes are made, ones that might allow Padgett to get away."

So Becky and Wilson began conspiring in earnest to get Padgett. They both shared a common interest. Wilson wanted to bust Padgett, while Becky just wanted to save herself. Wilson drilled Becky about what had happened and when it had happened. Even though he hadn't been there, he was quite convincing. Becky found herself actually believing nearly everything he said. Wilson seemed to be enjoying himself as he corrected Becky about a particular item.

When they were finished, they both felt better about the chances of trapping Tom. Becky still wasn't fit to drive. Would she need to come to Carlisle? Wilson assured her not to worry about that just yet. He planned on having another go at Padgett soon.

● ● ●

Jimmy wasn't much happier now than he'd been when he was locked up. Woozy still hadn't learned how to cook, so what was she good for? He flipped through the stations on the cable. What is this shit? Nothing on here's worth watching. The first night had been 'so so', but as he expected, the thrill of it all quickly faded.

He walked into the kitchen and peered into the fridge, nothing but crap. What was he supposed to eat? He was containing himself pretty well in light of what she'd put him through. He'd only slapped her once, and it'd been almost four days since he'd been home. Oh yeah, he had roughed her up a little bit the other night. But, she understood he was doing it for her own good.

Jimmy thought it might be good to go out that evening, let the people in town know that he was back. Maybe he could even catch Woozy up to her old tricks of flirting with any available man. She probably would be on her best behavior though, especially since she felt obligated to him for having him put in jail. She hadn't apologized for it yet, but Jimmy was sure that soon she'd be crying to him about how sorry she was for the way she'd done him. He'd like that and it would show that she was learning some of the lessons. Maybe there was hope for Woozy yet. All she needed to do was learn not to talk back, question anything he said, or dress in anything revealing. That was one of his biggest gripes. Sometimes she'd wear a low cut blouse. That was a really bad thing to do.

• • •

When Tom and Nick sat down, O'Rourke's was crowded. Woozy brought their drinks and then spun around to help other thirsty customers.

"Tom, on my first day, I got an at-a-boy from management because I spotted a potential shoplifter."

"Wait a minute. I thought you were a greeter?"

"That is what the job title is, but if I can help Wal-mart reduce shoplifting, I can earn a bonus."

"Well good for you. How many thousands of dollars do you think your bonus will be?"

"I'm not sure, but I'll buy the next round. How 'bout that?"

Tom just shook his head and smiled at his friend.

"Oh, I see someone from work. I'll be right back." Nick maneuvered over a few tables and started talking with a younger lady.

Tom watched Woozy move about. She didn't look happy tonight. He wondered if her husband had gotten released. Maybe he had. That might explain the sad demeanor.

The door opened and a gruff, angry looking man walked in. Tom watched him pass as he walked to the other end of the bar before he sat down. Woozy glanced up at the man and quickly looked away. The man just stared at Woozy, almost as if they had some unfinished business that needed doing. Tom studied the man closely as Nick returned.

"Hey, Nick, do you know that guy at the far end of the bar?"

"Oh my God, I think that's Woozy's jailbird husband."

Tom continued to watch as Woozy intentionally ignored the man. This was something she never did.

Jimmy was getting pissed as his wife continued to ignore him. He didn't want to make a scene, but he deserved respect. He stood and reached across the bar and grabbed her by the elbow. Woozy shrugged off his aggressiveness and asked what he wanted.

"I want a whiskey," he yelled.

Tom looked more closely at Woozy. He now noticed a mark on her face that he hadn't seen earlier. She had covered it with makeup. That bastard, Tom thought to himself. Woozy was extra careful as she sat the whiskey glass in front of Jimmy, making sure to keep her distance.

"Nick, are you sure that's Woozy's husband?"

"I've only seen him a couple times, but I'm positive that's him." Nick said something to Tom, but Tom couldn't hear him. Once again he was intent on Woozy and her man.

Woozy brought them two more beers and quickly left. No small talk tonight. Tom understood she was being watched by a wife beater.

Jimmy again grabbed at Woozy and she avoided him, but he called out, "I want another whiskey."

Woozy looked down the bar and momentarily held Tom's eyes. He could see the fear in her look. Nick wandered about visiting tables here and there while Tom watched the drama unfolding at the end of the bar. Tom noted the obvious agitation in Jimmy's eyes, as he angrily watched his wife doing her job. He was getting madder by the minute. It was just a matter of time before he totally lost it.

Jimmy picked up the glass then tossed his head back, downing it. He stood and let the stool fall backward, crashing loudly to the floor. Then, he defiantly walked to the toilet.

Nick returned and sat down. "Tom, did you see that? He didn't even pick up that stool."

"Yes, I saw it. The guy has some serious issues."

"How can you tell that from just looking at him?"

Sometimes Tom was surprised at how naive his friend could be, "Trust me, Nick. I can tell something to do with years of experience."

Jimmy came out of the bathroom and the bar went a little bit quieter. He looked at Woozy as he walked slowly toward the door. At the door, he turned and gave her another long look.

Nick looked at Tom before speaking, "Man, I think he looked really mad."

Tom was already moving. "I forgot something in my truck. I'll be right back."

By the time Tom figured out which way Jimmy had gone, he was halfway down the block. He must be heading home. Tom closed the distance quickly as Jimmy slowed to light a cigarette.

When Tom was ten feet away he stopped and yelled, "Hey Asshole."

Jimmy stopped and turned around, "You got some kind of problem man?"

Tom looked directly at Jimmy and said, "Yes, as a matter of fact I do."

Jimmy smiled before speaking, "So what are you going to do about it, old man?"

Tom cut the distance between them in half. That caused Jimmy's expression to immediately change. He hesitated as if considering his options, and then he lunged at Tom.

Even if Tom was an old man, Jimmy would soon regret calling him that. Tom stepped left and delivered a right upper-cut to Jimmy's mid-section. Jimmy doubled over and Tom quickly spun and gave him a knee to the face. Jimmy landed on his back, hard, and lay sprawled on the pavement. Tom gave him a couple of kicks to the ribs. Tom stood over him and looked down at Jimmy as he gasped for breath. Jimmy didn't look so tough now. His smirk was missing.

Tom spoke softly and slowly, "If you even think about abusing your wife again, I'll come get you." Tom turned and headed back to the bar. He needed a beer.

Tom walked into the bar and Nick said, "I was beginning to get worried about you."

"Sorry about that. I had some unfinished business I had to attend to."

A few minutes later, Jimmy staggered in. He had a large gash in his forehead and had difficulty walking. He appeared to be a different man.

Nick watched as he walked by, "Boy oh boy, I wonder what happened to him?"

Woozy watched Jimmy as he meekly pulled his stool up to the bar. She set a whiskey in front of him. Jimmy didn't even have to ask. Woozy brought Tom and Nick each a beer and looked into Tom's eyes. Tom gave her a slight nod. A few minutes later, Jimmy looked down to where Tom sat and locked eyes for a moment before he stared back down into his drink.

"So, Nick, when are you scheduled to do that greeter/security job again?"

"I'm off for the weekend, but I work two days next week."

• • •

Wilson knew he was preoccupied with Padgett. If he hoped to be re-elected, he better concentrate on some more immediate county concerns. He should let the dust settle. Wilson was positive that Becky wasn't going anywhere. Maybe Padgett would be more agreeable if he left him alone for a few days.

There were still major issues in the county that he hadn't gotten a handle on. There were the ever-present marijuana growers, all the meth labs, and there were even some guys in the boonies organizing cock fights. Sometimes, he wished he was just a city cop so he could clean up the streets. He despised all the loafing hoods that spent all day long standing on the street corners around Carlisle. He had plenty to keep him busy. Maybe a change of scenery would do him some good.

A week of county road trips would be productive. He could drive around and let the people out there know that he was still thinking of them. Too much time in the office, or focusing too many hours on too few issues resulted in many things going unfinished. He'd get the Padgett business taken care of soon enough. Patience is the key to most problems. He just had to keep that in mind. He had allowed himself to become careless. He'd even dropped his guard and nearly became friends with Padgett. Luckily, he saw the error of his ways before it was too late. He needed to stay on track. He glanced at the liquor cabinet as he walked down the hall to the bedroom. Not tonight *big boy*. We don't need another scandal.

•   •   •

Tom woke with a start. He was sweating and his head was pounding. He sat up and looked at the clock, 5am. He usually slept 'till six, but there was no way he could sleep now. He just had a wildly disturbing dream. He could clearly see his partner, Cole Bishop, climb out of the cruiser. He followed, shadowing Cole's movements, just a few feet behind him. Then, all those shots, Cole dropped instantly, and instead of reacting, Tom stood and looked as his best friend lay in front of him, dying. He turned, as if in slow motion, and began to fire in the direction where the shots originated. For the first time, he could see the shooter's face, something he'd never remembered before. He emptied his gun, but the guy didn't fall.

Tom shook his head, as if it would help the dream vanish. But, it was only a dream because the man he'd shot in the dream wouldn't even have been a teenager twenty years ago. Wilson couldn't possibly have shot Bishop.

He put coffee on and let Bella out, then he jumped in the shower. He let cold water course over his head, trying desperately to shake the dream. For the first time in years, the dream wouldn't fade. It was like it had just happened, like it had somehow happened again. He dried himself off, pulled on a pair of jeans, then grabbed his coffee and went outside to join Bella.

It was quite cool and clear that morning, but he didn't seem to notice. He looked at the stars, hoping to somehow purge his thoughts. He petted Bella and talked to her for a few moments, trying to erase the dream. But, it didn't help. It was still there, stuck in his head, like it had happened yesterday.

● ● ●

Albert entered Carlisle and stopped at the Marathon station, near the school. He had texted the buyer earlier and after they exchanged goods, Albert headed downtown. The man he'd met lived nearby and refused to do business in town. He thought that the police presence was too strong. Albert was okay with that. He could make exceptions, sometimes. Especially, if there was no additional risk and the money was right. He wondered how the addicts came up with their cash. He didn't care, as long as they paid. Albert knew that they obtained money in illegal ways. But, these were tough economic times. At least that's what Albert had been hearing lately.

The next drops would be more challenging. But, as long as no one did anything stupid, he should be fine. He had texted his customers about the deliveries earlier and was ready. He parked by the old train depot. From here, he walked a half-block toward the court house. There, he met his next customer. They did their business and Albert proceeded up the alley. A guy stepped out of the shadows. Another exchange completed. At the end of the block, he turned right, heading back toward his car, where he met the last drop in town. A quick hand shake maneuver and he was finished. In his car, he breathed a sigh of relief, only one more delivery.

Albert was early when he got to the East End. He didn't see his guy. That was ok. In order to remain inconspicuous, he'd go inside and buy a soft drink. Talk about good cover. He stood near the corner of the East End and sucked from the straw in his Dr. Pepper. His client approached and got his attention, then ducked behind the building. Business completed. Not one word exchanged with any of the junkies. Who said conversation was necessary? He got back in his car and finished the huge fountain drink. Albert thought about how smoothly things had gone. Conducting business in town had its drawbacks. But, you could take care of things and do it quickly.

Wilson pulled into the East End lot. He watched the Buick Century closely as it pulled out. He'd seen the driver on several occasions. For some reason, Wilson had a bad feeling about him. He scribbled the license number down before getting out of his truck. He was thirsty. Maybe an Ale 8 would hit the spot. Thankfully, no one had mentioned his video lately. Wilson felt that was definitely a good thing. He didn't think he'd ever live that down.

He paid for his drink, sat in his truck, and looked at the license number he'd written down. He'd check it on the DMV website later, when he returned to the office. He'd find out if the guy had any problems.

Wilson thought about where he might venture to today. He hadn't driven out Moorefield Road in a while. He cruised into Moorefield and pulled off the road and onto the shoulder. He watched as cars sped in his direction. He could pull some people over. Actually he was quite content watching the drivers' reactions as they jammed on their brakes, after they noticed his truck. Wilson tired of this game after a few minutes.

He decided to follow Route 57 west 'till it dead-ended at Route 32. From there, he could head back to town for lunch. As he drove along, he noted how depressed much of the county was. Had it always been this bad? He wasn't sure, but it probably had. Nicholas County had never been wealthy, not in his lifetime anyway.

Wilson had been driving along Cassidy Creek Road for a couple of miles when he noticed the Buick he'd seen in town earlier pass, going the opposite direction. He watched in his rear view mirror and saw the driver turn off into a driveway. So, this is where the guy lives.

Wilson suddenly had a change of plan. He would still drive out to Route 32. But, from there, he'd circle back the way he'd come and head back to Carlisle. That way, he could have a look at the guy's house without raising suspicion. He slowed as he approached the driveway. Wilson saw a clean mobile home situated a hundred yards or so off the road. Well, the trailer looked okay. Maybe he wasn't a bad guy after all.

•　　•　　•

Albert watched from the living room window as the sheriff slowly rolled past his trailer. What was he looking for? He wondered if the sheriff had taken his license number down and found out where he lived. Maybe that's why he was here. He couldn't suspect him of anything, could he? If he did suspect him, then he would have stopped.

After the sheriff was gone, Albert thought about his options. He could start using the old abandoned house again. Hell, he only moved here a few days ago. But, maybe he should move back to Robertson County, just as a precautionary measure. It was a hassle and all, but it was better being a little inconvenienced than it was getting caught.

He had kept all the boxes from his earlier move here. All he needed to do was pack up. Better safe than sorry. He heard from some of the local cannabis growers that the Sheriff was becoming a real pain in the ass. He wasn't planning on becoming one of his trophies. After he had all his chemicals and utensils packed, Albert stepped onto the back porch for a smoke. So, the lawman thought he was going to catch him, he chuckled. He toked repeatedly on his joint, attempting to calm himself. Maybe this will work out better in the long run. Albert was relieved he hadn't done anything foolish. The cop was probably driving around just killing time.

•　　　•　　　•

Tom drank his coffee and thought. He'd had a dream about Woozy's husband last night. He didn't think much about it. He had good reason to dream about him, especially after their encounter the other night. He had no regrets about laying the scumbag out. He deserved it. The thing that bothered him was a feeling deep inside; as if part of him wanted the guy dead. It felt as if there was some unfinished business.

He pulled his boots on and walked out the door. He wasn't really in the mood to check out hunting territory, but it would be good to get out of the house. Of course Bella was game.

They stopped at a high point. It offered a breathtaking vista, which overlooked the surrounding countryside. The fields hadn't been mowed in years, but as of yet, they hadn't totally been reclaimed by cedars or honey locusts. Tom watched as a couple of deer appeared. They were approximately two hundred yards away. They were just starting their day.

Bella sat next to him and they both watched more and more deer exit the safety of the nearby woods. Six or seven does wandered out. Now, their fawns were following, hopping in order to clear the brush. Bella sat patiently, but her feet were dancing left and right. She wanted to chase.

CHAPTER 14

It had been several days since she had the last coaching session with Wilson. She was feeling better, at least better physically. Becky had done some soul searching over the past two weeks. And she was once again thinking about escape. She felt she needed to get away from Kentucky. She didn't trust Wilson. Any cop that would fabricate a story to entrap another person, especially another cop, probably shouldn't be trusted. Her mobility was improving daily. Her ribs weren't hurting nearly as badly as they had been. She still wasn't sure that she could drive, soon though. The more Becky thought about things, the more worried she became.

It just wasn't like Wilson to leave anyone alone for any length of time. What could he be scheming now? Becky obviously had managed to survive mixing the medications that the Doctor had so strongly advised her against doing. She couldn't have imagined living the last two weeks without real meds. She was supposed to return to the clinic for a check-up. She sure as hell wasn't doing that. If she was well enough to return to the hospital, she'd just keep driving. South, Tennessee was sounding better every day. She had all her stuff together. She could leave on a moment's notice. All she needed to do was decide, decide if she was staying or going. It was beginning to feel that leaving was her only option.

•   •   •

Tom was enjoying a cup of coffee when he heard the engine noise. He moved to the window and watched as the sheriff's truck rolled to a stop. Oh shit, what does the bastard want now? Tom stepped outside to greet his nemesis. Wilson climbed out of the truck and smiled as he held his hat in his hands. Tom could tell that

Wilson's wheels were turning. He was apparently trying to come up with an appropriate greeting.

But Tom beat him to it, "What do you want, Wilson?"

"Now that's not very friendly, Padgett. I thought you and I were trying to bury the hatchet."

"Were we, Wilson? Was that before or after your little interrogation?" Wilson acted hurt. Tom wondered how long Wilson had spent practicing that wounded look. Tom opened the door and Bella quickly bound outside and jumped up on Wilson. Tom realized then that he needed to give her some additional training. She needed to understand the difference between friends and enemies. "Wilson, you want some coffee?"

"That'd be good, Padgett."

"Black alright?"

"I wouldn't have it any other way."

Tom returned with two cups and handed one to Wilson. He stood for a second before taking a seat. "Ok, Wilson, what can I do for you?"

Wilson leaned back and sipped his coffee. "It sure is peaceful out here."

Tom waited for Wilson to get to the point. Tom remembered that Wilson mentioned the Oxycontin the last time they'd spoken. He was still curious about that.

"Padgett, when we last spoke, we were just getting to the heart of the matter, until you suddenly decided to leave."

Tom considered Wilson for a moment, is this guy for real? "I'm a lot more comfortable here in my front yard, than I was in the police interrogation room. Tell you what; I'll give you the benefit of doubt, but strictly off the record."

"Good, Padgett. That'll be good." Can we talk about the drugs that happened to be in Becky's car the night she crashed?"

"We can talk about anything you want, and I'll tell you what I know."

Wilson liked that. Now they seemed to be getting somewhere. "Padgett, you know I found a bottle of Oxycontin in Becky's car the night of the accident."

"You mentioned Oxycontin, but that was all you said about it."

"Well, Becky believes that you might have laced her drink the night she crashed. And, she believes you planted the pills in her purse."

"Are you kidding me? She actually told you that?"

"Yes, more or less."

"What do you mean more or less? Did she tell you that I laced her drink and planted pills in her purse, yes or no?"

"Yes, that's what we've been able to piece together on the occasions that I've spoken with her."

"Wait a minute, Wilson. Piece together. Are you telling me that you've been coaching Becky about what to do and say?"

"No, Padgett, nothing like that. I've just been working with her, helping her to remember events of the evening."

"Back to my question, have you been coaching her?"

"No. She's just a little sketchy on some items, and I'm helping her reconstruct the evening."

"Do you realize that you could be prosecuted for what you're doing? Helping her to remember the evening's events, that's big of you."

Wilson had nothing to say.

"Why don't you tell me about this grand scheme of yours? Maybe I can help you sort it out?"

Wilson knew he was in a spot, so he decided to share part of his information with Padgett. Tom knew he'd get only half-truths from Wilson. That was fine, because two could play the deception game.

Wilson started, "Becky told me that she came to your house that Friday night."

"Go on."

"She told me that you were upset about her wanting to end the relationship. When you were in the trailer getting drinks, she believes you drugged her drink."

"What reason would I have for doing that Wilson?"

"She said you put the pills in her purse, to set her up."

Tom looked closely at Wilson. He knew that most of what Wilson had just said was a lie, but right now he needed to resolve this issue. He began his explanation, "Wilson, let me tell you how things really happened."

Of course, Wilson liked the sound of this.

"The week before Becky's accident, she came home with me. She'd been drinking and had obviously done some drugs before she came here. Anyway, to make a long story short, she tripped walking up the steps and spilled her purse. She must have dropped the bottle of Oxycontin." Tom took a sip of coffee then continued. "Bella found the bottle the next morning. I didn't know what to say to Becky, so I said nothing. When she came here the night of the crash, I had the pills sitting on the table, so she'd be sure and see them. Obviously, she did and then she must have gone crazy thinking that I thought all kinds of terrible things about her." Tom watched Wilson's face, and then proceeded. "She left in a state that night, the Friday she wrecked. When I went back inside to get a beer after she left, I noticed that the Oxycontin bottle was gone."

Wilson sat quietly, considering everything he'd just heard. "So the pills weren't yours? They were hers, is that what you're saying?"

"Wilson, do you honestly believe that I would be dealing drugs?"

"Maybe not, but, weren't you upset about your relationship ending?"

"We slept together two times, that's all. I've been around the block a time or two. It takes more than a couple of tumbles to make me fall in love."

"Becky said that she knew her limits, and wouldn't have taken too many pills."

"Come on Wilson, don't you know anything about addicts?"

"What do you mean; do I know anything about addicts?"

"Addicts always believe they're in control, that they actually know their limits. But, in reality, they hardly ever do."

Wilson thought about Padgett's story. It sounded convincing enough. But Wilson knew that Padgett was a smooth operator and he needed to be sure.

Wilson regarded Padgett, "Why do you think Becky would be carrying around such a big bottle of pills?"

"I can think of a couple of reasons. One, she likes to share them with friends, if they hit it off, maybe just to make an evening more enjoyable. Two, she needs them, and she also keeps them on hand for planned and unplanned transactions."

"You suspect she might be selling pills here in Nicholas County?"

"I've told you my side of the story, Wilson. Now it should be easy for you to figure the rest of it out on your own."

"What are you talking about now, Padgett? Figure what out?"

"Why should I even consider helping you? You'll probably turn on me at the first opportunity."

"Padgett, I'm just trying to get to the bottom of what happened."

"Ok, I'll give you a few more hints, to help you get to the bottom of things. Becky is a user. She obviously has been for a while, and she was probably high every time you interviewed her. Also, she probably sells pills on the streets, right here in Nicholas County."

"Wait a minute. That's quite an assumption, don't you think?"

"No I don't. Ok, one last bit of advice. Why don't you obtain a photograph of Becky Adkins and run it by Miranda Johnson, to see how much the girl remembers?"

● ● ●

Becky made her mind up. She was heading south. Wilson hadn't bothered to come back and that was really beginning to bother her. She felt like a sitting duck, waiting for something to pounce. Her Mustang was loaded with everything she needed. She had a little money in a checking account. She could go to Wal-mart and buy some supplies, then write a check to liquidate the account. She had her car title. It was a good thing that the car was paid off. She paused at the door which led into the garage. Becky smiled when she decided what else she'd do. She went back to the front door and unlocked it. She even left the inside door standing wide open.

She winced slightly as she climbed into the car. Backing out of the garage, she laughed at the thought of leaving the garage door standing open. She tossed the garage door opener out the window. Its case cracked as it landed on the gravel driveway. Her pain wasn't too bad. She should be okay. Besides, it would only be a three hour drive.

Three hours and she'd be at her new home in Clinton, Tennessee. She remembered reading the name Clinton on an exit on one of her drug runs down I-75. Clinton was a half hour north of Knoxville. Maybe she'd be able to find a real job and get herself straightened out. That was just it, though. She wasn't sure if she wanted a real job. She didn't know if she wanted to change her lifestyle. Sure, there were plenty of risks. But she had really begun to appreciate the benefits.

●　　●　　●

Tom poured himself another cup of coffee and watched as Wilson drove off. He almost hated helping the guy. The only reason he did, was because Wilson seemed so damned determined to blame him for something. Tom wondered whether Wilson would act in a timely manner with this new information. Or, would he do the usual and drag his feet? He recalled the conversation that he and Wilson had with Miranda Johnson. Miranda remembered that the woman she bought the Oxy from had been both good looking and fairly young. She was about the right height and had similar hair color. Why couldn't Wilson figure that out? Tom shook his head. Unfortunately, it seemed that Wilson could ignore much in his attempt to frame him.

That afternoon

Tom decided to go grocery shopping, one of his least favorite things. He would head over to Maysville. Good old Wal-mart, the largest retailer in the world, with several locations near you. Tom never bothered with a shopping list. Today's most important items were coffee and dog food. He also needed staples such as beer, milk, eggs and bread. Entering the store, an overly friendly man pushed a cart his way.

The man smiled and said, "Welcome to Wal-Mart, Tom."

"Nick, you are so cute in your little blue vest."

They talked for a few moments then Nick added, "Hey, I'm off in twenty minutes. Maybe we can stop by O'Rourke's for a couple?"

●　　●　　●

Wilson wasn't ready to give up just yet. What if Padgett was making everything up? What if he was just trying to do a cover-up? What if he was trying to shift the blame? Wilson realized much of what he'd been feeding Becky was also by design. He wanted Padgett's *head on a stick.* He wanted it so badly that he could almost taste it.

He thought about the girl in Carlisle, Miranda Johnson. Would she really be able to remember Becky's face? What if she said that she didn't recognize her? Then, he'd be back at square one. Was it worth the try? He could easily get a photo of Becky from the DMV and then he'd run it by the Johnson girl. Then, he would be a hero for solving the year old crime. He'd get Padgett later.

Wilson printed Becky Adkins' photo. He thought, not bad looking when she's not banged up. Well, Miranda would surely remember her. He called Miranda's cell and the girl picked up after several rings. Damn, Miranda was visiting her grandmother in Tennessee and wouldn't be home until next week. Wilson would have to be patient. Miranda told him that she would be home late Wednesday. She said that he could come over anytime the following day. He wondered about the additional delay, and then shrugged it off. Becky wasn't going anywhere. Not before he visited Miranda anyway. He recalled how gingerly Becky was moving around the last time he'd seen her.

●　　●　　●

Becky backed the car into the drive. The house wasn't nearly as nice as hers in Kentucky, but at least it was furnished. At first she wasn't sure if she liked having a fenced-in yard. But now, with her car safely tucked away she had more appreciation for it. A furnished two-bedroom house for five-hundred a month wasn't bad. She was sure that her battered wife story had helped her get a reduced rental agreement.

The house was on Coward Road. She thought about how she'd just run away from Kentucky and laughed at the appropriateness of the road's name. Becky backed in because she didn't want her license plate, 'HOTBABE', raising any red flags. She needed to get all that paperwork stuff sorted out on Monday. She would go down to the license branch, get her title transferred, and get a new drivers license.

She wondered if she could switch her driver's license back to her maiden name. That's what the title showed. She could tell the license branch that she had filed for a divorce and was waiting for the paperwork. Maybe after seeing her face, they'd show increased sympathy. She hoped so, it would make any attempt at tracking her more difficult.

Walking into her new home, she felt a sense of relief wash over her. She was sore and tired, but this whole change of scene felt good. There was one other house nearby, but it was almost a quarter mile away. There was enough privacy. Clinton wasn't a huge city, less than ten-thousand people. She could easily hide here. Becky sat on the worn recliner and felt her pills begin to kick in. She considered her dilemma. Work a legitimate job, or continue doing the illegal route?

•　　•　　•

O'Rourke's was busy again. Tom walked in and bellied up to the bar. Nick hadn't made it yet. He was probably getting a couple more attaboy's for another job well done. Woozy was taking care of business and appeared in good spirits. She brought Tom a beer and placed it in front of him, "On the house, Tom, and thank you."

"How are things, Woozy, everything ok at home?"

Woozy smiled widely and said, "Yes, things are the best they've been in years."

Tom felt a great deal of satisfaction as he watched Woozy spin around to serve other customers. The door opened and in walked the man, Nick the Greeter. Nick wore his typical ear to ear grin, as Woozy placed a napkin and beer in front of him.

"Tom, you know how it is, another day another dollar." They clinked they're cans.

"And how was your shopping experience today at the mart?"

"What, are you still on the clock?"

"Have you heard from Becky?"

"No, and I don't expect too either. I think she wiped the slate clean, of me, anyway."

"She seemed to be such a nice girl, too."

Tom didn't want to contradict Nick's assessment of Becky, so he just nodded. He recalled the short time they had shared. Yes, she was a *nice girl*. Yes she was a *nice wild young girl*.

"Hey, Tom, are you hungry what about a pizza?"

"OK, but after that, I've got to be going. Remember, I've got groceries in the truck."

As Tom drove home, he felt happy for Woozy. He knew he couldn't be Woozy's guardian angel forever. But maybe Jimmy wouldn't know that.

•　　　•　　　•

After Wilson arrived home, he walked past the liquor cabinet, trying not to look at it. But, he felt that ever present pull that always seemed to be there. This evening it happened to be stronger. He hung up his clothes and placed his gun on the dresser. Hell, why not? He'd been good. He put on a sweat shirt and some sweat pants, then carried an empty glass and bottle out onto the back porch. It was cool outside tonight. Autumn was already here. How could summer already be over? If his nosey neighbor was out and about, he might just have to invite her over. He chuckled, even though she was old, maybe she'd still be a good time. He studied the Jim Beam in his glass for a moment before taking his first sip. This sip seemed to have been months in coming. Smooth, just the way it always was, smooth as silk.

Another week behind him, the days seemed to fly by. Wilson thought about things, Padgett, Becky, and Miranda. Why did he have so few things on his plate? He was sheriff of the county. There were seven-thousand citizens counting on him to take care of business.

He thought about some of his past relationships, most of them ended up being mistakes. Drinking generally became the issue that destroyed whatever relationship had developed. At least that's what he'd been told. He hardly remembered any of them. He thought about Becky Adkins' photo. She was a nice looking woman. Maybe that could end up developing into something. He took a long drink, holding the whiskey in his mouth. He thought of Becky without her clothes on, and then he swallowed. He was sure she'd look good. Yeah, she'd look real good, especially naked.

• • •

Becky was actually quite comfortable, lying on the beat up old sofa. It seemed to fit the contours of her body perfectly. She looked around the living room. It was sparsely appointed but she didn't care.

She really missed having a man around. She missed having sex even more than that. She wasn't particular about partners. She went both ways. She actually preferred men, but flexibility wasn't a bad thing. She'd had a few relationships with women. But, they always ended abruptly, because women talked too much. That's what she liked about men. They didn't talk much, especially during sex. Another advantage with men was that they almost always went right to sleep after sex. Not all men, but most of them.

Becky wondered what would happen to Tom now that she wasn't around conspiring with Wilson. It was just as well, she could have easily gone down for something she hadn't done. She just noticed there wasn't a TV. It'd be nice to have one. She knew that she needed to eat some food, but she was worn out from the drive. Tomorrow will be here before she knew it. Maybe she should close her eyes. A man, that's what she hoped to dream about once she drifted off to sleep. Her medication was making her more tired than normal. Becky realized that maybe she needed a larger dose, something that would give her a better jolt. Her medicinal regimen was supposed to lift her up, not put her to sleep.

CHAPTER 15

Steve Caudill thought about all the things that had happened over the last four or five years. His life had been busy. It had been much busier than he'd wished. His parents had gotten divorced, he moved in with his dad in Carlisle, and he dropped out of high school in his sophomore year. He'd started doing methamphetamines. There was always something new going on.

He had spent his first fourteen years in Ripley, Ohio. He lived a normal life there. Now that he was living with his dad, things weren't as normal anymore. He felt he kind of lived with his dad, anyway, the five or six days per month when he was actually home. That was alright with Steve, though. He had just turned nineteen and could take care of himself. His dad was a long haul trucker, driving for J.B. Hunt Transport.

He thought about his mom sometimes. Not often, just sometimes. He hadn't seen her in years. That's what it felt like, anyway. His mother had a booth at the flea market in Ripley. That's where she tried to make money. Steve remembered how ridiculous it'd been to sit there in that old tobacco warehouse for hours on end. He had sat there with her sometimes and watched her try to sell some of her junk. Some days she wouldn't make a sale. He never understood why she bothered.

He understood why his dad asked her for the divorce. He'd seen his mother take many different men into her bedroom over the years. She always did that when his dad was away driving. He didn't care, at least they kept her occupied and out of his hair. He never talked to his dad about it. Maybe he should have.

Looking back, he wished he had tried more when he was in school. It was just so hard when he started his freshman year at Nicholas County. It didn't help that he didn't know anybody. Most of the kids wore UK clothing all the time, blue this or that. He never understood any of it. He could care less about sports. He spent his first semester trying to get to know people, but he struggled. He really didn't have much to talk about.

He became more and more of a loner. He had just a few friends. They hung out sometimes, in town on the street corners. After he dropped out of school he hung out more often with his friends around town. It was good. They never talked much. That was where he had his first experience with drugs.

Steve lived a few blocks from downtown. He could walk there easily and then just stand around with everybody else. He knew there must be a hidden purpose for all of the standing around. He soon found out what it was. That was where he met his new soon-to-be best friend.

Buzz taught him some of the street's hang out ways. He liked to talk even less than Steve did. But, he took him under his wing for some street style mentoring. Steve thought back to their first conversation. He remembered the difficulty he had in understanding him.

Buzz said, "New ere uh?"

Steve looked at him for a bit and replied, "Yeah."

"Gad a name?"

"Yeah, it's Steve."

"Uh."

So, he did understand Buzz. He was a man of few words. He watched as Buzz milled around some of the other people. They all just stood about, which seemed to be some sort of communication.

It took him a while, but soon he was hanging out like a pro. It was actually kind of like playing a hand-held video game. They all wore zoned out expressions on their faces and they were constantly checking their phones for texts or missed calls. Buzz had also taught him how to do his first drug exchange. When he succeeded, he got a sample of the product. He was fifteen.

His first experience with meth still floated around in his memory now, four years later. He had some close calls over the years, especially when he was new to drugs. Drugs, he realized were just like anything else. He needed to get a handle on them. He needed to learn more about his own limitations.

Steve was thinking more than usual lately. He wasn't sure why, maybe it was the weather. He wondered why he was only something like 5'8". He was the same height as his mom. His dad was 6'2". Could his growth have already been stunted from drug use? Maybe it was his diet. It had gone downhill lately. His dad usually left him a check to buy groceries when he went on the road. He made it out to the local IGA, usually for forty dollars, not a lot for two weeks. Steve used to go to the store and spend almost the entire amount on groceries. But lately, he bought something of little value, and then pocketed the rest. It helped that he knew which cashier would be the most likely not to raise any questions. He saw this was what people did with their welfare checks.

•   •   •

Albert was once again working in Robertson County. It seemed that no one had messed with the abandoned house in his absence. The roof had developed a new leak and the floor seemed spongier. But, there didn't seem to be any rodents about. Maybe the fact that meth had so many of the same active ingredients as d-Con had something to do with that.

He just finished a long night of cooking. He was beat. Running a meth lab was harder than people realized. He was concerned about the approaching deer season. Even though bow hunting was in full swing, not many people around here cared much for bow hunting. Now gun season, that was another story. Guns got Kentucky hunters' blood boiling.

He thought more about some of his clients of late. Some were younger than usual. How did they find him? They were probably just runners for the older users. Some of his older users were beginning to look really bad. In fact, they looked terrible. Not just in the face, their teeth were slowly rotting away.

He also noticed how the eyes of users began to take on similar appearances. It didn't matter if the people were white, black or yellow. Their eyes all started to look the same, strangely similar to people with Down syndrome. In many ways he felt sorry for them. Albert knew about the addictiveness of meth. Marijuana could become addictive. Luckily for him, it seemed to be less so.

The batch that he finished may not have been his best. Albert was slightly preoccupied as he was multi-tasking. He was setting up his makeshift lab while also trying to cook. He wasn't clear on some of the mixtures he had incorporated. They were probably alright. His clients would take damned near anything he made. He wasn't sure if they just totally trusted him, or desperately needed the fix. He assumed the latter.

He usually didn't smoke as much weed as he had last night, but the lab was stuffy, so he spent more time outside. He'd have to be careful about his habit. He had to drive around to make deliveries and he usually liked being fairly straight.

●　　●　　●

Wilson continued to sip his whiskey. He couldn't stop thinking about Becky. He almost wished he hadn't printed out the DMV photo. He hadn't paid any attention to her until he saw that photo. Now she was looking better and better to him, especially the more he sipped on the Jim Beam. After the last swallow, he had illusions of even tasting Becky, smooth, really smooth. Why had Becky been interested in old man like Padgett anyway? She needed a real man, one that was alive and kicking.

He drained his glass and closed his eyes. *He could see her walking toward him now. Yes, there she was. She was walking down the hallway. She was removing her blouse as she approached. She let it hang on her hand momentarily before she dropped it to the floor.*

Now she reached behind to undo her bra. The straps were loose, she was about to slip it off... Wilson's phone rang.

He looked at the number and cursed. It was nobody. He was in no condition to talk on the damned thing, anyway. Wilson poured himself some more whiskey and tried to recreate the vision of Becky's approach, but he'd lost it. Damn, if he left now, he could be at her house in fifteen minutes. He had only drunk half a bottle of whiskey, so he should be alright to drive. Why recreate the scene, when the real thing was just minutes away?

He closed his eyes again. There she was. *He watched as Becky walked down the hallway toward him. Man, this was some vision, especially since he was sitting on the back porch. Here she comes, she's unbuttoning her blouse. She's slipping it off.*

"Hey, Wilson, what are you doing over there, you pervert?" His nosey ass neighbor yelled, as she peered over the fence.

•　　•　　•

Bella wasn't particularly happy. She went outside to do her business, then right back into the trailer. Tom was getting dressed up to go somewhere without her. She didn't like being excluded, not one bit. Tom applied face paint, laced his boots, and then grabbed his bow before stepping out into the early morning darkness. He knew Bella would be listening to every step as he walked off into the woods, without her. She was getting possessive, almost like a wife.

He smiled knowing how Bella would pout when he returned, but just for a little while. It was a nice morning and there was plenty of moonlight. He made his way up into the woods. Tom had his mini Maglite with him so he could make sure everything was in order before he climbed the tree he'd chosen.

He got situated and began the climb, pulling the stand up as he went. Tom settled on a height about fifteen feet up. He tightened his safety harness and waited for daylight. He was sure he'd see deer this morning, but maybe not any bucks. It was still a little early in the season, and he wasn't overly impressed with the sign he'd found so far. He probably wouldn't take a doe today.

It felt good being in the woods. It was quiet and still as the first light began to seep through the trees. He watched movement in the distance, unable to determine exactly what it was. He knew the morning light can play tricks on the eyes. He remembered a time he'd watched a particular spot with much anticipation for at least an hour, only to find it was a leaf fluttering in the breeze after the sun had risen.

•   •   •

Becky woke early and found she was more stiff than usual. She looked around and realized where she was and that she had spent the first night in her new home on the sofa. It felt much more comfortable last night. She made her way to the bathroom. She filled a glass from the tap to wash down her morning pick me up.

Becky's new life was starting. She was a Tennessean now. She had a dream about Adam last night. *He had come home to Fleming County and found the house standing wide open and thought it had been burglarized. Then he went crazy and started throwing furniture through the windows. He smashed the flat screen television.* Boy, she wished she had that TV now. *Then he called the police and told them that his wife could be found in Clinton, Tennessee.* He couldn't possibly know that. It was only a dream, but it seemed so real.

She walked around the outside of the house while she drank her coffee. She noticed the house had an outside aerial. This was good. She might be able to get some local stations. It made sense to keep abreast of things going on around here. She needed to do some shopping and then relax until Monday. Because Monday, she knew would be busy.

Even though she woke feeling stiff, Becky felt well rested. She probably felt relieved just being out of that hotbed of activity over in Kentucky. She still had a pretty good stash of meds, but her cash was getting low. She needed to figure out what to do, and soon. She wondered what Adam could possibly be doing. She thought about calling, but decided she really didn't care to talk with him.

•   •   •

Wilson had survived the weekend, and probably hadn't done anything stupid. He vaguely recalled the nosey neighbor yelling something at him, but that didn't matter. He noticed the bottle of Jim Beam sitting on the kitchen counter. Not even empty, that was a plus.

He poured himself some coffee and stepped outside onto the porch. It was another beautiful fall day. He loved fall. So, he had made it through the weekend intact. Maybe he could control this bout with alcoholism after all. He took comfort in that and slowly sipped his coffee. He heard the neighbor's screen door open. Hell, he thought. He rose, attempting to get inside before the bitch saw him.

Too late, she yelled, "Wilson, I don't know what you were doing to yourself out there the other night, but next time, do it in the privacy of your own home or I'll call the cops."

Great, he silently groaned. Obviously, I'm not out of the alcoholic woods yet. He dressed quickly, and then headed to the station. Maybe it'd be a good idea to invest in some privacy fencing?

At his desk, he thought about the day as Deputy Leland walked in. "Hey, boss, how's it going?"

"I don't like being called boss, damn it. What are you doing here, Leland?"

"You told me to report in this morning, something about some additional training."

What in the hell is he talking about? Wilson had no idea what he was going on about, but Leland probably hadn't made it up.

"Ok, Deputy, ok. Give me a few minutes while I gather my thoughts." So much for any of his other plans, they'd just have to wait.

•　　•　　•

Steve was on the corner early. He was surprised to find it empty. He wondered where all his buddies were. Slowly, they started to appear, crawling out of this or that hole that they called home.

Steve had an okay weekend. At least his dad stopped by the house for a day and a half. He left Sunday afternoon on another two week road trip. Fortunately for Steve, his dad left another check for groceries, fifty dollars. He must have thought Steve looked thin and in need of more nourishment. He could get additional nourishment with that alright. Buzz wandered over and said some barely discernible words, before finally mouthing for him to follow.

They were going to do a pickup, but the location had changed. That wasn't all that unusual. It kept the cops from being able to follow any patterns. Buzz had received a text and he instructed Steve as to where and when the drop was going to be made. It was a fairly big drop, based on the cash that Buzz laid in his hand.

Steve wasn't bothered with other people as he walked toward the drop zone. He had his instructions, and his alone. If the guy delivering the stuff was more than a few minutes late, the deal was off. At that point, he would just walk away. Steve was more than a little nervous as he walked the last two blocks to the remote location, which was nearly a half mile from the square. At a predetermined time, he left the shadows and began to mill about on the sidewalk. A guy quickly walked past, they exchanged packages, and the deal was done.

•　　•　　•

Albert was pretty hyped up. He really hated being stoned and out of it while conducting business. He had no one to blame but himself, unless it was maybe the sheriff. He didn't like the fact that he was once again operating out of that shack in Robertson County. But now, he had to focus on his task.

He texted the location for the next drop. This time, it was the younger guy that he had seen around town a few times that he made the exchange with. As he walked off, Albert realized the kid was pretty smooth, probably not a big user yet. Once he finished his business in Carlisle, he was going to head back home for some sleep. He was dead tired.

As Albert drove northeast on Route 32, it finally dawned on him what he had mixed improperly last night. He remembered that he had stepped outside to take a leak. When he returned, he'd forgotten where he was in the mixing process. So, he mistakenly doubled up on drain cleaner and anti-freeze.

He realized that it shouldn't have too adverse of an effect on his more chronic users. But, to a newbie, that might be a little different. He was mad at himself for the mistake, but it wasn't like he could do anything about it now. Luckily for him, the concoction hadn't blown up in his face. Tonight, he'd be sure to keep to the recipe, not too much smoking, and he would definitely pay more attention.

• • •

Wilson needed to get rid of his deputy because he had other things he wanted to do. As Leland refreshed his memory about their task, Wilson realized the necessity of it. He would just have to curtail his other mission until tomorrow. Wilson explained some of the details about obtaining a search warrant.

"Sheriff, you mean if I suspect somebody of a crime, I need a warrant to enter their home?"

"That's right, Leland, unless they invite you inside to have a look."

"You mean, like if they say come on in for a cup of coffee, I can bust them?"

"Listen, Deputy, first there has to be probable cause. Then you need to be in possession of a warrant that states the specifics of the search."

"Sheriff that seems kind of backward giving the criminals all the time to get rid of whatever it is that they're hiding."

Wilson sighed; he knew he was in for a long day. "Let's talk about basics for the moment, Leland. There are things called rights. Everyone is entitled to them."

"Even criminals have the same rights?"

"Yes, criminals are not criminals until it's proven that they are. Ok, now what about pulling somebody over for a violation? Leland, what's the first thing you do?"

"Call for backup?"

"No, you don't call for backup. Besides, I'm the only other backup."

"I approach the car, pull out my gun, and ask for their license and registration?"

Wilson ran his fingers through his hair. "Deputy, you don't need to draw your weapon for a traffic stop."

CHAPTER 16

Becky realized that getting the right person at the license branch was absolutely critical. She watched the interaction between people as they got to the counter and received help with whatever they needed. One woman in particular seemed to be the friendliest. Becky waited until she was available before she stepped up to state her needs. She told the clerk she needed to transfer her car title and also needed a Tennessee driver's license. The title would be easy enough, but the driver's license and plates would prove more difficult. The clerk listened as Becky told her story. Becky said she needed her driver's license to reflect her maiden name, just like her car title did.

"Ma'am, I'm sorry that you're going through a divorce. But you'll still need the divorce decree before I can issue a name change."

Becky was prepared for that response. "My husband beat me. That's why we're getting divorced. If my married name shows up on my Tennessee license, he'll track me down. He has connections. I'm scared to death that he'll find me."

The clerk seemed to consider this more seriously as she looked at the marks on Becky's face. She leaned closer to the counter and spoke in a hushed tone, "Ok honey. I'll do the name change on the license for you, but you'll need to bring proof of the divorce after you get it, so we have it for our records."

"Oh, thank you so much. You don't realize how much this means to me."

• • •

Steve felt incredibly powerful. That was the most meth he'd ever taken. He was curious why Buzz was being so generous. Steve

169

was usually content to put his meth into a drink, and enjoy it that way. But now, Buzz was showing him some of the finer arts of smoking the chalk, as Buzz referred to it.

Steve sat on a chair in someone's apartment. It offered a clear view of the courthouse through its front window. They all laughed as they watched the city police stand outside by the station. He wasn't sure what was so funny, but it seemed like the thing to do, so he laughed along. Buzz was really wound up. He offered some more chalk to Steve. This meth was good. Steve could even understand most of what Buzz said.

He wasn't sure, but he thought he heard that Buzz had rounded up a car. Now, they were speeding down some road out in the countryside. Steve felt his heart rate had increased greatly and he was getting sick to his stomach. But, he couldn't really talk as he lay and watched while Buzz drove. He had no idea where they were or where they were headed. Steve had never seen Buzz drive a car. He didn't know if he even had a license. Buzz pulled the car into a tree-lined drive and stopped. He stopped so they could enjoy some more chalk. Steve didn't believe he could handle any more. But Buzz encouraged him, "Come on."

●　　●　　●

Albert cruised along Abners Mill Road on his way to the lab. He wasn't really in the mood for his whole cooking episode tonight. But, he knew he still had a job to do. He arrived earlier than normal.

As he approached the house, he saw a vehicle sitting in the lane and wondered why. People wandered around off in the distance. They seemed to be searching for property boundaries. They probably wouldn't have gone inside the ruin, so his laboratory shouldn't have been discovered. He backed out the way he came. That's when he noticed the *For Sale* sign that'd been attached to the fence. Shit, that surely changed things. He drove a few hundred feet farther up the road and pulled onto the shoulder to wait.

He didn't have to wait long. Ten minutes later, the car backed out the drive and left, going in the opposite direction. Albert had to move fast. He quickly backed up to the abandoned home and began to fill the trunk of his car. He threw things in the car much more roughly than was probably safe. But, under the circumstances, it seemed necessary.

He wondered if he was over-reacting. Maybe no one would even consider buying the derelict property, but he couldn't take that chance. He was drenched in sweat when he finished loading. He would go back to Cassidy Creek and re-establish operations there. Hell, maybe he should just quit the business. But how would he be able to afford his cannabis? A smoke was definitely needed when he got home, maybe more than one.

• • •

Wilson took the call from the State boys. A car had run off the road into a ditch near the intersection of Route 36 and Route 68. The accident happened halfway between Carlisle and Millersburg. The driver had sustained minor injuries. The passenger hadn't been so lucky. He had been air-lifted to Lexington and it appeared he might not make it. Wilson was told that drugs were involved. Both victims were residents of Carlisle.

He thanked the officer before clicking off. Another drug related accident in this sleepy little county? He'd stop by the hospital to have a chat with the driver. Maybe they were part of the crowd that hung around on the street corners in town.

At the hospital, Wilson asked about the accident victim. He was given the room number, and as he made his way there, a nurse met him in the hallway. She told him that he probably wouldn't be able to get much out of the patient.

"Well, thank you for that, young lady. But I'm the sheriff and I'll make that determination." Wilson pulled a chair close to Buzz and looked at him for a moment. The young man stared blankly at Wilson but said nothing. He could tell he wasn't about to talk freely, so he began, "So, you were driving the car last night when it crashed?"

Buzz shook his head.

"Do you know what happened to your friend?"

"Dun no."

"Looks like you've got a problem, based on the drugs that were found in your system."

•　•　•

Tom had scouted the area near his trailer with little success, and decided he'd give the wildlife reserve a try. The season for bow hunting was nearly five months in length, but getting a good-sized buck during bow season could prove difficult. It's especially difficult before the rut begins. His plan was to familiarize himself with Clay WMA well before that happened.

There were two entrances into the reserve in Nicholas County. Clay WMA Rd. Lower Unit, allowed access to approximately one third of the acreage, while the Upper Unit allowed access to the remainder.

Tom decided to hunt the Upper Unit acreage, primarily because it had a large section of woods that bordered Cassidy Creek. Once again, Bella was locked up in the trailer as Tom drove off.

•　•　•

Wilson was happy that the training session with Leland was finally finished. He didn't think it would ever end. Now he could get back to serious policing. He needed to check in on Becky Adkins. He wanted to see if she was a fit for some counseling. He could have called and asked her to come by the station, but stopping by unannounced always worked well. That would also give him an excuse for visiting her. He planned to drop in on Miranda Johnson the next day, but that was no concern of Becky's.

As of yet, the kid that had been in the car wreck with Buzz was hanging in there. However, he was still in intensive care. Wilson suddenly realized he had more irons in the fire than he wanted.

He hummed to himself as he drove northeast on Route 32 toward Flemingsburg. When he pulled into Becky's drive, he was surprised to see the garage door open. He was equally surprised seeing no car. Did Adkins have another car? As he climbed from the cab of his truck, he nearly stepped on the broken garage door opener lying at his feet. He also noticed that the front door was standing open. He relaxed, thinking that Becky was probably inside. He knocked and waited a moment but received no answer. He tried the handle, it was unlocked.

Sticking his head in the door, he called, "Mrs. Adkins?"

No one was home. Maybe she ran to the grocery. He didn't really need to be concerned. This was Kentucky and people don't usually lock their houses.

•   •   •

Tom turned into the main unit at Clay's and parked in the lot. He pulled his bow out of the truck, and then knocked an arrow before he stepped into the woods. He hoped to see more sign here at Clay, more than he had near his place.

The trails that led back toward the creek were much more defined than around his trailer. That was promising. He didn't really need to bring his bow this morning, but you never know what you might spook when scouting. There were several rubs on the trees. That was encouraging. Tom felt better about his chances here. He pulled out his GPS and made his way back toward Cassidy Creek.

Tom had stopped his truck earlier at a spot he liked the looks of, on Cassidy Creek Road. He set a way point on his GPS and now he walked toward that point. From the road, the woods had looked perfect for game. Tom was even more impressed with them now, as he scared various animals out of hiding. Driving to Clay from his trailer had taken only fifteen minutes. He didn't want to invest hours driving around looking for bigger game. He'd love to score a trophy buck, but he wasn't really worried about getting a record on Boone and Crockett.

A little over an hour later, Tom walked through the edge of the woods which bordered Cassidy Creek Road, where he'd set the waypoint. Now, he would backtrack and head to his truck. Hopefully, he'd find a perfect tree along the way.

• • •

Steve was completely unaware of himself. He was in a hospital bed and didn't even know it. He would never get his GED, he would never marry. He'd made a major mistake and had no way of correcting it. It would have been nice to turn back time, but that only works in the movies or the music scene. He would never see his mom or dad again. There were numerous things that he would have changed if he had one more chance. But that chance seemed to be slipping away as he lay in the intensive care unit at Saint Joseph Lexington. He had no knowledge of the helicopter ride. He probably would have enjoyed it. Steve had made a terrible mistake, a mistake that would cost him his life.

Even though his father had never been around, it didn't mean that he didn't care for the boy, but that was another story. On the outside, Steve's injuries looked minimal, but looks were deceiving. This was one of those times, looks had been very deceiving.

Unfortunately for Steve, he'd been on the receiving end of a bad batch of crystal meth. Maybe a more hardened user would have shrugged it off. But he wasn't a hard user and he hadn't built up his tolerance level yet. His body couldn't handle all the drugs he'd ingested. Steve didn't make it. Just nineteen, he died of a heart attack.

• • •

Keith Poole was notified about Steve Caudill's death. Since the cause of death had been undetermined, an autopsy was necessary. The doctors at the ICU obviously knew the probable cause of death, but by law, the County Coroner needed to be involved. He was responsible for contacting the next of kin.

Keith was not anxious to tell the parents of a nineteen year old boy that their son was dead, but at least Wilson would accompany him on that task. Wilson was responsible for getting in touch with the deceased's immediate family. Then, both men would go visit the home and explain what had happened to their son.

It was Wilson's job to track down Steve's father, Bruce Caudill. He had found out that he worked for J.B. Hunt Transport and was able to get in touch with him through the company's dispatcher. It would be another day before Bruce could get back to Carlisle as he was finishing a delivery in St. Louis. Protocol demanded that the family wasn't informed about the death over the phone. As soon as Bruce arrived home, he'd learn of the details. This would be Wilson's first NOK notification and he wasn't looking forward to it. He really hoped that Keith would handle the explanation since he had more experience. Besides, he was the funeral director, wasn't he?

●　　　●　　　●

Tom got up and made a nice breakfast of bacon, eggs and wheat toast. He was hungry, probably because of all his trekking around in the woods. Bella gave him the cold shoulder. She was still mad about all the time he'd been spending in the woods, without her.

After cooking the bacon, he poured the excess grease on Bella's food, but she just turned up her nose. She was going to teach him a lesson. It didn't matter to Tom. She'd eat when she got hungry. Bella had managed to chew a batch of hair from her haunches. Tom referred to it as Bella's Mohawk look. They were going to the vet for her damned monthly allergy shot. Tom wasn't sure if Bella's condition was really due to allergies, but as of yet he'd been unsuccessful in trying to locate a dog psychologist in Nicholas County.

The trip to the vet would probably help Bella appreciate her master again. If she could only remember back in her dog brain to the time she'd been spayed, when she had to stay overnight for observation, all night in that horrible place with all those smells. When he brought her home, she cried, and then rolled over onto her back to show him her shaved belly. She wanted Tom to appreciate the amount of trauma she'd been through.

This visit would be brief and then back to the homestead. That should make Bella very happy, until Tom deserted her and went off to the woods. Maybe they'd go out on a long hike this afternoon. That would make her feel that she was still part of everything. Tom really didn't want to come home one day after hunting to find that Bella had gone crazy and chewed off one of her paws.

CHAPTER 17

Wilson was just about to knock on the door as Miranda Johnson opened it. She invited him in and then spun around in her electric wheelchair, as she made her way into the living room. Wilson had decided to try a little small talk. Maybe that would help Miranda be more cooperative.

"So, Miranda how's your grandmother?"

"My grandmother's fine. She's seventy years old and uses a walker. We have a whole lot of fun together, you know, just rolling around the house."

Wilson didn't care much for her attitude, but guessed he couldn't blame her. It must be hard to be in the prime of your life and then suddenly finding yourself confined to a wheelchair. He wanted to know if Miranda recalled anything new, if she remembered any more about what happened the night of her accident.

"Miranda, it's been a while since Tom Padgett and I was here. Have you recalled anything new since the last time we talked?"

"Sheriff, you left me your business card. You asked me to call you if I remembered anything, right?"

"Yes, that's right."

"Have I called you?"

Wilson felt his face redden. "No, you haven't called."

"So the obvious answer must be no, I haven't had any revelations."

He managed to hold his temper. He was through with the small talk, might as well get to the matter at hand. He pulled the copy of Becky Adkins' photo from the folder that he'd been carrying and laid it on the coffee table between them.

•   •   •

Albert wasn't particularly happy about doing business in his trailer. But, what choice did he have? Luckily, he hadn't seen the sheriff around anymore. Maybe he just over-reacted and the sheriff didn't suspect him. Besides, the time it took to get to Robertson County and back was starting to add up. He suddenly had more customers than he could handle. Maybe he'd have to stop taking new patients, like doctors did.

One advantage of working at home was that he could set his own hours and he planned on changing them. He was going to start cooking a little later than he previously had. Something like 10pm, that way he'd be finishing up around 6am. Then he could clean up and deliver his product.

Albert wasn't happy about some of the price increases for marijuana that a few of suppliers were asking for. Unfortunately, the sheriff had confiscated more crops. He'd even shut down a couple of operations. Luckily, that was only in Nicholas County. He was still getting favorable prices over in Fleming County. The sheriff in Fleming must have bigger fish to fry, not as much free time as the Nicholas County Sheriff. Pursuing simple little pot growers, didn't he have other things to do?

He thought about what a pain the sheriff was becoming and shook his head. Albert figured he'd have to adjust his meth prices in order to pay for the higher prices he was being forced to pay for his marijuana. Just like everything else, it all boiled down to the cost of doing business and competitive advantage.

•   •   •

Tom just finished lunch and remembered that he'd promised Bella a hike in the woods. "Bella, do you want to go for a walk?"

Her tail made a good thump on the kitchen linoleum floor. She was ready for a big romp. Tom pulled the door closed and turned around to see her bound through the gap in the fence. She turned and waited for Tom to catch up with her. "Good girl, Bella."

He wore a light jacket. It was cool outside now with a chance of frost tonight. Tomorrow would be a great time to see what kind of activity was in the woods at Clay's. This would need to be a long hike in order to keep Bella satisfied.

There were a lot more leaves off the trees since the last time he'd been through here. One more sign of the approaching winter. The chipmunks and squirrels had been busy. Shells of acorn and hickory nuts were everywhere. It was generally quiet in the woods, with only occasional disturbances of chain saws or shot gun blasts.

About an hour into the hike Tom turned for home. "Come on Bella." Now she noticed a squirrel challenging her in the distance, at least a hundred yards away. She was off.

● ● ●

Becky Adkins' photo lay on the coffee table between them. Wilson noticed the shocked expression on Miranda's face. She stared down at the photo but said nothing. Wilson tried to refrain from saying anything for fear of further chastising by the snippy girl. He waited. She was still silent. Only her mouth was open. He could just make out her lips mouth three words.

"Oh my God."

Wilson remained silent and waited for any additional reaction.

"Where did you get this?"

Wilson was never one to readily share credit, "Oh, I did some checking around and came up with it."

Miranda tried to recover, "It's her. That's the lady that sold me the pills at the football game."

"Are you absolutely sure?"

"Of course I'm sure. Do you think I would ever forget that face?"

Wilson contemplated the gravity of the situation. "Would you be willing to testify in a court of law that this is the woman that sold you the Oxycontin?"

"Yes, are you crazy? Of course I would."

Wilson, seeing that she was getting worked up, pulled the photo away from her.

"Why'd you take that?"

He couldn't think of an appropriate reply, but managed, "because the photo belongs in the police record."

"Can I get a copy of it?"

He was in control of himself again. "No, Miranda. I don't believe that would be a good idea." He told her that he would be in touch and walked out the door.

•   •   •

Tom enjoyed the first beer of the afternoon. His phone rang. Recognizing the number, he laughed before answering, "Hello Nick."

"Well, I'll be, if it isn't my old pal Tom."

"Hey, Nick, how you been doing?"

"I'm doing just great. I was awarded the Wal-mart greeter of the month trophy."

"You've got to be kidding me, right?"

"Yeah, but I did get a ten cent raise."

"What have you been up to?"

"Oh you know this and that. Why don't we meet over at the Gyp for a beer, in about half an hour?"

Tom glanced at his watch and noticed that it was three o'clock, "Its five o'clock somewhere," he reasoned.

When he arrived at the Gyp Joint, Nick was entertaining everyone that was sitting at the bar. He hoped that he wasn't keeping them riveted with more tales of the *greeter*. Nick paused for breath when Tom approached.

"Hey stranger, long time no see."

"Yeah, Nick, what's it been seven or eight days?"

"Has it only been that long? It sure seemed longer than that to me."

"So tell me, how in the world have you been doing? Have you been keeping out of trouble?"

"You know me, Tom. Trouble follows me where ever I go."

They both laughed. Tom offered a toast, "To friendship."

"Have you heard from Becky?"

"Not a word."

"Seems odd, don't you think, that she'd just disappear like that?"

"No, it's probably not that odd. The lady had plenty of issues. Hopefully, she's working her way through some of them. And how's Woozy doing? I'm assuming you've been to O'Rourke's?"

"Oh, she seems to be doing alright. At least she was the last time I was there. Which was, let me think, oh right, it was yesterday."

"Your memory's sharp as ever, Nick."

"Hey Steve, could you get Tom and me another round?"

• • •

Bruce Caudill reluctantly opened the front door and invited the two men inside. Wilson immediately noticed Caudill's eyes. They looked exhausted and worried. Bruce slouched over to a chair and indicated for them to sit opposite him. Wilson was hoping that Poole would take the lead. The main reason was that he didn't know what to say. Luckily for Wilson, Keith began.

"Mr. Caudill, I'm afraid we've got some very bad news."

Bruce leaned forward in his chair and rested his elbows on his knees. He held his head in his hands while he shook his head.

Poole continued, "Sir, your son is dead. He died of a heart attack."

Bruce Caudill's head snapped up, "How in the hell can a nineteen year old boy have a heart attack, you mind explaining that?"

Both Keith and Wilson were surprised by the sudden aggression from the boy's father. Neither had expected this type of reaction.

Keith cleared his throat before continuing, "Sir, the reason he had a heart attack was the result of taking an overdose of methamphetamines."

Caudill was on his feet, "My son didn't do drugs. He just didn't."

Wilson, now on edge, placed a hand on his holster. Keith put a calming hand on Wilson's knee. He looked at Wilson and shook his head. Wilson understood he needed to stay level headed.

Keith waited a moment before speaking, "Mr. Caudill, we don't fully understand the circumstances surrounding your son's death. But, drugs definitely played a part. Hopefully, the investigation that follows will help shine some light on the events which led to your son's death."

Caudill shook his head in regret and disbelief.

•　　•　　•

Albert had been giving consideration to a new pricing structure. He mulled some things over as he inhaled the joint from his latest stash. According to his estimates, his suppliers seemed to have raised their prices by nearly twenty percent. He felt that was entirely unreasonable given the circumstances. What, just because of a little police pressure? Hadn't there always been police pressure?

Albert realized that his clients would pay more, even a dramatic increase. He thought about the methods some of his customers employed to raise cash. He didn't need to create any more problems than he already had. He decided he needed to keep his prices reasonable. Maybe by using alternative ingredients in the cooking process, he could lower his production costs.

He'd always disagreed with cheapening the cooking process, but Albert was running a business. He knew one of the simplest ways to lower costs was to change the chemical composition. However, that paved the way for more dangerous crap for his clients. At the end of the day, what it meant was lower cost to him but more toxicity for his customers. They would still receive the same high or euphoria, which, after all, was their only goal. He knew that as long as that high was attained, the addicts would be happy. It didn't matter if their teeth rotted out a year or two earlier. Most of them weren't worried much with their looks anymore, anyway.

•   •   •

Tom got up early and immediately noticed the frost that had formed on the inside of his windows. He already knew that the trailer wasn't energy efficient. But, he'd been optimistic about keeping some of the cold out. As he enjoyed a second cup of coffee, the little electric heater clicked away by his feet. His thoughts turned to the Clay WMA. He felt good about where he planned on setting up. Bella lay at his feet next to the heater. She intently watched every move he made.

He let her outside and felt the crisp cold early morning air. The night had been clear, and at the moment, the temperature was probably in the upper twenties. Bella plopped herself down on the floor as Tom let her back inside. She could see that he had gotten dressed in his hunting attire. She realized that she wasn't going to be invited. Let the sulking begin.

He bent down and scratched her stomach, "It's alright girl. I won't be gone long."

Finding little encouragement in his words, she released a loud frustrated sigh. Tom laughed out loud as he looked down at her; the look on her face was pitiful.

•   •   •

Wilson hadn't slept well. He'd had too many things churning around in his head. He suddenly realized he had too many things to do. He needed to find Becky Adkins and he also had to address the Buzz problem. There seemed to be an unlimited number of drugs available, right under his nose. He had just finished his shower and sat at the kitchen table, drinking a cup of coffee.

Wilson began ticking things off on his fingers. One, Becky Adkins was most likely selling drugs, which was probably the cause for Miranda Johnson's accident. Two, Buzz. He had been wacked out on drugs, which contributed to Steve Caudill's death. Three, despite his continued efforts, there seemed to be an abundance of drugs available, whether it was meth, pills or marijuana.

He finished dressing and considered his plan of attack for the day. First, he'd stop by the station and see if Deputy Leland had any issues that required his attention. Afterward, he would drive over to Becky's place and deliver the bad news to her.

As he headed up Route 32 toward Fleming County, he wrestled with pangs of regret. Maybe he and Becky could have hit it off, but not now. As he turned the truck into her driveway, his regrets immediately vanished. The house was exactly as he'd left it on the previous visit. Every door to the house stood wide open. He sat in the truck and looked at the empty house. He realized that Becky Adkins had done a runner.

•   •   •

Albert was pleased with the results of his new formula. This process should help save him enough money to offset some of the recent price increases for his marijuana. The most obvious downside to the new cooking process was the increased toxicity. Because of the heightened toxicity, he had to spend greater amounts of time outdoors. This caused him to smoke more weed. He would need to fix that problem.

Another downside to his new formulation was the stronger sulfurous smell. When he stood quite far from the trailer, he could still smell the powerful odor. If the smell reached the neighbors, he hoped it would be less strong. Fortunately, there was just one neighbor in close proximity and the trailer was usually upwind.

Regardless of the issues with toxicity and the sulfurous smell, the new batch had delivered a good yield. He looked around the cook area and was very pleased with the order of the lab. He had to give himself a pat on the back for that. He was definitely a neat cook. One of the good things about this location was the ease of waste disposal. Two sides of the property joined the Clay WMA, so houses could never be built there. Since meth production caused an abundance of chemical waste, it was handy having a disposal site nearby. Just a few minutes till six, time to call it a night and make the laboratory disappear. Albert had a large fold-up table where he prepared the concoctions. Now that he was finished, he put all the potions safely out of site and folded the table.

•　　•　　•

Tom pulled his truck off Cassidy Creek Road and over onto the shoulder. He got out and started getting organized for the hunt. He parked near the main entrance to Clay. Parking on Cassidy Creek Road, eliminated at least a two-hundred yard hike to his stand. He had all his gear; tree stand, bow, knife, light, string and safety harness. He was set.

It was six o'clock, early, but he needed to get into the woods and up into his tree as soon as possible. Getting into the woods early would allow time for calm to return, and wouldn't totally interrupt the animals' routines. Like humans, animals are creatures of habit. As long as things are fairly normal, they maintain predictable behavior.

Tom was a hundred yards into the woods when the odor assaulted his nose. He hadn't smelled anything like it since he'd worked for the Mt. Sterling Police Department. He tried to ignore the smell and the memories that came flooding in. He needed to focus on today's hunt.

He slowly made his way through the woods, occasionally turning on his Maglite to verify that he was on the right trail. Fifteen minutes later, he was at his tree. He got all his gear together and placed the stand onto the tree and began his climb. When he was in position, wearing his safety harness, he pulled the bow up from the ground and knocked an arrow and waited. He listened for calm to return. He also tried to forget the smell. It was definitely the unmistakable stench of a meth lab.

• • •

Wilson was in a quandary. Becky was most likely the person that had sold Miranda Johnson the illegal drugs last fall. But, he hadn't charged her with anything when she'd wrecked her car, even though she'd been under the influence of alcohol and drugs. He'd been so anxious to get Padgett, he wasn't thinking. Now she had fled, maybe even fled the state, what should he do? He tried to think.

It's not as if he could go and ask advice from the County Attorney or anything. He was angry at himself for possibly messing up the chance to catch the person who sold Miranda the drugs. He sat at his desk, drummed his fingers and thought, what to do, what to do?

A smile slowly crept over his face. He didn't need to mention the car wreck and his attempt at *helping* Becky implicate Padgett. He could act as if that chapter had never even happened. If he could locate Becky Adkins and bring her to trial for selling drugs to Miranda, he would be a hero. He could kill two birds with one stone. He could put an old unsolved crime to bed, and at the same time get another drug dealer off the street. He'd obviously have to let Padgett off the hook for his supposed involvement in Becky Adkins' drug possession. Padgett would just have to wait. He was going to mess up sooner or later and Wilson was going to be there waiting, waiting to bring him down. Now, it was time to find out where Becky Adkins had disappeared to.

●　　●　　●

Albert had finished cleaning up and was ready to start his deliveries. It was early, actually too early. Maybe he'd go into town and grab a bite to eat. That might be a good idea. He rarely frequented Carlisle, except when he was doing deliveries. This might give him a little more credibility, being seen out and about in town. He might as well go to Garrett's. That seemed like an excellent idea, right across the street from the sheriff's office and the police station. He smiled at the irony of it.

Albert looked at the menu and realized how hungry he was. He'd forgotten about the additional marijuana he'd smoked last night. He decided on some eggs and coffee, hell maybe he'd even spring for some sausage. He'd picked up a copy of the Carlisle Courier and was just preparing to read it when both his breakfast and the sheriff arrived.

Albert quickly became consumed with the paper, holding it mere inches from his face. Sheriff Wilson had stopped in for a cup of coffee to go. Luckily, he left as quickly as he'd arrived. As Albert lowered the paper, he noticed the photo on the front page. What a shock. It was the kid from the drug exchange last week. Right there, on the front page. The nineteen year old had apparently died of a heart attack. The autopsy had confirmed that drugs were involved. Albert quickly lost his appetite. Being visible in Carlisle suddenly didn't seem like such a good idea.

●　　●　　●

Tom decided to call it a morning. Today's hunt had been somewhat successful. He'd managed to see several does and a young buck. Since this was the first time in an unfamiliar hunting site, that wasn't bad. As he walked out, he followed a different trail than the one he'd taken in. He saw plenty of fresh sign and also located the spot where the waste from the meth lab was buried on the edge of a clearing. The path was clearly evident. It ended at a trailer nearby.

Someone was going through a lot of trouble to hide the waste, but the effort was pointless based on the toxic ingredients.

He shook his head with the knowledge of what the person cooking or pushing this junk was doing to him or herself. The biggest crime though, was the damage done to the victims, the users that the drugs brought down. Tom wasn't a policeman anymore. Telling Wilson about what he found was a waste of time. It would end with Wilson trying to implicate him.

He drove slowly on the way home. Bella would be excited. It was nearly noon when he walked in the trailer and found Bella sulking on the couch.

He grabbed a beer and headed outside, "Come on, girl."

She slowly climbed off the couch, a little performance to show Tom just how upset she was. He waited patiently as she stretched and took her time. "Hurry up, Bella or I'll leave you inside."

That must have convinced her to get it together. She came out, but that didn't mean she was going to pay any attention to him.

•　　•　　•

Wilson was pretty sure he recognized the man that tried to hide behind the newspaper in Garrett's. He racked his brain, attempting to remember when and where he had seen him. He wasn't one of the drug users that hung around on half the street corners in town. Wilson also didn't believe he was a resident of Carlisle. At least he didn't think he was.

Where had he seen the guy? Then, something clicked in his head. He had seen him at the East End last week or so. He remembered that he had passed him out on Cassidy Creek Road. Wilson had circled around and checked out his trailer and thought it looked alright. Why did he act so suspicious? He might be worth taking a closer look at.

But he couldn't get bogged down with him right now. He had to determine what the best approach was to locate Becky Adkins. Buzz, the druggy that had been driving the car when Steve Caudill had died, was scheduled in court next week. If Wilson could somehow come up with Becky Adkins' whereabouts, he'd be looking good. He wasn't sure how to approach searching for Becky with some of the assets at his disposal, especially since he'd been messing with evidence.

Maybe Padgett would be willing to help him sort things out if Wilson agreed to some kind of truce. On second thought, that probably wasn't a good idea. He had most likely already burned all his bridges with Tom Padgett. Besides, he really didn't want his help, anyway.

●　　　●　　　●

Albert was furious with himself for being so stupid. What had he been thinking? Going into town to eat breakfast, at Garrett's? He was damned lucky the sheriff hadn't recognized him. Well, one thing was certain. He wouldn't ever do that ridiculous maneuver again.

He had managed to get his act together after he'd left Garrett's. He left Carlisle to text his clients from a remote location, a few miles from town. When he had everyone scheduled, he rolled back into town and efficiently delivered his goods. Then Albert just as efficiently headed to Fleming County, where he would lay low until later in the evening. The way his luck had gone in town, Albert felt that the sheriff just might be waiting in his driveway if he went straight home.

But he was still hungry. Albert found himself at McDonalds where he wolfed down a couple of double cheeseburgers and drank a Dr. Pepper. He must be getting careless. He had always prided himself for being in control. What was happening? Why was he suddenly on edge all the time? Maybe he should disappear for a while. He had some cash. But if he disappeared, would he have any customers to come back to?

Albert hated problems and now it seemed as if he was creating about half of his own. Was he losing it? As he chewed on his burger, he thought about the kid that had died. He probably died from an overdose. That was the second death that he could potentially be connected to, the second one that he was aware of, anyway. He needed to come to grips with himself.

CHAPTER 18

Tom had gotten into his stand fifteen minutes later than he liked, but there was still plenty of time for the area to settle down. He listened to all the noises nearby, fully appreciating how quiet the woods could sometimes be. He thought back to when he'd been a younger hunter, back when his hearing was far better. Sometimes, the woods could get downright noisy as various game wandered about. The squirrels could definitely make a bunch of racket. If there were squirrels playing and running around chasing one another, it was surprisingly loud. They probably weren't playing, really. The male was hopeful, but the female that was being chased, played hard to get. On especially dry mornings, two squirrels romping around could almost make a hunter believe a herd of deer were heading his way.

This morning it wasn't noisy. Tom thought about the active competition between dew and frost. As the sun broke through the trees, the frost was quickly losing. This morning, animals would be moving stealthily. Even the squirrels would be quiet. Tom was sure that the deer could easily sneak up on him today, part of the problem with his inevitable hearing loss. But, at least his eyesight was still strong. As his hearing strained and his eyes scanned the woods, he managed to spy the buck he'd spotted yesterday as it strolled in his direction. Tom was pleased with this development. He knew that as the rut got closer, the older and stronger bucks would come. This little guy was paving the way for a larger buck that soon would muscle its way into the woods.

● ● ●

Wilson was frustrated. He really didn't know the best way to proceed. But it was his own damned fault, this mess that he found himself in. Maybe he should just forget about trying to track down

Becky. He suddenly had plenty of other issues to focus on. He thought about poor Steve Caudill, just nineteen years old and now dead. Where had he gotten his drugs from? Had he gotten them from his joy riding partner, Buzz? Somehow Wilson shook this thought off. Buzz wasn't the sharpest blade in the block. He couldn't imagine him being able to mix up a batch of meth. And, he surely couldn't see him being successful at selling drugs on the street. No, Wilson felt confident. There had to be someone else.

He decided to give Buzz a courtesy call. He would drop in on him in that rundown apartment that Buzz called home. Of course, the visit would be off the record, just a test of the waters.

Buzz happened to be home and answered the door. Wilson could see by the glazed look in his eyes, that maybe he wasn't home after all. But he was here, so he had to try, "I want to ask you some questions about the day Steve Caudill died."

Buzz managed, "Wus dat?"

"Steve, the kid that was in the car with you the night you crashed."

"I dinn't kno hes nem."

"Let me get this straight. You drove around out in the country high as a kite, and you didn't even know the name of the guy sitting next to you?"

Buzz slowly shook his head.

•   •   •

Albert wasn't having a particularly good night. He was having a very hard time focusing and the toxicity of the mix was beginning to get to him. Even though he wore adequate protection, the latest batch was still burning his eyes and throat. He also spent too much time behind the trailer smoking weed. This was something he needed to address, and soon. He knew he would need to increase his prices more if he couldn't get his habit under control. Maybe he didn't care. His customers would still buy his drugs. They weren't a discerning bunch. He could substitute almost anything he wanted in order to cut costs and they wouldn't notice. Albert laughed out loud. He could use the cheapest chemicals, as long as their ultimate high was attainable. That's all that mattered.

Albert left the trailer later than usual. Clean-up had taken longer, mainly because of the additional chemical containers that he had to put away. But, the place was now pristine. He locked the door. As he walked to his car carrying the day's deliveries, he whistled to himself. He didn't like being late for his rounds. No telling what kind of trouble a stressed out junkie could get into. That wasn't his problem. All he needed to do was get this stuff into their hands. He had other business to attend to that afternoon. He needed to go see his own suppliers and get his pot. He hoped there hadn't been any more unexpected price hikes. He was looking forward to some much needed relaxation later tonight.

•   •   •

Tom enjoyed the sunlight as it filtered through the trees while he watched the little buck amble around, just below his stand. A couple of does walked by and one of them paused to urinate. The little buck's nose went crazy. Tom laughed silently as he watched the spectacle unfold beneath him, thinking *it must be love.* He watched as the does walked on through the woods. The little guy seemed content to just hang out beneath Tom's tree stand.

Ok, it was getting late, time to call it a day. But, the buck wasn't going anywhere fast. This is unbelievable, Tom thought. What to do? Spook the little buck in order to climb down from the tree? He didn't want to draw unwanted attention to himself in the tree, although he was considering it because the buck seemed to have found his favorite playground. He would be patient and wait the little guy out. As Tom watched, the buck heard something and was now on high alert. It looked off into the distance a moment before it turned and bounded off in the opposite direction.

Tom thought he would call Nick to see what he had been up to lately. He was just preparing to climb down, when a huge buck appeared out of nowhere. That was what had frightened the little guy. Tom's bow lay on the ground fifteen feet beneath him as the buck defiantly walked by.

• • •

Wilson had a new outlook. He'd decided to let Becky Adkins slide for the moment. He was still curious about that character that he'd seen in Garrett's the other morning, so he decided to go have another look at his trailer. As he drove out through the country, he felt relaxed. It felt good to have a renewed purpose. He had spent way too much time on that dead end Becky Adkins. He wouldn't make a mistake like that again.

Wilson glanced at the mail box as he slowly rolled past Albert's trailer. A. Rankin, Cassidy Creek Road. That should be easy to check out, Wilson thought. The place still looked the same, absolutely neat as a pin.

He was just about to the entrance of Clay WMA and was preparing to turn around, went he noticed a familiar truck. Well, if it isn't Tom Padgett's F-150, parked right across from the WMA entrance. That's interesting. Wilson wondered, is Padgett hunting, fishing or just hiking with that dog of his? He thought it seemed odd that Padgett felt compelled to come way out here to do any of that. He had plenty of places to hunt over on Abners Mill. Well, the wildlife area is noted for its hunting, fishing and hiking, so maybe I shouldn't draw too many conclusions. Just in case, he pulled up alongside Padgett's truck, got out and took a look inside. Wilson could see face paint and buck lure containers lying on the seat. Hmmm, he must be hunting.

• • •

Nick was in his usual spot, bellied up to the bar as Tom walked in. He yelled out, "Hey Tom, How's things been going?"

"Everything's been great!"

Nick spun around, "Hey Woozy, could you round up a couple for Tom and me?"

Woozy seemed tired to Tom, but at least she didn't appear to have any visible marks. Maybe the threat that he had laid on Jimmy

Fugate was still holding. He hoped so, anyway. Woozy returned with the beer and gave Tom a quick smile.

"How are you holding up, Woozy?"

"Oh, you know, I can't complain." She turned and went back to take care of business farther down the bar.

Nick was beaming, "So tell me. What have you been doing with yourself?"

"Not a great deal, you know how retirement can be."

"Yes sir, I surely do. They've asked me to work an extra day over at Wal-mart."

"Nick, aren't you supposed to be enjoying your retirement?"

"I'm only sixty. You know I get bored sitting around the house."

Tom smiled and slowly shook his head before he replied, "It sounds like you need to find yourself a hobby."

"Now there's an idea. You mean something other than eating and drinking beer?"

"Yes, I mean a real hobby, something that you're interested in, which keeps you engaged. You know something like hunting. That might just be the ticket. Think of it, plenty of fresh air, and all kinds of exercise."

Nick seemed to consider this for a moment before responding, "Now that you mention it, I guess eating and beer drinking will have to suffice. Besides I'd really hate to lose my beer belly. I've become quite attached to it. You could say we're inseparable."

●　　●　　●

Wilson found nothing on file for Albert Rankin. So, if he had no record, why did he behave so weirdly the other morning at Garrett's? This was one of Wilson's foolproof indicators of guilt. When someone appeared nervous for little or no reason, they must be hiding something. Some things seemed to finally be sorting themselves out.

Buzz was definitely going to go down for drug activity and also for reckless vehicular operation. Steve, well he got what he had coming, unfortunately. But who were the suppliers? He'd asked the city cops. They seemed to have few leads into the drug activity. That was unacceptable. The drugs were being pushed right under their noses. Wilson knew better than to get into some kind of pissing contest in Carlisle. That would just get the Mayor riled up. He needed to think outside the box. If Wilson had been making and selling drugs, how would he have done it?

Friday night finally

Wilson couldn't remember the last time he'd been so anxious for Friday night. He didn't have any grand plans. It would just be nice to forget about hoods for a while. He climbed out of his truck, just as his nosey neighbor stepped out to get her mail. He acted like he hadn't seen her and quickly walked to his door.

"Hey, Wilson, you got any more weird ideas or plans this weekend?"

God, if he wasn't a law enforcement officer, he just might wander over and smack her, right upside the head. He slammed the door behind him. Maybe he should look for another place? He hadn't planned on hitting the bottle tonight, but maybe it wasn't such a bad idea. He hadn't gotten into any trouble the last time.

•   •   •

Albert had managed to get through his drug dealings in town without any problems. Maybe he wasn't losing it after all. His marijuana buys had gone ok, also. Nicholas County's prices were still higher, but he needed every one of his suppliers in order to fulfill his increased needs. He thought how funny it was that the business world worked, from Wall Street to pot growers on Mexico Road in Fleming County. They all adhered to the same principles. Albert leaned back in his recliner and enjoyed his first smoke of the evening. The first smoke or the first drink, those were always the best. He wasn't going to rush tonight. No, tonight he was going to take his time and enjoy himself.

He wondered why his clients seem to use less meth on the weekend. That didn't make any sense. He usually cooked meth on Friday night and then did nothing on Saturday night, so why no complaints? Maybe the users saved some of their stash for big weekend blowouts? That didn't make sense to him either. Maybe there was some brotherly love happening, some sharing that happened only on weekends, like parties or something. He had absolutely no idea. The more he thought about it, the less sense it made. But, he wasn't complaining. He welcomed the downtime, but these were chronic users. They should be desperate for everything they could get. Albert let out a loud guffaw, after inhaling more of his reefer. Why in the hell did he even care? Why should he care at all?

● ● ●

Tom laughed at himself as he told his tale, "My bow lay down there on the ground and a twelve point buck slowly meandered by. To add insult to injury, the buck even gave the bow a big sniff."

Nick laughed so hard he cried as Tom recited his unfortunate hunting tale. "You mean the deer waited for you to let your bow down to the ground before it decided to walk from cover?"

Tom looked down at his beer can, "I guess it did. That's exactly how it happened."

Nick was on a roll now, "Tom, you mean the big old stupid buck outsmarted you?"

"Yes, stuff like that happens more than I like to think about."

"Hey, Woozy honey, could you bring Tom a fresh beer? I think he's ruined this one, with all those tears he's been crying."

Tom held up a hand, "Enough talk about all my misfortunes with animals, two legged and four legged. Can I be serious for a moment?"

Showing concern, Nick prompted, "Go ahead."

"Nick, I've got to ask you a serious question. This might be a little bit personal, are you up for that?"

Looking really worried, Nick seriously said, "I hope I am, Tom."

Tom took a slow, deep swallow of beer. "It's come to my attention that Wal-mart has big plans for you. I've been told they've got huge plans."

"Where'd you hear that from?"

"I have my connections. I've been appointed by Wal-mart to offer you a promotion. Will you accept the position to Chief Operating Greeter?"

Nick let out a huge sigh and tried to catch his breath. Tom leaned on the bar laughing.

"You really had me going. I thought something terrible had happened."

Tom got Woozy's attention, "Hey Woozy, I think Nick could use a fresh beer. This one's all foamy from his shaking hand."

Tom stopped laughing when he looked over at Nick. He had suddenly gotten pale.

"Nick, are you ok?"

"I think so. It's just that my heart hasn't been quite right today."

"You should have said something, Nick."

"It's alright. I'll just take my nitro tablet and go home."

Tom was worried now. He watched Nick as he feebly reached into his pocket and pulled out a tiny prescription bottle. Tom hung his head and stared into his beer.

Nick turned, faced Tom, and then winked, "Got you back, ass hole."

• • •

Wilson kicked off his shoes and leaned back in his recliner. He was relishing his first drink of the night. A nice slow sip of whiskey was about as good as life gets. That's the way Wilson felt right now. He thought about the neighbor lady and wondered what to do. It wasn't as if he could file a complaint or anything like that. Didn't she have anything better to do? Why was she always worrying about him? He decided right then and there not to do anything stupid tonight. No way was he giving her anything else to get excited about.

Excited, now that was a rarely used word, rarely used by him lately. When was the last time he had any real excitement? DVDs filled one complete shelf of his bookcase, but he'd seen them all multiple times. As he took another sip, he thought about the last woman he'd been with.

Her name was Susan. They'd broken up two years ago. That was the last relationship of any substance that he'd been involved in. Two years, he sipped and reflected. Two years is a long time. He knew he had some problems which caused undue stress in relationships. But didn't everyone? Susan, she was some woman. She was quite a looker. He wondered what had happened to her. He tried to remember if he still had her number. As he looked through his contact list, he saw that he did and hit the call button. The phone rang several times before going to voicemail. He hung up. What was he thinking? What would he even say to her after all this time? He glanced over at the DVDs. Wilson read the familiar titles, Penitentiary Babes, Crazy Wild Sara, Hot Lady in the City, etc. None piqued his interest.

• • •

Tom was on the road home. He didn't like driving after he'd drunk so much beer, but they'd gotten a bit carried away. He and Nick had been having way too much fun. He cruised down Route 68, speed control locked on fifty-eight in a fifty-five zone. Everyone passed him, and that was fine.

Tom hoped Bella was ok. It had been hours since she'd been outside. He chuckled to himself as he thought about how she would demonstrate her level of displeasure. He wondered what it'd be like if Bella could talk. No, that wouldn't be a good thing. He probably wouldn't enjoy some of the things she'd have to say. One thing was certain; he didn't need a woman in his life. Bella provided more than enough drama.

He opened the trailer door and expected Bella to sprint outside to relieve herself. No Bella. She was in the bedroom and he tried to coax her outside. She really looked like she was pouting.

"Come on Bella, don't you have to go to the bathroom?"

She just turned her head and laid it on the floor. Ok, Tom thought, I might as well have one more beer. Maybe Bella will recognize a sense of normalcy. As he pulled a beer from the fridge, Bella padded into the living room.

"Are you ready to go outside now?"

Tom watched her do her business for some time. Holding it for so long would have killed him. She was finally finished, but not finished punishing him. She lay down several feet away from where he sat.

"Bella, you are somethin' else. Sometimes you're a real handful."

•　　•　　•

When Wilson woke up, he immediately noticed the pounding in his head. Maybe I should just close my eyes again and try to sleep until tomorrow. Hangovers aren't very forgiving though, and this one isn't going to let me off the hook. So why fight it?

He pulled himself upright and wandered into the kitchen. He grabbed the aspirin bottle and poured out four tablets, then stuck his head under the faucet to wash them down. Coffee, I need some coffee. After his coffee finished brewing, he moved to the living room, back to the comfort of his recliner. He remembered most of the evening, which was a very good thing. He took a sip of coffee, closed his eyes, and tried to will the pounding in his brain to stop.

As the pain lessened, Wilson opened his eyes and glanced around the room. Nothing seemed to be out of place. The karaoke machine wasn't hooked up, thank God, so there shouldn't be a surprise YouTube video. He finished his coffee and walked to the kitchen for another cup. When he returned, he noticed that many of his movies were scattered about on top of the DVD player. All of them were removed from their cases and were lying haphazardly around. He didn't remember watching any movies last night. Had someone else visited him? He moved out onto the back porch. Wilson breathed in the crisp morning air. Thank God that meddlesome old neighbor wasn't out, poking her head in his business.

●   ●   ●

Tom got up early and Bella was ready for the new day. She had totally forgotten how angry she'd been last night. Tom thought if only his ex-wife had had such short term memory. Maybe they'd still be together. No, that life was ancient history. He was even glad with the way it turned out.

He poured some coffee and stepped outside. He wouldn't hunt today, but a hike in the woods would be good. Tom whipped up some breakfast and read the paper. Nothing exciting had been happening around town. He thought about the article he'd read in the paper last week. It was about a nineteen year old that had died from a heart attack, but drugs seemed to be a factor. Tom shook his head.

He got dressed and ready to go. Now he could make the announcement. "Bella, do you want to go for a walk?"

He knew that if she could speak she'd probably say *hell yeah, and why'd you take so long to ask me*? Bella darted around the back of the trailer and into the woods. She knew where she wanted to go. Tom followed while she led. She jumped a squirrel and chased it before it escaped up a large maple. Then she waited for Tom to catch up, wagging her tail in triumph. A moment later, she saw a group of deer a hundred yards in the distance; she was after them in a flash. This was definitely Bella's kind of day. Chasing was one of the most enjoyable things in life.

●   ●   ●

The weekend had come and gone. Albert had finished another long night of cooking in his toxic kitchen. He was tired of the game. He needed a change. He couldn't figure out how it had gotten this way.

He thought of his mother. He hadn't seen her in years. He wondered if she was still living. Somehow, he knew that she probably was. She was *too damned mean* to die. He thought about the recent death of Jack Estep and felt a boost of confidence. Yes, he had bucked tradition. He was making meth in his own home. So far, he hadn't made any mistakes. If Estep had still been alive, he'd proudly show him how his operation worked. But Estep wasn't living, and Albert worried about his own mortality.

Albert had a lot of shopping to do this afternoon. He needed more chemicals and for those, he generally shopped in Lexington. He would spread the wealth around to many stores. That way nobody would question his large chemical purchases.

He finished around noon with his deliveries and rolled down the four-lane, making his way to Fayette Mall. Albert didn't actually shop in the mall, but the stores he frequented were nearby. He would go to Lowes, Home Depot and of course, Wal-mart, where everyone shopped. Oh, and he couldn't forget CVS. He needed more medication. He pulled out of Thornton's after reluctantly dropping nearly $4 a gallon. It seemed as if everyone was trying to get rich off of everybody else.

•　　•　　•

The following morning

Tom was in the woods alone, much to Bella's displeasure. He had promised her that he'd return early and that seemed to appease her. He felt lucky this morning and the conditions felt right. It was cold with swirling wind. The deer should definitely be moving, so he might have an advantage.

Bucks got more careless as the rut approached and the wind messed with their normally keen senses. The wind was also messing with Tom's senses. He felt the chilly blast of a twenty mile per hour gust. He hoped he'd be able to hear the animals moving around with all the noise. He pulled his collar higher, attempting to cover his ears and waited.

He watched the does come into the clearing at around 8:30. There were four of them, two large and two smaller, mamas with their fawns. They all ambled about for a while before one of the group tensed, alerting the others. They started to leave. Something they weren't interested in was coming their way. It was the big buck that had surprised Tom earlier. The does apparently didn't want anything to do with the big guy. Tom waited patiently as the buck came straight at him. He looked bigger, bigger than he remembered. Tom whispered to himself, come on big boy, come on. The buck suddenly stopped and turned to give Tom a perfect broadside shot.

Tom had already drawn his bow and was holding steady on the buck while he tried to get control of his breathing. The shot was approximately fifty yards with no obstructions. The buck took another tentative step and Tom released the arrow. The bow was so quiet; the buck didn't even flinch, that is, until the arrow hit something. The buck spun and bounded off in the direction he'd just come from.

Tom couldn't believe it, he missed? What could have happened? His hunt was finished today. He quickly climbed down from the tree and walked to the spot where his arrow should have been. He looked back at the tree and approximated the track of the arrow. That's when he noticed the small sapling that had changed the arrow's course. The arrow was buried in the soil. It had been deflected, and landed under the buck's chest.

●   ●   ●

Wilson was in relatively good spirits. Buzz had gotten sentenced for reckless operation of a vehicle and also for being under the influence of drugs. The penalty wasn't severe because he was a first time offender, and that usually meant a less harsh sentence. Wilson still wasn't satisfied, because Buzz hadn't given up the name of his supplier. It seemed that he might not have even known who his supplier was. How can you buy drugs from a person you've never met? How can you drive around in a car, and then have an accident in which the person next to you dies, and you don't even know his name? Wilson was not a man that liked mysteries. He intended to solve this one.

He stepped out onto the courthouse steps and could see people milling about on a couple of the corners nearby. Well, there are *two less people* hanging about this morning, he thought. Those were just the cold hard facts.

He drove down to the East End. He was just killing time. He got a large coffee and climbed back into his truck. As he sat in the parking lot, it dawned on him. He realized how busy this little gas station/diner was. Wilson ate here on occasion, but he usually ate at Garrett's. All sorts of people wandered in and out. It might be a good idea to eat here every once and a while. You never know, he might crack some big case while relaxing in the East End parking lot.

●   ●   ●

His phone rang. Tom stared at the number before answering. "Hello."

"Hello dad," his son said nervously.

Tom hadn't received a call from Andy in two years and was totally stunned. He sat down at the kitchen table. "Hey, Andy, how have you been doing?" The conversation would be a struggle if Andy didn't have anything to contribute.

"Oh, all right, I guess. Dad, the reason I called, is to tell you that I'm getting married."

Tom nearly dropped the phone. "Well, great Andy. Who's the lucky lady?"

"Her name is Nancy. We've been dating for three months."

"When's the wedding planned?"

"Not for a while yet, we've really just begun to talk about it." Andy told his father that he'd like to bring Nancy around to meet him.

"Well, my place in the country isn't so nice. Maybe we could meet at a restaurant or something."

"We don't care about where you live. Nancy's parents aren't well off either."

Tom wasn't sure what not well off either was all about, but he didn't want to blow it. "When are you planning on coming?"

"We're gonna spend the night with Mom on Friday night, so how about Saturday morning?"

"That sounds good, Andy. And how long will you be able to stay?"

"Oh, not very long, we need to be back in Lexington by early afternoon."

"Okay, son, I guess I'll see you on Saturday. Do you need directions?"

"No, I got your address from Mom. See you Saturday, Dad."

Tom was shocked to have received a call from his son. He was even more shocked that Andy was coming to visit and his claim to have gotten his address from Darlene. He'd never given Darlene any information about where he was living. Maybe some of his pension paperwork that had gone through the Mt. Sterling Police Department had found its way across the Mayor's desk. Old Bud Blankenship must be supplying Darlene with information on him, like where he lived for instance. Well, isn't that just sweet? Why would Darlene care about where he lived anyway? Hopefully she wasn't planning to visit.

Tom looked around the trailer and wondered how to make it a little more hospitable. He didn't wonder long. He realized there was no way to make a worn out trailer nice. Besides, Nancy's parents were just like him, *not well off.*

• • •

Albert had done well with his shopping. He'd been economical and managed to find many ingredients on sale. Now, for the dreaded drive back home. He hated driving in Lexington, especially on New Circle Road. The lights were so poorly timed. He wondered what genius traffic light engineer had programmed all the lights. He laughed at the thought. He thought about Jack Estep. Estep was going to have become an engineer. Maybe if he'd still been living, he could have become the traffic light czar.

Finally, he was through the New Circle mess and headed northeast. Another hour and he'd be home. He had a car full of supplies. Hopefully, they'd last at least two weeks. He couldn't stand dealing with Lexington traffic. Just the thought of it made him crazy.

He turned into his drive and parked. Albert grabbed two gallons of paint thinner from the trunk and made his way to his trailer. He unlocked the front door, pushed it open with his hip and made his way inside. The room reeked of gas. Albert's initial reaction was slow. Did he leave the gas on? He dropped the cans of thinner, and quickly shut off the burner of the stove. He threw open the back door in order to help clear the air. Normally, this might have been the right decision. Tonight however, it happened to be the worst thing Albert could have done. The igniter on the door's threshold quickly did its job. Albert wasn't sure exactly what happened. What he remembered, was that it was loud and bright.

CHAPTER 19

Wilson had just stepped from the shower when he heard his phone ringing. He wrapped a towel around himself, but by the time he reached his cell, it had gone to voice mail. He turned and walked to the bathroom to finish getting dressed. Looking in the mirror, he was disappointed. Had he put on more weight? He was going to have to either get serious about exercise, or go on a diet. Neither of the options pleased him. He decided that doing nothing was the most logical plan.

After he slipped into some comfortable clothes, he picked up his cell. There was a voicemail waiting, from the State Police. He played the message back and listened as an officer reported on a mobile home fire with injuries, on Cassidy Creek Road.

He returned the call and got the State Police dispatch and was told that the trailer fire was still in progress. Address in hand, Wilson hung up and walked back to the bedroom to change, so much for a quiet evening.

He thought about the houses on Cassidy Creek Road. He believed most of them were trailers. He continued to mull things over in his mind as he got into his truck. Could the fire be at Albert Rankin's trailer? That didn't seem likely based on the outside appearance of the trailer. Wilson suspected the possibility of a meth lab gone awry somewhere. He knew he was jumping to conclusions, but every once in a while, his instincts were dead on. Wilson flipped on his indicator and turned onto Cassidy Creek Road.

• • •

Tom remained seated for a long while. It was dark outside. He hadn't moved from the spot since he'd talked with Andy earlier in the afternoon. He needed to move. He needed to get circulation going in his legs. He couldn't believe that Andy was coming to introduce his bride-to-be. Maybe the boy was growing up, and finally going to give Tom the time of day.

Tom didn't understand how to deal with or how to feel about this turn of events. He welcomed reconciliation with his son, but would it really happen? Sure, it could happen, but both parties would need to do their fair share. Tom felt that he could give some, he hoped Andy could.

He recalled past arguments that he and Darlene had, all too often, concerning Andy. She'd always be sure to throw out the 'he's just like you' line. Tom hated hearing that. Besides, if Andy was just like him, why was he so damned difficult to get along with? Tom didn't like to dwell on the past.

He walked to the fridge and snatched a Bud. Andy wants to get married, well good for him. I hope this Nancy turns out to be a better wife than Andy's mother was. Tom was moping and he knew it. He took a long pull from his beer. Maybe Nancy would be a nice girl. Maybe she'd be able to help them deal with their difficult relationship. Tom hoped so, but he had no idea why they insisted on coming to his trailer.

●   ●   ●

Wilson moved over to the side of the road to give the ambulance room. Well, at least its lights are on, that's a good sign. Wilson could tell that the fire was nearly under control. It was Albert Rankin's trailer. One end had been heavily damaged by the flames.

He climbed out of his truck and was met by the State policeman in charge, Sergeant Thompson. He shook Wilson's hand in introduction. "Well, Sheriff. It's a little early to tell, but my suspicions would lean toward a meth lab."

"Yes, Sergeant, I think I'd agree with that assessment."

"Sheriff, do you have the necessary manpower? Can you handle this investigation, or would you like some State help?"

"Normally, I'd take all the help I can get, but I've already got some insight as to what happened here tonight. If you guys could help me with the crime scene tape, I'll take it from here."

After the fire department had finished and the state boys were gone, Wilson wandered around and shined his Maglite over the scene. He couldn't see very well and he didn't want to contaminate the area. He called Deputy Leland and told him keep an eye on the place overnight.

As he walked to his truck, he noticed something odd about Rankin's car. Was the trunk lid open? Wilson walked over. He lifted the lid on the old Buick. Well, what do we have here? He saw bleach, paint thinner, lye, iodine crystals, and drain cleaner. Wilson smiled looks like we got us the makings of a lab. The cars doors were locked but Wilson shone the light inside and saw that the backseat was loaded with chemicals. The passenger floorboard was full with bags from various drug stores. Well, Mr. Rankin, it looks like I'll be paying you a visit, come morning.

•   •   •

Albert was at the Nicholas County Hospital. His burns were only second degree. The doctor had informed him that they were keeping him overnight for observation. Albert had been lucky. His injuries could have been much worse. That's what the doctor had told him. He had nothing to do but think as he lay there and looked at the four walls.

He wondered how the doctor knew that he'd been lucky. Did medical training include course work that dealt with explosions? He tried to remember what had happened. He had gone to the door, unlocked it, and walked in and then smelled gas. He turned off the gas and opened the door to clear the air, and BOOM. Maybe he had been lucky. The blast had blown him right through the door. He ended up in the back yard.

He remembered watching the trailer burn. He also remembered trying to scoot away as he lay on his back. He managed to move further away before the second explosion occurred. He thought of the cans of thinner he'd dropped, that might have done it.

He could hear sirens in the distance. He had nowhere to run. He was so tired.

Albert lay back and waited as the trailer burned. What could have happened? He was always so careful. He always cleaned up and put everything in its place. How could the gas have been left on? Could the gas valve have failed, malfunctioned somehow? He didn't think so. Again he asked himself, what could have happened? Help arrived. The EMTs tore his clothing off, stabilized him and prepared him for the ambulance ride.

•   •   •

Tom was up early, but he was always up early. He had no intention of hunting today, especially after missing that buck. Back to the drawing board, he needed to practice. He knew that things like saplings deflecting your shot happened, but he still felt he'd failed. He had always been his toughest critic. He wasn't about to let up now. An hour of shooting should do it.

He sipped on his coffee and thought about all the shots he'd missed over the years. There hadn't been a great deal of them, but that didn't change the facts. When you blow a shot, you've nobody to blame but yourself. People that make excuses for their shortcomings are just kidding themselves.

Bella watched Tom put arrow after arrow inside the two inch circle, from fifty yards. He couldn't hope for much better than that. He needed to run to Maysville to go shopping. He needed groceries and he'd get some things to brighten up the place. Tom didn't have a woman's touch, but he was going to try and make the place more inviting, more feminine. After Andy and Nancy's visit, he could file the frilly stuff back in a drawer until it was needed again.

He looked around the trailer and tried to figure out what it lacked. This was going to be a pain. He hated shopping. He hadn't thought about it much, but that was one thing he missed about Darlene. She did all the shopping.

•   •   •

Wilson stopped at the hospital to check on his latest patient. The nurse gave him the room number and he knocked on the door. After he entered, he found Albert enjoying his breakfast. Albert had been told he was to be released soon, so he needed to arrange for a ride. Albert wondered where he was supposed to go.

Wilson waited for Albert to finish chewing, "Well, Mr. Rankin, it seems you had quite an eventful evening. And, I'm glad that you seem to be doing alright."

"Why thank you, Sheriff."

"Albert, do you mind if I call you Albert?"

Albert shook his head, "Not at all, Sheriff."

"I'd like to ask you some questions about you're unfortunate accident. Is that all right with you?"

"I guess so. Do I have a choice?"

"No, I'm afraid you don't." Can you tell me exactly what happened last night?"

"Well, I'd just gotten home and when I opened the door, boom."

"Just like that, huh? You opened the door and boom?"

"Yeah, I don't know what could have happened."

"You didn't smell gas or anything like that?"

"Not that I remember, maybe something mechanical happened, I don't know."

"Albert, I'm going to have another look around your trailer, just to be sure everything looks on the up and up. You sure there's nothing else you want to tell me?"

"I wish there was, Sheriff, but that's what happened."

Wilson looked at him for a bit. "Albert, do you have somewhere you can go, someone you can stay with?"

He thought for a moment, "Yeah, I do."

"That's good. Now don't you be thinking about taking off until you hear from me, ok?"

● ● ●

Albert clicked off his phone. Funny, but no one wanted to put him up for a few days. His two best friends, his suppliers from Mexico Road, said they had no room. Another supposed friend had an equally lame excuse. He didn't have a whole lot of options. His trailer was ruined. Then, he remembered his car. If he could get a ride over to Cassidy Creek, he'd have wheels. He thought of all the people he knew around the county and couldn't come up with one person that would be willing to help him out. His old burned clothes were in a bag sitting on the floor. He rooted through the pockets and found thirty dollars in cash. Surely he'd be able to bribe somebody for a ride over to the trailer.

With his so-called friends search exhausted, he called a number he hadn't called in over five years. "Mom," he uttered when she answered.

Albert's mom didn't drive, but she had a neighbor that agreed to give him a ride to her house, for $20, of course. Albert checked himself in the mirror. He had miscellaneous bandages on his face and hands. He wondered why they hadn't just wrapped gauze all the way around his head. At least that would have given him the appearance of a sheik or something. They wheeled him out the door, in spite of his protests. It was hospital policy that patients were taken out in a wheel chair, how ridiculous.

● ● ●

Wilson learned of Albert Rankin's pending release. He watched from an adjacent lot as they wheeled Albert out. Albert climbed into an old beater Toyota driven by an equally beaten old man. They slowly moved on. Either they didn't know one another or they were angry with each other. From Wilson's vantage point, it was hard to tell, but that's how it looked.

Wilson hadn't been able to locate anyone that knew much about Rankin. It seemed that he was a loner. Wilson knew something about loners. He didn't want Rankin to follow Becky Adkins' example and disappear. He followed the unlikely pair into town and from there, to a subdivision just east of downtown. They pulled into a driveway on Mockingbird Lane. Albert climbed out. The beater backed out and rolled two houses down the road and parked.

So, that old man had gone to pick up Rankin. After Albert was inside, Wilson checked the address to verify who lived here. He hung up his cell. Wilson was satisfied to know that Rankin was home, at his mother's house. It was obvious that Rankin didn't have many options for making an escape. His car had been impounded.

Wilson was happy with the Rankin situation, so he decided to join Deputy Leland at the crime scene. He hoped that Leland hadn't tried to take on some sort of mini investigation on his own. That's all he needed, for Leland to screw things up. He breathed a sigh of relief as he pulled into the drive at Albert's burned out trailer. Leland popped up from the cruiser's front seat, trying to make it appear as if he hadn't been asleep.

●　　●　　●

Tom was confident that if given the same shot again at the buck, it would yield entirely different results. It had been years since he'd hunted and he was obviously rusty. He had failed to take all the variables into account. He wouldn't make the same mistake twice, but it would be a good idea to allow the area to calm down, especially after he'd given the buck such a fright.

Tom had learned a few things about himself since he'd begun his solitary, retirement lifestyle. One thing he felt was that he seemed to be getting weird. He asked Bella if she wanted to go for a walk. He spelled the word out, W A L K. He said it slowly, so it sounded like four individual words. Yes, he was getting very weird. After he spelled walk for Bella, she went out the door like a shot. Maybe she couldn't spell, but she certainly understood consonants. Tom realized he might need a night out, a night out amongst people.

The leaves in the wooded acreage were turning and beginning to fall. Winter was two months away. He thought about his drafty trailer and prayed for a mild winter. It might be a good idea to pick up some plastic window covering to help insulate the place. He'd do that today. The woods were quiet and Bella was at his heels for the moment. She was funny about that, sometimes she had to lead, and sometimes she needed to follow.

After a while, Bella stopped and looked southward. Tom listened, as an obviously large animal approached. A young girl on horseback stopped and looked their way.

Tom called out, "Hi there."

"Hello."

Bella was leery. This was one big dog.

"My name's Tom Padgett. I live down the way on Abners Mill."

"I know. I've seen you around." The girl replied.

Did everyone know where he lived and what he did? "What's your name?"

"Oh, I'm Lisa and this is Miss Annie."

"Well, it's nice to meet you Lisa. Do you ride out in these woods often?"

"Yeah I do, all the time."

"Doesn't it scare you being out here alone?"

"No my dogs are always with me. They're out here somewhere."

Bella inched closer to Miss Annie, trying to figure out exactly what she was.

"This is Bella, my ever faithful companion. She seems to be afraid of horses."

Lisa laughed and started to turn Miss Annie, "Well, I've got to be going. Bye, see you around."

"Bye, Lisa. We'll see you later."

Tom watched as they rode off. What a confident young lady. She couldn't be any older than twelve. "Ok Bella, excitement is over. Let's go home."

Just thinking about shopping was making him tired.

He'd go home, and lie down before going to Maysville. A few minutes into sleep, he woke up. He was in a cold sweat. He'd had another dream. Why did he continue having these dreams? In his one, he saw a trailer on fire. Something about the trailer was familiar. What was it about the trailer that bothered him? It was a repeat of the other dreams, this aspect of familiarity. He didn't understand what any of it meant.

• • •

"Leland, has anything happened while you've been guarding the scene?"

"No, Sheriff, everything's been quiet here."

Wilson stared at his deputy with frustration. "Leland, obviously it's been quiet, otherwise how could you have slept so soundly?"

Leland turned red but said nothing.

"Deputy, I'm going to show you some techniques today, things that might prove valuable for you in the future. So, open your ears and not your mouth and maybe you'll learn something."

Leland really hated it when the sheriff made him feel like a child. Wilson walked around the burned up trailer and tried to get a handle on what could have happened.

From the chemicals and medication found in Rankin's car, Wilson assumed that a meth lab had exploded. He would need to be careful in the search for evidence. When he finished gathering his evidence, the Aftermath team would come to clean up the remains. Watching the Aftermath team work would be on the job training for both him and his deputy.

Wilson asked Leland to grab respirators, gloves and booties from his vehicle. "Leland, have you got the camera with you?"

"Yes Sheriff."

"Are there fresh batteries in it?"

"I think so. I haven't used it since the meth lab accident over near Abners Mill."

The sheriff shook his head. "That was months ago.

The batteries were probably dead by now. They'd have to make due. He thought that it sure is hard to find good help.

"I want you to follow me around the crime scene. I'll tell you when and what I'd like photos of, is that clear?"

"Yes Sheriff."

"Good, now take a shot of the entrance door."

"How can you tell which door is the entrance Sheriff?"

"Deputy, what are you talking about? The door that faces the road is usually the front door."

"But around these parts, people usually knock on the back door. So does that make it the front door?"

Wilson could feel himself getting angry. He realized he needed to keep his temper in check. He'd be spending a great deal of time over the coming days with his deputy. "Leland, let's assume the front door faces the road, okay? So would you take a photo of that door, please?"

They walked around the trailer as Wilson told his deputy what to take photos of. After they finished with the photos, Wilson asked Leland to get a pad and pencil from his truck. "I'm going to poke around inside and tell you what I find. I'd like you to record what I tell you."

"All right, Sheriff."

Wilson put on a respirator as well as gloves and booties. He stepped through what was left of the back door.

"Leland, there are two cans on the kitchen floor, both empty. They might have contained thinner. There are remnants of paint cans, chemical containers, propane tanks, portable cookers, pots and pans under what's left of a cabinet. It looks to me, that there were all the components for a lab in this kitchen. It's hard to make out all the descriptions, but most of the remains appear toxic in nature."

"Sheriff, how do you spell remnants?"

•   •   •

Albert couldn't believe the recent turn of events. He stood in his mother's living room as she sat in her big comfortable chair staring at him.

She shook her head before speaking, "So, you messed up again and come home to mama with your tail between your legs. What truck ran over you this time, boy?"

Albert had no choice but to stand and take whatever this woman, *his mother*, threw at him.

"Look at you, what the hell happened to you? You look worse than the last time you came crawling back home. I asked you a question, boy. What happened to you?"

Albert hated being here. He hated being scrutinized by the fat old woman sitting in the chair directly in front of him.

"My trailer caught fire."

"Oh, so your trailer caught fire, did it? What'd you do? Have the wood stove cranked up too high?"

"No, I didn't have a wood stove. The trailer just blew up."

"Wait a minute, Albert. You're saying the trailer blew up. Just blew up for no good reason, did it?"

"You might not believe me, but that's what happened."

"And why wouldn't I believe you, Albert? You've always been such an honest boy, always been truthful."

This reunion was far worse than he could have imagined. His mother had actually gotten bitterer over the past five years.

"So, you want to stay with your mama until you get your insurance settlement? I might be able to make room for you, but it'll cost you."

Albert really didn't want to mention the next fact, but he didn't know any way around it. "My trailer wasn't insured."

His Mom's mouth gaped open. "How can you tell me that your trailer burned up and you don't have insurance? Where's your brain at, boy? And, I suppose you want to come live with me until you get back on your feet?"

"Mom, I don't know what else to do."

"Well, you should have thought of that, boy. You should have thought of that before you went and blew yourself up."

"I didn't blow myself up."

"I'm not stupid, boy. I know that trailers don't blow up without a reason, and you can bet the sheriff knows that, too."

Albert looked down at the floor. "What are you talking about? What about the sheriff? Why are you even mentioning him?"

"Are you that stupid, boy? The sheriff drove by the house a minute after you walked in. I saw him with my own eyes."

"Well, what makes you think the sheriff's concerned with me?"

"In all the years I've lived in this house, I've never once seen the sheriff drive down this road. Now you walk in, and a minute later, here he comes. That's just too big of a coincidence for my way of thinking."

Albert again looked at his Mom, "Can I stay here for awhile?"

"You still get your disability checks?"

Albert shuffled his feet, "Yeah, I do."

"Well good, Albert. I guess I'll be able to put you up for a while."

CHAPTER 20

Tom wandered aimlessly around the house wares department at Wal-mart. He walked up and down the aisles. Forget about anyone asking if you needed help, unless you didn't need help, then they'd be on you like flies. He decided to get some curtains to cover up his terrible looking windows. He also thought some little throw rugs scattered here and there might help cover some of the cracks and tears in the linoleum.

He had already finished all his other shopping. He pushed his cart around and tried desperately to finish up. Luckily, there were two or three cold beers in the fridge at home. The beer in his cart was surely getting warm from his prolonged browsing session. Glassware always impresses women, for some reason. Would they stay for lunch? Should he get a matching set of dishes, for those special occasions? It was beginning to feel like déjà vu, like one of the shopping sprees spent with Darlene years ago, like the one where everything he'd owned as a bachelor was replaced by everything she wanted.

Tom remembered something about a tablecloth, supposedly an important item. Normally, if you spilled something on the table, you could wipe it up and be finished. Not so with a tablecloth. If you spilled something on a tablecloth, it needed to be washed. Then, you need to have backup tablecloths. Whoever came up with this tablecloth idea must have gotten rich. Disposable table cloths, Tom was positive Wal-mart would have those.

He found them and picked up two, red and blue and suddenly remembered what his silverware looked like. This little shopping spree was going to set him back a bit and he wouldn't be surprised if Andy called him Saturday morning saying that they couldn't make it.

The cart was full, nearly overflowing. Tom had a rule. If it didn't fit in the cart, then you didn't need it. After he paid and was leaving the store, he heard a familiar voice.

"Can I see your receipt, sir?" Nick wore his usual grin and his blue Wal-mart vest.

"Hey, Nick, how are you?"

"Great. I get off in twenty minutes. Want to go have a couple?"

"I'd love to, Nick, but I've got some domestic stuff that needs doing. You can come by my house if you'd like. I've got plenty of beer."

"I tell you what, I need to swing by home for a bit and then I'll be over."

"That'll be great. I'll see you then."

Tom pushed the cart out to his F-150 and began to throw all the house ware junk in the back.

• • •

Wilson was in a good mood. He was going to give Albert Rankin some bad news. He enjoyed that. He liked it when he got to deliver bad news. He climbed in his truck and drove to Mockingbird Lane. When Albert answered the door, Wilson told him the news.

"You're under arrest for suspicion of running a meth lab in your residence on Cassidy Creek Road in Nicholas County." Wilson handcuffed Albert and led him to the truck.

Albert's Mother stuck her head out the door and yelled, "Hey, Albert, what about my money?"

Albert glanced back at his mother, shook his head, and then smiled. She won't get my money, he thought, even if I go to prison for the long haul. I'll never give her my money.

Nicholas County didn't have a jail anymore, although they still had a jailer. The jailer's responsibility was to take suspects to the facility where they'd be held until arraignment. In Albert's case, this was Bourbon County. But, before Albert got shipped out, Wilson wanted to ask him some additional questions in the interrogation room at the police department. He was hoping to find out more about the explosion.

"Albert, explain it to me one more time. What happened the night of the fire?"

"Sheriff, I already told you what happened."

"I understand that, Albert. I just want to hear it again. That is, your account of what happened that night. See if anything new comes to light."

Albert looked at Wilson before continuing. "What's in it for me, Sheriff? Why should I help you?"

"There might be nothing in it for you, but we don't want to leave any stones unturned, now do we? So refresh my memory, will you?"

"Okay, I walked into the house and smelled gas. I turned the gas off and opened the back door. Then the explosion happened."

"Wait a minute, the last time we spoke, you said you didn't smell gas."

"I guess I didn't notice it at the time Sheriff, everything happened so fast."

"You say the explosion happened when you opened the back door."

"Yes, it seemed to happen at about the same time."

"And you're sure you wouldn't have left the gas on? Maybe you just forgot to turn it off?"

"Sheriff, I'm positive the gas was turned off. I worked in the kitchen cleaning up for an hour before I left the house."

Wilson smiled as he rose from his chair, "Thank you Albert."

Wilson drove back to Albert's trailer to check on something, something that was bothering him. He went to the rear of the trailer and began probing through the remains around the door. He didn't see anything odd. He noticed a worn trail leading away from the trailer which led to the woods. He followed it and came to the waste dump that Albert had been using. He checked the ground for tracks, tracks that could have come from other locations. He found none.

Wilson went over what Albert had told him. So, Rankin turned the gas off and then opened the door. That's when the explosion occurred. What was on the door? Wilson returned to the trailer. He lifted the remains of the threshold. As he did, a small piece of metal rolled onto the charred floor. Wilson picked it up in his gloved hand and smiled. It looked like some kind of sparking device.

•　　•　　•

Tom got up late, which was unusual. He slept in because he and Nick had stayed up late, too late. As a matter of fact, Nick was still sleeping in the guest bedroom. Tom recalled some of stories Nick had told him last night. Nick was funny; he was even funnier when he was half drunk. But, Nick probably wouldn't feel funny this morning. Tom had brewed coffee and he and Bella played outside while they waited for Nick to wake up. They returned from a walk to find Nick sitting at the kitchen table drinking a cup of coffee.

"Morning Nick, are you feeling okay?"

"I will be. You wouldn't have any aspirin around, would you?"

"Of course I do. I know all about aches, pains and hangovers."

Tom was relieved when Nick finally made his way out the door. Nick had gotten his strength back after breakfast. Nick drove off, and Tom began to finish his trailer beautification project. Last night, he had barely managed to get the dishes and silverware put away before Nick arrived. Andy was coming and he wanted the place to be presentable. He had already hung the curtains on the back windows. He thought they looked cheerful.

He was starting to hang the front curtains, when he heard and saw the truck roll into the drive. Wilson, what could he want now? At the last meeting he'd had with Wilson, he'd finally gotten Wilson to pursue the connection between Becky Adkins and Miranda Johnson. So for a while, it'd been relatively peaceful around here. He opened the door and Wilson stepped inside.

"Morning Padgett," Wilson stuck out his hand.

"Morning Wilson, would you like a cup of coffee?"

"Yeah, I don't mind if I do."

While Tom was in the kitchen getting coffee, Wilson looked around the living room.

"Looks like you're sprucing the place up. There isn't a new lady in your life, is there Padgett?

"No, Wilson, there aren't any new ladies in my life. I'm not in the market at present."

Wilson nodded in understanding.

"So, what brings you out here? Are you doing a community service social call?"

Wilson chuckled. "No, I just happened to be in the area and thought I'd stop in. So, you're fixing the place up. Are you planning on selling?"

Tom waited for the other shoe to drop but carried on. "No, actually my son is visiting tomorrow. He's bringing his fiancé."

"Well congratulations, Padgett. Maybe someday soon you'll be a grandpa."

"I'm not holding my breath waiting for that to happen."

Tom could tell that Wilson's wheels were spinning. This might be a good time to throw him off balance. "So, Wilson, whatever happened with Miranda Johnson? Did you ever get to show her Becky Adkins' photo?"

That seemed to wipe the gleam from Wilson's eyes. "Oh right, I was meaning to tell you about that. It appears that Becky Adkins left town, she's gone."

Tom studied him for a second, "Did you get a chance to show Miranda Becky's picture?"

"Yes, I showed it to her."

"Well, did she recognize Becky Adkins?"

Wilson fidgeted with his coffee cup. "Miranda wasn't quite sure. She wasn't certain."

Tom could tell that Wilson was in his fabrication mode again and decided to drop it. Tom thought, good thing Wilson's a cop, because he's a terrible liar. "Want another cup of coffee?"

"No, not for me," Wilson stood, reached for the door, and then paused. He turned and faced Tom. "Did you hear anything about that trailer fire over on Cassidy Creek Road?"

Tom tensed slightly, as he recalled his last dream. "No I didn't. Should I have?"

"No, maybe not, I just remembered seeing your truck parked there last week."

• • •

Woozy wiped the bar down, out of habit more than anything. She hadn't slept well in two weeks. Things had been okay with Jimmy for quite some time, but, he was beginning to get difficult again. Last night he threw his dinner plate at the wall because his food wasn't hot enough. The night before that, Jimmy had punched a hole in the wall, because his favorite shirt was in the wash.

Since the night Tom had given Jimmy that talking to, he hadn't touched her. But, he was getting more and more volatile. It was probably only a matter of time. He could just raise his voice slightly and it would make her nearly cower. Woozy knew she couldn't continue like this, but she couldn't say anything about it to Jimmy.

She didn't have any place of refuge. Her friends still stayed with their abusive men. They just didn't relate to Woozy's dilemma. There was one bright spot on the horizon, though. Her daughter Charlene had moved out and had moved in with her boyfriend. Woozy knew it probably wouldn't work out. Her daughter was only eighteen, but at least now she was out of the house.

So, if Woozy could figure out a plan to leave town, Charlene wouldn't be a problem. Bartenders were needed all over the place. She could leave the state, maybe end up in Florida. Jimmy wouldn't be able to find her there. But, she didn't have that kind of money. That didn't mean she couldn't start saving, though. She'd start to sock a little aside each night.

• • •

Jimmy had been doing a lot of thinking. Mainly, he'd been thinking about what he needed to do about Woozy. She didn't seem to get it. Why should she be surprised when he threw his dinner plate at the wall? The meal was ice cold. Any other man would have reacted the same way. Why should she be surprised that he punched a hole in the wall? His favorite shirt was in the wash, wasn't it? And all he had to do was raise his voice and she acted all afraid. She acted as if he was gonna hit her. He hadn't hit her once since that knight in shining armor had stood up for her ass. Maybe that was part of the problem.

That Good Samaritan son of a bitch hadn't been around lately. So why should Jimmy be worried about him anyway? As far as he was concerned, he needed to get control of things again. He had allowed some hero to interfere in his life. Well, Jimmy was sure of one thing, things were going to change. They were going to change real damn soon.

Jimmy picked up a glass of whiskey and downed it in one gulp. Boy, that stuff was good. He remembered another thing. Woozy claimed that tips weren't as good as they used to be. Why are tips less than they used to be? That didn't make sense. Maybe she's keeping some money hidden away. Well if she was, he'd find out.

• • •

Tom sat at the kitchen table after Wilson left. Déjà vu, that's what this was. Wilson just couldn't help himself. The guy is obviously obsessed with hounding me.

He finished hanging the curtains and then put the disposable table cloth on the table. There, the place looked better already. He placed the throw rugs strategically over the most obviously worn spots. Bella quickly claimed one of them in a sunny spot in the living room.

Tom stood back and observed the room, not too bad. The trailer didn't really have the woman's touch, why should it? Tom was pleased with his creativity and felt that he'd earned a beer. Whether he really earned a beer didn't matter, he was thirsty. He half expected his cell to ring with Andy offering up an excuse for not being able to make it, but it remained quiet.

• • •

Wilson was having little luck with his search for a witness. When he left Padgett's, he drove back to Rankin's burned out trailer. Then, he walked around the area and knocked on doors. Not one of the neighbors even knew Albert. It was almost as if he didn't even live on Cassidy Creek. As a matter of fact, many of the neighbors hadn't even known the trailer was there. Not until they saw the fire. How can people live in an area for five years and not know their neighbors? Well, if he was honest with himself, the same thing applied to him. Wilson was convinced that somebody had an axe to grind with Rankin, and the only suspect he had at the moment was Padgett.

His evidence was weak. All he had was Tom's truck that had been parked in the vicinity of the crime scene. That was even questionable, because it was two hundred yards away. But, the fact that someone had deliberately placed an igniter on the door of the trailer couldn't be denied.

What else could he do to prove Tom's guilt? Maybe he could flash Albert's picture around town and see if any of those street people recognized him. He could ask the Carlisle Police for help. He could even have Leland make some inquiries. Someone must know Albert Rankin. Wilson felt his pulse quicken at the thought of being able to get Padgett. This cat and mouse game they'd been playing was going to end, for Padgett, that is.

•   •   •

Friday night

Woozy hoped it would be productive. She needed to get dressed. Jimmy wasn't around, which was great. She didn't need him staring over her shoulder telling her what she could or couldn't wear. She wasn't dead yet and tonight she was going to dress like she wanted. When she dressed in a more suggestive outfit, her tips were better, sometimes a lot better. When she dressed in Jimmy's imposed conservative outfits, she'd get twenty-five percent less in tips.

Tonight, she planned to start her *get out of town slush fund.* She pulled a V-neck blouse from the closet, a little sheer, but not totally revealing. Woozy smiled as she looked at herself in the mirror.

She felt confident. Woozy, this is the first day of the rest of your life. She actually felt different, she almost felt sexy. She felt that a tremendous weight had been lifted from her shoulders. She hadn't felt like this in years. It's going to be a great night. She rounded out her ensemble with some of her favorite jewelry. She felt happy as she turned around and looked in the full length mirror. She'd almost forgotten what it felt like being a woman. Well, she was feeling it and seeing it now. She was even going to pull out the stops on her choice of shoes. No bland flats tonight. She would wear something with heels, maybe open toes. As she turned out the light and walked toward the door, Jimmy walked in.

• • •

Tonight, Tom was going to relax. He hadn't fully recovered from partying last night with Nick. It had turned into a beautiful day after starting off cool and it was unusually mild for the time of year. He and Bella sat in the yard as he enjoyed some coffee. The leaves fell from the trees as a gentle breeze blew. He relished autumn and appreciated the variety of the colors in the woods all around him. He had never been to New England, but had heard that the autumn leaves there were supposed to be the best. Well as far as he was concerned, some of the fall colors he'd witnessed this year would be tough to beat. He wasn't sure how you could improve on some things.

He wondered how Andy and Nancy were getting on with Darlene. He was glad that he wasn't there. He'd get his turn tomorrow morning. Maybe it'd be just fine. Tom went inside for one last cup of coffee and grabbed a big rawhide bone for Bella. She could make short work of them if she was in the mood. He held the big bone out and Bella grabbed it and began to chew with a vengeance. It looked like this was going to be another *short work* bone. He heard a coyote in the distance and thought how coyotes can sure make a bunch of noise. Bella listened too, but had no intention of joining any pack. She had it made right where she was.

• • •

Wilson swirled Jim Beam in his glass and thought of his successes this week. Overall, it had been a pretty good week. There were still some stones unturned, but he could be patient. So far, none of the people that stood around town on the street corners had offered much help. How could none of them know Albert Rankin? On second thought, most of them were probably doing meth. So they might not be able to recognize their dealer.

Wilson was convinced that Rankin was selling meth in town. He just needed someone to admit it. What is all this crap, solidarity within the methamphetamine community? Buzz had gotten sentenced earlier in the week. When Wilson asked, he claimed he didn't know Rankin either.

He went to the kitchen and poured himself another drink. Maybe he'd take the bottle out to the back porch. It was a nice night, probably very few were remaining. He remembered his neighbor. To hell with her, he was entitled to his privacy. Why was she always sticking her nose in his business, anyway?

Wilson had just gotten comfortable on the porch when he heard the neighbor's door open. The old woman walked over to the fence and just glared at him. Wilson just stared back at her. Two can play this game. Neither one spoke.

Finally the old woman broke the stalemate, "Wilson, I'll be keeping my eye on you tonight. Don't you be playing any of your sick games?"

He watched her in disbelief as she turned and walked back inside.

CHAPTER 21

Tom laughed out loud as he reread the article in the Lexington *Herald-Leader*. Bella watched him as he went to refill his coffee. She couldn't understand what he was laughing about. He returned and looked at the article again and found it just as entertaining.

There was a new type of theft that was growing in popularity around Lexington. Several people had driven their cars into store fronts to steal cartons of cigarettes. Tom chuckled, at least the jokers waited until the stores were closed. He wasn't sure if the fact that he found this amusing was normal or not. Maybe he was losing it. The first idiot had driven a late model Ford pick-up through a brick store front. Then, the driver ran into the store and escaped with two cartons of cigarettes. It was all captured on video.

The second genius was obviously the smarter of the two. This nut knew better than to ram his truck head-on into a brick framed doorway. He had lowered his tailgate and slammed into the doorway while driving in reverse. Tom wasn't sure if the intention was to save money by only damaging the back of his truck, as opposed to the front end. Or, maybe he had a spare tailgate lying around somewhere which he could use to replace the ruined one. Maybe he lowered the tailgate so his license plate number wouldn't be visible? Whatever the clever rationale for this maneuver was, it failed badly because the video image clearly showed the license plate number. The thief did manage to get twenty cartons of cigarettes, though. If he could take them into jail with him, at least he'd have a few weeks' smokes. Sometimes Tom wished he was still a policeman. Criminals seemed to be getting dumber all the time.

●　　●　　●

Wilson wanted to get out of Carlisle. It felt as if he hadn't been out of town for months. He planned to go to the mall in Lexington. He thought he'd just wander around and watch people. He didn't need anything from the store, but maybe the change of scenery would do him good. He turned into Hamburg Pavilion. He hadn't intended on going all the way to Lexington to look for music, but he was here now, and so was Best Buy. As he climbed out of his truck and made his way into the store, it dawned on him that maybe some new karaoke CDs would be in order. His music collection at home was dated. It'd be good to have some new tunes.

As Wilson browsed through the CDs, he hummed some of the songs listed on the CD jackets. They had quite a selection. There were many songs that he was unfamiliar with. Was he that out of touch? He wouldn't worry about things like top forty and such. If he was going to sing, he wanted to sing songs that he knew. He definitely had no intention of uploading anymore of his performances to YouTube. That chapter in his life was behind him.

He was surprised at the number of CDs that passed over the cashier's scanner. He looked at some of the titles, A Boy Named Sue, by Johnny Cash; Bad, Bad Leroy Brown, Jim Croce; Crazy Little Thing Called Love, Queen; The Devil Went Down To Georgia, The Charlie Daniels Band. This was some good stuff, some classics.

●　　●　　●

It was a few minutes after ten when Tom heard the car pull into the drive. He peered through the curtains and noticed a shining BMW convertible rolling to a stop, a 328i. Well, Andy must be doing better than he'd thought. Bella led the way as Tom opened the door and walked out to greet Andy and his fiancé. He hugged his son after Andy closed the car door.

"Good to see you, son, so you're Nancy. It's nice to meet you."

Nancy didn't reply.

It was a beautiful day, but there was still a chill in the air, so Tom invited them inside.

Andy looked around as they approached the trailer, "So, this is where you live?"

"Yes, this is the place that Bella and I call home. It might not be much, but it's paid for," Tom laughed. Once inside, Tom asked if they'd like anything, coffee, beer, water.

Nancy hesitatingly moved around the living room, "I'd prefer some bottled water."

"I'm sorry, Nancy. I don't have any bottled water. Is tap water okay?"

"No, I don't drink tap water. That's alright. I guess I don't need anything then, thank you."

Andy agreed to coffee and Tom joined him.

"Have a seat, both of you. That's quite the car you're driving, Andy. You must have landed a good job."

"No, it's not mine. That's Nancy's car. Her parents gave it to her for graduation."

"Well that's some graduation gift. What was your major?"

"I majored in cosmetology. I graduated from The Salon Professional Academy of Lexington."

Nancy was critiquing the trailer. "Do you plan on staying here long?"

Tom didn't like the tone of that question. "Oh, I'm not sure, but for the short term, it's quite alright."

"I had a friend that I graduated from the Academy with who grew up living in a trailer. He told me he couldn't wait to move away from home. He said living his life in a trailer made him feel like a complete loser. Does it affect you in that way Mr. Padgett?"

What was this girl's problem? "Actually, I'm quite comfortable living here. I don't really have that many options with my current income and all."

Andy looked a little nervous as the conversation continued, but he didn't have anything to contribute.

Nancy set her sights on Bella, "Does that dog stay in the house all the time?"

"Yes, that dog is Bella, and why shouldn't she stay in the house?"

"Well they have fleas and things like that. They're usually not very clean."

Tom could feel himself getting angry. He needed to change the subject.

"Andy, how is your Mother doing?"

"Oh, Mom's doing well. Last night she made us quite the dinner. I was surprised when the Mayor joined us."

Nancy again endeared herself, "Mr. Padgett I assume these curtains were already here when you moved in. You surely didn't buy them?"

Tom wasn't going to subject himself to any more ridicule. "You know, Nancy, to tell you the truth, I really can't remember if they were here or not."

Andy got to his feet, "Well, I think we'd better be going."

Tom watched from the door as they drove off. "Wow, that was quite the good time, wasn't it Bella?" He opened a beer and quickly drained about half of it. He remembered what Andy had told him on the phone, about Nancy's parents. Andy had said 'they aren't well off either'. Maybe her parents weren't well off, but buying her that new BMW convertible couldn't have been cheap. She had exuded an air of confidence, or was it superiority? Tom couldn't believe that Andy would be attracted to such an obnoxious, spoiled girl. Hopefully, he'll come to his senses before it's too late. Tom drank the remainder of his beer and wished that she had kept her mouth shut for a moment; maybe they could have had a conversation.

• • •

Wilson decided he might as well swing by the Liquor Barn since he was in Lexington. His Jim Beam Black stash was getting low. Plus, at the Barn, he could get a case discount. It had been a great idea to get out of Carlisle. Now he had some music and whiskey. Let the good times roll. He got back in the truck and unwrapped one of his karaoke CDs. Even though it only played the background music on his stereo, it didn't matter. He knew all the lyrics. He sang along with 'The Devil Went Down To Georgia' as he rolled up Route 68. He hadn't sung in a while, but no one could have guessed it. At least that's what Wilson thought. He believed he sounded pretty damned good.

Back in Carlisle, Wilson slowly drove around the courthouse square. All the usual street people were out and milling about. Don't they have any place to go? Didn't any of them have anything to do? It put him in a bad mood to see the same people day in and day out just stand around downtown. The city should find something for them to do. Maybe have them pick up trash, or sweep the sidewalks, anything but just stand around and make the town look bad. But, it was Saturday and he wasn't gonna let these people bother him. No, nobody was going to screw up his weekend. He had new music, plenty of whiskey and his voice sounded stellar.

• • •

Tom and Bella had just finished an enjoyable hike. Bella settled in on her favorite rug. Tom took a shower and dressed. It had been an exciting day, maybe awful would be a better description. It'd be nice to relax this evening. His phone rang and Tom noticed his caller ID, Nick.

"Hello Nick, how's it going?"

Tom's cheerful mood evaporated as he listened to what Nick had to say. He stepped over to the fridge and pulled out a beer. "Ok, I'll see you there about six."

After disconnecting, Tom took a long drink and sat at the kitchen table. It looked like a relaxing evening was no longer an option. He couldn't believe what Nick had just told him. He shook his head and ran his fingers through his damp hair. Nick had called from O'Rourke's, but that's not where they were planning to meet.

He tried to figure out what could have happened. What could Woozy have done in order to end up in Meadowview Regional Medical Center? Nick told him that he'd stopped in at O'Rourke's for a beer. When he asked where Woozy was, he was told that she'd been admitted to the emergency room the previous night.

Tom removed his slippers, and then put on his shoes. He checked himself in the bathroom's cracked mirror and realized that it still needed to be replaced. Bella watched him as he finished getting ready. She knew that he was going someplace, but she was unconcerned. Tonight, she was ready for sleep. She didn't care if he went out, as long as he made plenty of time for her tomorrow.

● ● ●

Wilson unloaded his truck. He carried things into the house. He returned for the last load, his case of Jim Beam, it felt like he was being watched. He glanced left, over to the neighbor's front door, and noticed her standing there. She stood and shook her head while she glared at him. Wilson thought it would do her some good to lighten up. Maybe he should ask her to come over later and sing some karaoke? Not a chance of that. He didn't have any church hymns or spiritual music in his collection. Once inside, he poured a glass of whiskey, then went to the freezer and grabbed a pizza. Whiskey, karaoke and a large meat lover's pizza, that would be tough to beat.

He turned the stereo up loud and sang along with some CDs, and then set it to random play. He was amazed at the selections that came on. They were absolutely perfect. Did his stereo have some of that intuitive stuff built into it or something? He thought about how there were so many intuitive things everywhere today. If you did a search on Google, it tried to predict your next thoughts. If you watched a movie on Netflix, they suggested what other movies you'd like. If you purchased things on line, companies would email you with ideas about what else you needed. Whatever happened to individuals thinking for themselves? He took a drink and wondered if Google knew what he was doing right now.

• • •

Tom found Nick in the lobby and together they walked to Woozy's room. Neither of them knew what to expect, nor were they prepared for what they found. Entering the room first, Tom found Woozy lying on her back with the head of the bed tilted about thirty degrees. Both her eyes were blackened and swollen shut. Her nose must have been broken, because it had been set. Her mouth was swollen and cut. Tom couldn't tell if her arm was broken, but it was wrapped in a sling. He stepped out into the hall and found a nurse. He wanted to know the extent of her injuries.

"Are you a member of her family?"

Tom didn't need this nonsense. "Yes, I am. I'm her brother."

Tom returned to the room and found Nick sitting in a chair next to Woozy's bed. She wasn't awake. She'd been given a strong sedative so she'd be able to sleep. Tom relayed to Nick what the nurse had told him. It was obvious that something terrible had happened, but as of yet, Woozy hadn't spoken.

She had a broken nose. She also had several stitches in her lips, both inside and out. Her arm was broken, but the doctor would determine later if a hard cast would be necessary. She had multiple broken ribs which they hoped would heal naturally. She had been given a brain scan and the possibility of any permanent damage had been eliminated. The nurse also added that based on the medication she'd been given, she probably wouldn't wake up 'til morning.

Tom and Nick walked out through the lobby to the parking lot. Tom noticed that Nick was quieter than he'd ever seen him.

Finally, Nick asked, "What do you think happened, Tom? Do you think she was in a car accident?"

They stopped next to Nick's car. "She wasn't in an accident. I'm sure the police are looking for a suspect. I would bet her lowlife husband is on the run."

"How can you be sure about any of that? Maybe she was in an accident?"

"Listen, Nick, the combination of injuries doesn't add up to an auto accident. Her injuries are totally consistent with those received from a physical beating. I'm coming back in the morning. Hopefully, she'll be able to tell me what happened."

●　　●　　●

Wilson loved that last song. He remembered it from high school. He wasn't sure that it was from the nineties, but that's when he used to sing it. Come to think of it, high school hadn't been that long ago. He'd graduated when, was it fifteen years ago? Many of the songs Wilson sang along with were actually songs he'd heard his parents play. Back then, he felt like those songs were funky and old fashioned. But now, they were what he enjoyed. Songs from the seventies and eighties were some of his favorites. He took a large bite of pizza. The hot cheese slid off the crust and wrapped around his chin. He jerked and dropped it on the floor as he ran to the kitchen to grab a towel.

He finished the pizza, all but one piece. Maybe he'd eat it later. Wilson refilled his drink and danced his way into the living room. He unwrapped one of the karaoke CDs. The help of the onscreen lyrics was welcome. Wilson tried to decide on his first song. Let's see, this should be a good one to start with, *You Don't Mess Around With Jim*, by Jim Croce. Actually it would be a great warm up.

The music blared from the speakers. Wilson couldn't believe how close the music sounded to the original recording. And, with some great singing by yours truly, Bill Wilson, you'd swear that the performance was live. When the song ended, he took another well deserved swallow and looked for his next song. He found another tune and pressed the up arrow. He definitely needed more volume.

●　　●　　●

Tom walked into Woozy's room at 9:00 am the next morning. She tried unsuccessfully to drink some juice. He took the container in his hand and held it steady so she could drink.

"Hello, Woozy. Looks like you had a bit of bad luck."

Woozy tried to open her eyes. She managed to open one of them just a bit.

"Yeah, I really did it this time, didn't I?"

"Woozy, you've got to stop blaming yourself. Do you want to tell me what happened?"

"No, not really, I don't want to think about what happened."

"It was Jimmy. He did this, didn't he? Do you know where he went?"

"I'm sure he's long gone. I made him angry and that's why I'm here. It's my fault."

Tom wiped a tear from his cheek as he looked down at the battered woman.

Tom walked out of the hospital an hour later. Now he had a far better understanding of what had happened. Woozy told him of her plan for saving money with hopes of moving away. She said she had dressed for work and what she wore happened to be more provocative than Jimmy allowed. She really didn't care anymore. The hell with what Jimmy thought about the way she dressed. It was over. She told Tom that when she saw her reflection in the mirror, she felt great. She actually felt like a woman again. That had been something that she had nearly given up on. Unfortunately for her, luck hadn't been on her side. Jimmy had come home, just as she was about to walk out the door. She didn't make it, not until she was wheeled out by the medics later that evening.

• • •

When Wilson woke up, he realized that he'd spent another night in his recliner. His head pounded, but not as badly as it did sometimes. He looked around the room. He was relieved that nothing seemed terribly out of place. He glanced down and noticed that he only had on his underwear. No real harm in that. As he started to stand up, he noticed, that yes, he was wearing his underwear, but he also had on his cowboy boots. He quickly scanned the room to make sure his camera and tripod weren't visible. He sat back down and tried to remember. What was with the cowboy boots? He struggled to pull the boots off. He went to get his robe, wrapped it around himself and walked into the kitchen. He needed some coffee.

As he cradled a cup of hot coffee, Wilson wandered around last night's performance area. All the new karaoke CDs had been unwrapped. Could he have possibly played them all? He started to pick up the CDs and began to marry them up with their cases. They were scattered everywhere. Had there been other people here last night? He managed to find all the CDs and returned them to their cases. All but one, one CD seemed to be missing. He looked everywhere, then realized that it was probably still in the player. Before he removed it from the player, he wanted to know what the last song was that had been played, especially since he didn't remember any of it. Wilson was more than a little confused when he read, *I Am Woman*, by Helen Reddy.

CHAPTER 22

Jimmy had fled from Maysville. He didn't expect to have any difficulty hiding out, especially way out here. He was thirty miles and two counties away from Maysville, so the lousy, good for nothing cops, shouldn't find him. He thought about how Woozy had made him go crazy. He couldn't even begin to understand what she was thinking wearing that low cut v-neck blouse. It was even see through. She looked like she'd just walked out of some kind of whore house. She was sure surprised when she ran into him in the hallway. Lucky for Jimmy, he'd caught her before she'd totally disgraced him by going out in public. She wouldn't be doing anything like that again, any time soon, anyway.

He wondered where Woozy's knight in shining armor had gotten off to, but he wasn't worried one little bit about that hero of hers. Jimmy was safely holed up in a barn out in the middle of nowhere. He had fallen in with some Mexican guys that did odd jobs all around the area. They'd agreed to let him stay in the barn, out back of the doublewide they rented. They agreed to let him stay, if he paid them twenty bucks a week. He could also work with them wherever they worked, but they were only going to pay him crap. Thankfully, he knew the situation was just temporary.

One thing was in Jimmy's favor, his complexion. His olive-toned skin made it easy for him to blend in well with the group. He couldn't understand a damned thing they said, though. That, too, was only a temporary problem. As soon as the pressure died down, he would be long gone.

•   •   •

Tom got up early and walked the trail with Bella. She had run ahead a good distance, but he wasn't concerned. There didn't seem to be many hunters in the remote section behind this trailer. Tom thought that was just as well. He could enjoy long walks with Bella and not have to worry about her being mistaken for a deer.

It was nearly gun season. He hoped to get a couple more chances at the buck that he'd missed before gun season opened. Then, he noticed that Bella had stopped. She was standing perfectly still with her front paw raised. She looked like an English Pointer. The only difference between a pointer and Bella was patience. The pointer held a position to alert its master of the presence of whatever game they sought. Not so with Bella. She held her position for only a moment and then she was off. She hopped through the briars after a group of deer.

Tom laughed as she returned, holding her head high. "Good girl, Bella. You nearly had them."

She ran back to the spot where the chase had commenced and made sure that the deer hadn't returned. Bella loved her romps in the woods. With the flea and allergy seasons finally dying down, Tom was enjoying them more, also. It had been over a month since he'd taken her to the vet. That might just be a record.

They turned and began their walk back to the trailer. Tom had decided on two more hunts, an afternoon hunt and then one morning venture before the opening of gun season.

●　　●　　●

Wilson drove to town earlier than usual. He had something he needed to do. He hadn't done anything on Sunday and he was grateful for that. The hangover he was saddled with on Saturday morning had lasted well into the afternoon. But today he felt fantastic. He stopped and got a coffee before he opened up his office. He was anxious to find out about the evidence he'd sent to the lab. He almost wanted to shout out loud. He couldn't stop thinking about the pending lab results.

He phoned the lab at precisely 8:00 am. Wilson knew that he would receive notification when the tests were finished, but he wanted the results now. The person on the other end of the line didn't share Wilson's sense of urgency. He didn't make Wilson's day, either. Actually, he put quite a damper on Wilson's day.

"What do you mean the tests were inconclusive?"

The technician waited a moment to allow Wilson to calm down before repeating, "Sheriff, the items had no prints on them. There was nothing to suggest that they were associated with a crime."

Wilson could feel his face redden, "What do you mean not associated with a crime? They were in the remains of a burned door. They were most likely the ignition point for the gas explosion."

"I understand that, Sheriff. All I'm doing is stating the facts. There are no prints and no discernible evidence of tampering with the device."

"No tampering with the device? It was most likely attached to the door. It was what triggered the explosion. How could it not have been tampered with?"

"Sheriff, nearly every home in America has at least one BIC lighter, so they're quite common. Many times they show up in peculiar places."

•   •   •

Jimmy was going to have the pleasure of learning to strip tobacco. He looked up at the beams in the barn, noticing that it was one big barn. And since it was such a big barn, there was one hell of a bunch of tobacco hanging in it. Jimmy thought that stripping tobacco couldn't be all that hard. He thought that the guy's name was Pedro, or something like that, who was going to give him a lesson. Why was there any need for a lesson? It seemed like it should be pretty simple. Pull the damned leaves off and throw them in a pile. No, it seemed as if there was more to it than that. How in the hell is that guy Pedro going to explain it, if we can't talk? Now Pedro did some kind of sorting or something. Stripping the leaves seemed to depend on where the leaves were on the stalk. Jimmy thought he'd gotten the gist of it.

After about five hours, they stopped for lunch. Stripping tobacco was harder than Jimmy had imagined. He'd listened as the Mexicans talked and had learned a couple of their names, not that it would do him a bit of good. So what if he knew Pedro, Ricky and Juan? What could they talk about? They all seemed to laugh a lot. They found many things funny, probably something to do with him. Well as soon as he felt it was safe to leave, he was going to. He might even make one of these boys pay a price for making fun of him. He didn't know what they talked about. But, they were usually looking his way whenever they started laughing. Oh yeah, he would make one of these bastards pay.

●　　●　　●

Tom was in his tree stand at 3:00 pm. That would give him three and a half hours to hunt. It was quite breezy, which could work either for or against him. The buck may be careless with the wind blowing. That depended, however, on the timing of the rut. He watched as squirrels scurried about in preparation for winter. They surely were industrious little things. One of the squirrels climbed the tree Tom was in and stood on the toe of his boot. Tom looked down at it, just moving his eyes, and noticed that the squirrel realized something wasn't quite right, but couldn't understand what. Finally, it glanced up at Tom's shape and must have put two and two together. Back down the tree it went, quickly.

Now that the entertainment was finished, Tom could turn his attention back to the woods. He watched as several does walked toward him and then stopped at about sixty yards away, content to stand about and eat. Where was the buck? It was getting dark out, almost too dark to take a shot. Then the buck wandered in following the scent of the does. The buck wasn't going to give Tom another broadside shot tonight, but he was definitely distracted by the does. Eventually, the does wandered away in the opposite direction of Tom and the testosterone driven buck, blindly followed. When the deer were a good distance away, Tom climbed down. It hadn't been a total waste. Tom saw what he had hoped to see this evening. The buck was getting more careless.

•   •   •

Wilson was not a happy camper when he hung up the phone. That was basically the same answer that the lab had given him a while back. The pill bottle he'd sent to the lab was too hard to pull prints from, and now this. There weren't any prints to be found. What good is it having a lab at your disposal if they never find anything? So, the lighter just happened to somehow end up strategically wedged under the door?

Wilson was having a hard time buying the lack of prints. Rankin's trailer had been targeted, but with no witnesses or evidence, how could he prove anything? He had a gut feeling about Padgett. He had been in the vicinity of both meth lab explosions. He was confident that this was more than a coincidence. But without evidence, there was nothing he could do.

He schemed about the possibility of baiting Padgett somehow. How could he set the guy up, and do it convincingly? Wilson realized he'd already been down that road, unsuccessfully on other occasions, but he just wanted to get Padgett so badly.

The fact that Padgett lived in the area when the first meth lab explosion had occurred was a real stretch, as far as making any kind of connection to Padgett. And, the pill situation with Becky Adkins had also gone awry. He could have sworn that the ignition device was an iron-clad opportunity to bust Padgett. Wilson knew Padgett was no angel. But if he was going to ever be successful in bringing him down, it was going to have to be done with real evidence. He needed to catch Padgett with his guard down. How could he do it?

•   •   •

Jimmy was up in the rafters of the barn and handed down the stakes that held the tobacco. Even though it was cold out, he was already sweaty. He coughed from all the dust and dirt in the air. Finally, he had handed down enough tobacco stakes. The leaf pulling charade could begin. The same group was here again and it seemed like the same jokes were being told about him. He was going to get one of these bastards. He'd get one of them good.

Just after lunch, the situation improved greatly. It was still the same nasty dirty tobacco job, but a new hand showed up, quite an improvement as far as Jimmy was concerned. One of the men must have a daughter or a sister. The *senorita* was probably fifteen or sixteen and really put together.

Jimmy hoped he would work alongside the young lady at the leaf pulling game. Maybe she was here to give him some additional training. He hoped that was the case. But Pedro and Juan quickly took their places between him and the girl. Jimmy swore under his breath at his missed opportunity. He looked up at all the tobacco that hung in the barn and realized that there was still at least another week's worth of work. That wouldn't be bad at all, especially if he could get a little time alone with *la senorita*.

He glanced over at the young girl and smiled when she looked his way. She didn't smile back. She just went back to work. She was twice as fast at the leaf pulling game, but Jimmy didn't care. Jimmy had other thoughts about what she might be good at.

● ● ●

This was it, the last day before gun season opened. Tom wanted to take the big buck with his bow and he needed it to be this morning. He knew things would be different tomorrow when all the gun hunting idiots would be in the woods, shooting this way and that. He usually avoided opening day of gun season. It could be quite dangerous. Hunters with their semi-automatic shotguns would be shooting wildly, as the deer bounded away from errant shots. He'd been in the woods on an occasion when a hunter fired five or six slugs at an escaping buck. If anyone had happened to be walking in the vicinity, there would have been a fairly good chance of getting shot. Tomorrow he would sleep in and listen to all the nearby shooting. It would be clearly audible through his trailer's paper thin walls.

He settled into his tree stand and felt optimistic. The only downside about hunting this morning would be if a gun hunter decided to scout at the last minute. Tom hadn't seen anyone in this area since he'd been hunting here. Hopefully, the trend would continue.

As he thought about the things that could go wrong, he heard the snap of a branch over near a cedar thicket. He focused all his attention in that direction. He could make out part of the body through the cedars and realized it was a large deer. He couldn't see the animal's head, but the body that he could see was big, definitely a buck. It was still seventy yards out. The buck would need to be closer before he would shoot.

The buck displayed his rack as he stepped from behind the cedars. Tom wasn't totally sure, but he thought it was the same buck that he'd shot at before. His pulse quickened as the buck turned and took a step in his direction. Tom felt an adrenalin rush as the buck took one, then two steps toward him. The buck was walking straight at him, which didn't present Tom an opportunity to draw his bow. If he tried to pull his bow back, the buck would surely see the movement. He had to hope that the buck would turn and give him a perfect broadside opening. The buck was closer now. It was the same buck that he'd missed before. Tom wasn't planning to miss today.

At forty yards, the buck continued straight toward him. Tom hoped the buck didn't walk directly under his tree. Finally, thirty yards out, the buck paused and turned slightly to look back from where he'd come. This was Tom's chance. He quietly drew the bow, holding the sight on the buck's chest area. Then, the buck completed his movement and gave Tom another broadside offering. Tom was so surprised; he nearly failed to compensate for the change. Big bucks don't usually give hunters a second chance. Tom wouldn't let it slip away. He released the arrow. It flew silently and true. The arrow struck the buck exactly where Tom aimed. It dropped immediately. Tom took a deep breath, and then waited for the buck to expire before he climbed down from the tree.

●　　●　　●

Wilson was at Albert Rankin's trailer again. He tried to think of everything there was that could be gleaned from it. He needed the area to be cleaned up, but he had put off having the coroner call the

Aftermath team. He wanted to thoroughly exhaust his search before he gave up.

He looked at the contents again and learned nothing new. Before the blast, the trailer had been neat. Now, even in its ruined state, it was somehow orderly. He tried to put himself in the position of an arsonist. The fire department felt that the explosion was just another meth lab mistake. Why would anyone want to do this to another person?

There were only a couple of reasons. Maybe they'd had a bad experience with drugs that they'd bought, or maybe they had a deep hatred of people that manufactured drugs.

Wilson finished with the trailer and walked around the yard. Many more leaves had fallen and it was now nearly impossible to even see the chemical dump area. He was disappointed. He might as well have the Aftermath team come and do their thing. He climbed into the cab of his truck and as he backed out into the road, he noticed something in his rearview mirror.

He turned around and drove past Rankin's trailer. He stopped behind a parked truck and waited. He didn't have to wait long. He watched Padgett drag an enormous buck out of the woods. Well, he thought, looks like Padgett really was hunting here after all. But, in the back of his mind he knew Padgett had the ability and smarts to hunt and set traps at the same time. Wilson believed that Padgett was an extremely versatile man.

•　•　•

Tom struggled with the big deer. He didn't remember the first buck he'd shot being this hard to drag out of the woods. He huffed and puffed as he finally reached the edge of the woods. He leaned over, put his hands on his knees in an attempt to catch his breath. His truck was another fifty yards or so away. He looked across the road and noticed that Wilson stood next to his truck. He must have been watching as Tom wrestled with the deer. Tom left the buck lying where it was and walked across the road so that he could move his truck closer.

Wilson nodded as Tom approached, "So, Padgett it looks like your alibi about hunting could be solid."

Tom didn't have time for Wilson, "Yes, Wilson, what tipped you off allowing you to arrive at that conclusion?"

Tom moved his truck paralleling the big buck. He tried to muscle the monster into the truck bed. The buck probably weighed 220 lbs. or more. As he was about to close the tailgate, Wilson walked over and asked if he needed help.

"Thanks for nothing. Is there something you want with me this morning?"

Wilson looked closely at the deer.

Tom noticed his curiosity. "Yes, it's properly tagged. Are you covering for the game warden?"

Wilson smiled, "You know, Padgett, I was just at that trailer up the road again, you know, the one that somehow caught fire. I found a device that probably caused the explosion, but according to the lab there were no prints on it."

Tom looked at Wilson, "No prints, huh? Well that makes it kind of tough to try and pin the accident on someone who's innocent, doesn't it?"

●   ●   ●

Jimmy was exhausted. He walked into his temporary living area in the barn. He had washed up at a rusty old rain barrel that was under the downspout at the corner of the barn. When he finished, he glanced over at the doublewide and could see a shadow through the curtains. He thought it was the young girl. She moved around in front of the window. He watched her and wondered if she had just taken a shower. He wished he could have a shower, especially with her. He looked forward to working with her in the tobacco barn tomorrow. With a pretty girl like that in the barn, the day would be much more bearable. He moved deeper into the barn and tried to get warm beneath the feed sacks that served as his bedding.

The following morning

One of the Mexicans motioned for Jimmy to follow him into the doublewide. All the men were sat around the table eating breakfast. It smelled good. He was damned near starving. The girl offered him some coffee. So, she spoke some English. Quietly he enjoyed his coffee while the rest of the men ate a decent meal. But he shouldn't complain, at least he had some coffee.

She handed him a plate of bread. She said her name was Maria. He figured that her main job was to cook for the group and only worked in the tobacco barn on occasion. Unfortunately for Jimmy, she wouldn't be working in the barn today. She told him she was taking English lessons which were, apparently, every other day. Jimmy would just have to tolerate the *amigos* crap on his own today.

●   ●   ●

Tom let his deer hang for a couple days. Today he was going to process it. He had found a good chest freezer on Craigslist, for $50. It was fifteen cubic feet, which was larger than he needed, but he had managed to shuffle things around in the kitchen and dining area to make room. He planned to keep about half of the meat and give the remainder to a young man he'd met who lived just over the county line. His name was Chad Burnett; he was married with three young children. Chad had just lost his job. Tom used his filet knife to remove the scent glands before cutting the pieces into steaks. He wrapped them in freezer paper and then stored them in the freezer.

He had originally planned to let Chad cut the meat however he wanted to. But, then he figured, why not just cut it and package it for him. That way Chad and his wife wouldn't need to mess with it. It was a slow process in his cramped little trailer. Bella was quite attentive during the packaging.

When Tom had brought the buck home and hung it in the tree, Bella was initially afraid of it. The buck was a lot bigger than her, so she stood and watched from a safe distance. Finally, she got brave enough to move closer and smelled around. She found that there were benefits to smelling around. She really enjoyed the fat that Tom mixed in with her food. He planned to take the meat over to Chad's later that evening, when he was sure they'd be home.

• • •

Jimmy wasn't cut out to be a farmer, or whatever he was right now. His back hurt, his hands hurt, his feet hurt. He thought about the time he spent in the Maysville jail. It was a hell of a lot easier than this. He wondered about Woozy and the recent lesson he had given her. Did she learn anything from it? He was confident that she wouldn't wear that slutty looking outfit for a while. He'd put the kibosh to that with the beating that he'd given her. He still couldn't believe that she would do something like that. It was such intentional provocation. She was lucky that he didn't kill her. Then, Jimmy had another thought. Would Woozy try to divorce him?

She probably would, it wasn't as if he could stop her. If he went back home, they'd throw his ass in jail. He'd get at least five years for his latest stunt. The legal system was so screwed up. People do some terrible things and nothing happens to them. But, let a man discipline his wife, his right by marriage, and they nail him to the wall. Well, if Woozy planned to divorce him, there was nothing he could do to stop it. Besides, having her around for cooking, sex, or whatever, surely wasn't worth spending five years in jail for. Hell, maybe he was divorced already, by some super legal maneuver. He could care less. He would survive, and if everything went according to plan, he'd have a go at that sweet Maria real soon.

• • •

Tom removed half the meat from the chest freezer and put it into plastic shopping bags. There was probably around 50 lbs. of venison. That should help the Burnetts make it through their tough patch. He loaded it into the F-150. Bella gave him her 'are you going to leave me?' stare.

"Come on, Bella. Do you want to go for a ride?" Silly question, she jumped in the truck.

Tom knocked on the door and Chad opened it, "Evening, neighbor."

"Hey Chad, how are you doing? Listen, I shot a buck the other morning. It's big, with more meat than I'll eat. So, I brought some over and hoped you guys could use it?"

Chad was embarrassed. He wasn't used to accepting help from other people.

"Chad, this isn't a handout. You can help me out sometime if you feel obliged to pay me back, ok?"

They grabbed the venison from the truck, while Chad's wife moved stuff in the freezer to try to make room.

Tom noticed the challenge she faced. "If you don't have enough space, I can store it for you."

"Thanks Tom, we'll eat some now and more tomorrow night, so the problem's solved."

Tom smiled over at the kids in the living room. They were watching TV. Chad finally remembered he hadn't introduced his wife, Linda.

"Tom, would you stay for dinner? It's no bother."

"No thank you, Linda. I've got my baby in the truck. Her name's Bella and she's a jealous girl."

Linda smiled, "Another time then?"

Tom agreed and stepped out into the yard.

Chad followed, "Thanks for that, Tom, we really do appreciate it."

"I know you do, Chad. I'll be doing some more hunting and if I get another deer I'll bring some of it over."

As Tom got in his truck, he felt a tremendous sense of satisfaction. He hated seeing people struggle. It felt good to help out. On his way home, as he was about to cross back into Nicholas County, he passed a group of migrant workers as they climbed out of their van. He slowed down and did a double take. One of the men in the group wasn't a migrant worker. If Tom had never seen him before, he probably wouldn't have noticed because he was dressed similarly and was dirty and blended in with the other men. He could have easily passed for one of the group. He even had the same skin tone. Tom probably wouldn't have noticed him at all if he hadn't known the man, but he did. It was Woozy's waste of a husband, Jimmy.

CHAPTER 23

Wilson stepped out of his office in the courthouse, and stood on the sidewalk and looked around the square. On one corner was a group of women. They were always there. One of them always had a stroller. It's November, he thought. Why are they outside standing on the corner? Then he looked in the other direction and noticed that the other group was in place, also. Well, one thing had changed. There were now fewer of the corner people, as he'd begun to call them. One was in jail, one was dead, and the dealers were dwindling too. Jack Estep was dead and Albert Rankin was locked up. Wilson had no illusions though. He knew there were plenty of other people willing to step up to fill the void that had been created by Estep and Rankin's absence.

He took one last look at the corner people before he went back inside. The corner groupies just stared back at him with their blank looks. He didn't have time to worry about that clan this morning. He was going to meet the Aftermath team over at Cassidy Creek for the meth lab clean up. Keith Poole was too busy. He had funeral business to attend to. Wilson had told Poole that he would oversee the operation this morning. Maybe as the cleanup crew was taking care of business, some new bit of evidence would be uncovered. He didn't feel optimistic, but right about now it couldn't hurt. Wilson reluctantly dialed the number, and was disappointed when Deputy Leland answered on the second ring.

"Hey boss, what's up?"

Wilson and Leland waited, parked in front of the trailer when the Aftermath team finally arrived. They were dispatched out of Lexington and had gotten lost somewhere along the way. He silently cursed as he thought about the extra half hour that he'd sat in the truck and had to listen to Leland drone on about his latest girlfriend.

Wilson explained to Leland, "We're just here to observe and see if they uncover anything unusual. You know, during the course of the clean up."

"Like what, Sheriff? What unusual thing do you think they might find?"

Wilson was already at the end of his rope, "I don't know, Deputy. That's why it will be unusual."

Even though they'd gotten lost on their way to Carlisle, the Aftermath team worked efficiently. They were finished with the trailer in less than three hours. Wilson walked the team leader over to where the chemical dump was located and told him to be sure to clean it also. After four hours and a large amount of county funds later, the job was finished. The Aftermath team got into their truck and headed back to Lexington. Wilson hoped they didn't get lost this time. He stood and looked at the remains of the trailer. The chemicals were gone, but the shell remained. Wilson shook his head, another carcass of a trailer in good old Nicholas County.

●   ●   ●

Jimmy was really tired of the tobacco game. He wondered when it would be safe to come out of hiding. He was reasonably sure that it hadn't been long enough. That didn't change the fact that he desperately wanted to get out of here. Last night in the barn, he'd nearly frozen his cojones off. Now in the kitchen, he sipped on his coffee and watched as Maria quickly moved around the place clearing dishes. He thought that she looked exceptional today. She handed him some bread and returned to her task at the sink. Jimmy was disappointed when they began loading into the van, because Maria wasn't with them. That's when he remembered that she came at lunchtime. That would be all right then.

The Ford Econoline van was huge. It had seats for twelve people. Every morning it seemed to smell a little worse. It was one of Jimmy's least favorite times of the day, the commute. The van stank of body odor and farting. It didn't help that the Mexican boys probably existed solely on beans and tortillas. None of them seemed to be bothered with the stink in the van, but it nearly drove Jimmy nuts. This was another one of the things that he looked forward to leaving.

After he got out of the van, he looked up into the far reaches of the barn's rafters. Pedro nodded his head. That was Jimmy's cue to climb up and begin to hand the tobacco down. He hated this, also. There was little he didn't hate about the whole situation.

Just after noon, Jimmy heard the slam of a car door. Maria walked into the barn. She had brought lunch. Jimmy looked down from the rafters as everyone began to eat the burritos she brought. What he would give for a big greasy hamburger. But now, Maria was here and it distracted him. She didn't seem interested in him. However, that was of little concern to Jimmy. He could just steal glances at her as she moved around and stripped the tobacco. She was looking better every day. He needed to be alone with her, but how could he do that with eight Mexican guys constantly in attendance? Jimmy had to think of a way. He watched from high above as Maria bent over and picked up another stake. She sure looked good.

●　　●　　●

Tom hadn't fired his 870 in years, but he didn't feel the need to practice. He had a doe permit and he planned to do some still hunting around the trailer, now that the opening day fiasco was behind him. He wanted to get a good sized doe to help fill his freezer. Even though he had painstakingly removed all the scent glands from the buck, the meat was still gamier than doe meat was. Sure he had ways of preparing it to reduce the gamey taste, but good doe meat was tough to beat. Bella pouted as Tom stepped outside into the frosty morning. He laughed about Bella's attitude. She might actually be more difficult to get along with than a woman.

He felt nearly invisible with his camouflage coveralls and face paint. He had no intention of shooting a buck today. He just planned to fill one of his doe tags. He walked into the woods at a brisk pace, wanting to get into position. He'd located the spot a little more than a mile from the trailer, a place he'd found earlier over near the county line. It had an excellent stand of cedar trees with early sun exposure and a meadow, which offered a good amount of thicket. He knew there'd be plenty of deer here.

He was in position by 7:00 a.m. As he leaned against a cedar tree, he removed his gloves and put his hands in his pockets while he waited for the sunrise. He always wore thin camo gloves when he gun hunted, so that he wouldn't have any problems finding the trigger.

Just about 8:00, Tom noticed a deer in the meadow begin to rise. He watched as more and more deer stood up. He was surprised by the number. So far, he had counted eleven. As another yearling stood, there were now an equal number of fawns to does, all at a distance of about a hundred yards. He'd wait for them to move, hopefully in his direction. He could take a hundred yard shot, but he didn't have a rangefinder and didn't want to take a chance wounding a deer. He didn't believe in taking low percentage shots. Tom had known many hunters that took chances with low percentage shots. It was probably because they didn't know how to move quietly in the woods, which would allow them to get closer to the game. He could be patient.

They began to move, one by one, walking his way. Just a few more yards and he would have a clear shot on a nice doe. As he readied himself, the lead doe stopped. She stamped her foot and let out an all too familiar blow, and off they bounded away from him. That was frustrating. Tom was confident he hadn't been sighted. As he continued to watch them run and hop away, he suddenly heard footfalls behind him. That's what spooked the deer, two beagles and a blue heeler. The dogs had their noses glued to the ground, following the deer scent. They passed twenty feet from his position, so caught up in the chase none of them even noticed him. The morning's hunt was over.

•   •   •

Wilson had wrapped up another fine week of law enforcement. He was getting more confident with his abilities every day. That was a step in the right direction. He threw his feet up on his desk and lit a cigar. Smoking wasn't allowed in the city building, but nearly everyone had gone home for the day. Friday night. He needed to get out and burn off some steam. He hadn't gone out to socialize in quite some time. Now that he was sheriff, he supposedly had to keep his nose clean. Maybe he should go home first to change clothes. He could drive his truck, not his work vehicle. That's a great idea. It would enable him to keep a low profile.

After he'd gotten home and dressed, he looked in the mirror and admired his reflection. He thought he looked like a western outlaw and was pleased with that. He wore his cowboy boots, an oilskin duster and matching hat. All he needed to complete his ensemble was a six shooter, but he had better leave that at home. He could surely get in trouble tonight, especially with a gun strapped around his waist. He nodded to himself, gave his hat one final adjustment, before he strolled out the door.

He was looking forward to a nice relaxing night. Maybe he'd just drink a few beers with the boys, then head home. As he stood on the step outside his door and inhaled a great big, deep breath, he heard the neighbor's screen door open. He walked quickly toward his truck, but not quickly enough.

"Hey, Wilson, what is it, Halloween or something?"

• • •

Tom clicked his phone closed after he talked with Nick. Tonight, they were meeting at the Gyp. It'd been quite a while since they'd been there. Tom didn't bother to ask if Nick was already parked on a stool at the bar or not, he'd find out soon enough. Tom had been fairly subdued all week, especially after visiting Woozy in the hospital. Nick had told him that she was out of the hospital and resting at home. That was good news.

He still hadn't decided what to do about Jimmy. Seeing him with that group of migrant workers had been quite a shock. Jimmy, it appeared, was living nearly in Tom's backyard. Tom had given him fair warning, and look what had happened? He had damned near killed Woozy. Now that waste of a man was living right here, over by the county line. He was hiding in plain sight.

•　•　•

Jimmy was trapped in the back of the stinking van. He was three rows behind Maria. It seemed like the guys didn't want him anywhere near her. Protective bastards, as far as Jimmy could tell, she wasn't attached to any of them. The cold weather had done nothing to help the smell inside the van, but they'd be home soon.

The van stopped in front of the doublewide and Maria climbed out. She closed the door and waved as she walked inside the house. Where the hell are we going now? It was Friday; the work week was over as far as Jimmy was concerned. They rolled along in the same direction they'd just come from. He wasn't up for another round of tobacco. Don't these Mexicans know when to quit?

Jimmy didn't put up an argument. Besides, what could he say? He'd only learned about ten words of Spanish since he'd been working with this group. None of them spoke any English, either, and they seemed content to keep it that way. He watched out the window as they drove along the narrow, blacktopped road. They crossed a rail road track and rolled down a grade. He could see a river beneath them on his right. He tried to remember what it was called. The 'Licking', that was it. He remembered that he had read once that it flowed all the way to Cincinnati, a long way from where they were now.

The van pulled into a gravel parking lot and stopped. The Mexicans started climbing out. Jimmy looked at the place. It was a bar, the Gyp Joint. Well, well, the Mexicans might be human after all.

•　•　•

Wilson hadn't been inside the Gyp Joint for a while, not since being elected sheriff. It hadn't changed any, as far as he could tell. He sat with his back against the wall, drank his beer and people watched. He kept his coat and hat on with his hat pulled down low over his eyes. He felt kind of like Clint Eastwood in *High Plains*

Drifter. He was confident that he struck an imposing figure, with an air of mystery surrounding him. So far, nobody had recognized him. That was good. That was how he'd like to keep it. After he finished his first beer, he lifted the can slightly and got the bartender's attention. He quickly brought Wilson another. Now, that's a good bartender, he thought.

The door opened and a stream of Mexicans walked in. Wilson lifted his head slightly in order to get a better view. He wished he'd brought his gun along now. He wondered how many of them were legal. Finally, the stream that came through the door ended, nine in all. Good thing he hadn't brought his gun. He only had six shots. He noticed that the last Mexican through the door wasn't a Mexican at all. He was a white guy that was pretending to be a Mexican. Why the hell would a white guy be hanging around with this group? Was he hiding from somebody or something? The white guy was just as dirty as the rest of them. Maybe he was just working on the same farm, very interesting.

●　　●　　●

When they walked out of the Gyp Joint, Jimmy once again climbed into the back seat of the van. At least he had it to himself. Jimmy and his *compadres* had only gone into the bar to get beer and cigarettes, and now were just sitting in the cold stinking van. What the hell is wrong with this group? Jimmy was surprised at how the bartender's face glowed when the group wandered into the Gyp, but now he knew why. Out of the blue, nine guys walked in, each of them ordered a twelve pack of beer and a pack of cigarettes. The bartender charged fifteen bucks for a twelve pack and four or five bucks for smokes. They'd probably just made the guy's night. None of these Mexicans were drinking Corona. Wasn't that like the Mexican national beer? Every one of them had bought Budweiser.

As Jimmy sat in the back of the van and drank his beer, his feet kept getting colder. There was obviously no reason to turn the heater on. It was below freezing outside, but inside the van it must be warm, since all the windows were steamed up. But, Jimmy's feet didn't feel warm. He couldn't wait to get to the comfort of his feed sack bed. He could wrap a burlap sack tightly around his feet and have another restful, freezing evening.

The Mexicans laughed about something again. What he would give to know what the hell they were saying. He still hoped to be able to get a crack at one of these clowns, for all the crap they'd put him through. One of them rolled down a window and threw out a bunch of empties. Jimmy wished he could say *'close the damned window'* in Spanish.

●　　●　　●

Tom pulled into the lot at the Gyp just as Nick got out of his car. Tom was really glad to see that Nick wasn't wearing his Walmart vest. Tom hadn't noticed it when he'd first pulled in, but now he noticed that the migrants' van was parked in the lot. He couldn't tell if Jimmy was inside or not, because the windows were steamed over. Tom grabbed Nick's hand and gave it a good hard shake.

"Well, aren't you a sight for sore eyes?"

Nick laughed, "Sight for sore eyes, huh? I haven't heard that saying since I was knee-high to a grasshopper."

Tom opened the door and they both walked in. It seemed someone was sitting on Tom's favorite stool, but must have gone to the restroom. Steve brought Tom and Nick a couple of beers and they took the remaining stools.

Wilson walked back to his barstool. He looked in the mirror hanging over the bar in order to see the newest arrivals. Well, if it isn't Padgett. Wilson made a slight smirk as he sipped his beer. He was sure that Padgett didn't recognize him. He pulled his hat a little lower. He might just have to stay a little longer than he had planned.

Wilson watched Padgett and his fat friend talk about whatever. Wilson turned as Padgett glanced in the mirror at him. He figured staying for another couple wouldn't hurt. He lifted his can and the bartender was there, just like that with a fresh beer. He wondered if the bartender would consider a job in law enforcement. It would be nice to find a replacement deputy.

Something about the swagger was immediately recognizable to Tom. He could have recognized it a mile away. What the hell is Wilson up to now? Was he into some kind of half-assed undercover assignment? The men that had been sitting next to Nick got up to leave. That was Tom's chance to strike up a little conversation with Wilson. He moved down to the stool right next to Wilson.

"Hey Wilson, what's up with the *High Plains Drifter* outfit? Are you undercover or something?"

Wilson was stunned that Tom recognized him. He looked at Padgett and nodded, "I just stopped in for a beer, that's all."

Tom looked over Wilson's outfit, "Well, you sure got dressed up, for the old Gyp, anyway." "Hey, Steve, a beer for Nick and me, and give one to Clint here, also."

• • •

Jimmy was glad when he finally got out of the van. He'd drunk at least eight beers and hadn't been allowed to go to the bathroom. Well, he was taking care of that now. He stood outside the barn and urinated while he stared at the dark bedroom window where Maria slept.

This had been one great night. Was that how all Mexicans partied? Buying beer at a bar and then carrying it outside to drink? That didn't make any sense to Jimmy. If you pay the bar price for beer, then drink it in the damned bar. Half the toes on his right foot felt frozen. He looked at the curtains in Maria's window. Again he wished that he could curl up with Maria, if only to warm his feet. At least tomorrow would be a day off, for that he was thankful.

Jimmy fumbled his way into the dark barn, anxiously looking for his nest. He wasn't sure how much more of this shit he could take. Now both of his feet were numb. He tripped as he got closer to his little bedroom. He landed hard and hit his head on something. Damn it, that hurt. He stood and tried to get his bearings. The night was clear, but the moon wasn't visible. It's black as coal in this mouse infested barn. He began to feel his way along the wall, hoping to get there without falling again. Jimmy finally managed to feel his way to his make-shift bed.

He shook the sacks. A couple of mice tumbled out of them and scurried off. "Find your own damned bed." He sat on a feed sack and began the slow, painful process of wrapping his aching and freezing feet.

● ● ●

Wilson left the Gyp Joint immediately after he finished the beer that Padgett had bought him. He was pissed about the comments that Padgett had made about him that he looked like *High Plains Drifter*. Wilson dismissed that dig. He did look like him. Then Padgett had called him Clint, that smart ass. Wilson decided he was going to have the last laugh. He pulled his truck into the garage, entered his house and took off his duster and carefully hung it in the hall closet. However, he did keep his hat and boots on. He poured himself a large glass of whiskey. Who was that guy with Padgett, anyway? Were they partners, probably not. Wilson felt that there were a lot of strange things about Padgett, but him going both ways seemed highly unlikely.

He wasn't going to sing tonight. He wasn't in the mood. Padgett had really gotten under his skin. He was heartened by the idea that he might be able to return the favor someday. With any luck, that day would be very soon. He realized that he hadn't eaten dinner, but as he sipped on his whiskey, he forgot all about being hungry.

He walked over to his DVDs and looked at all the familiar titles. He had upgraded his karaoke collection, maybe he needed to consider doing the same for his movies. He found a title that he hadn't watched in a while and popped it in the player. He eased back into his recliner as the video started, another Naughty America Production. Yeah, this was gonna be a great movie.

● ● ●

Tom drove slowly along Abners Mill as he made his way home. He realized that he probably shouldn't have made fun of

Wilson, but it was just too hard to resist. Tom already knew that Wilson had issues. That getup he wore tonight just seemed to highlight more of them. Tom laughed as he remembered Wilson hunkered down under that big hat and wearing his cowboy wannabe coat. Nick had even noticed him. He'd also commented about Wilson's outfit. That was telling because Nick wasn't the sharpest dresser around.

Luckily for Tom, Nick had to work on Saturday. That had been a good reason to call it an early night. Tom was painfully aware of how much Nick liked to drink, so it was good to escape an evening unscathed.

Tom walked into the trailer and noticed how comfortable Bella looked lying on the sofa. The throw rugs she had seemed to enjoy were no longer good enough. Tom hung his coat up, grabbed a beer from the fridge and sat next to Bella on the couch. He looked at his sleepy little baby. He scratched her chin and she quickly rolled onto her back to make her stomach accessible. "Ok, Bella, I take it you'd like me to scratch your stomach?"

Tom still needed to get another deer. He thought he'd go out again in the morning. He was still wrestling with what to do about Jimmy. He slowly mulled the Jimmy problem around in his mind while he sipped his beer. He knew Jimmy wouldn't be stupid enough to return to Maysville, but you never know, maybe he would be.

CHAPTER 24

Jimmy woke up from a frozen, fit-full sleep to a barrage of Spanish coming from Pedro's mouth. Before he left the barn, Pedro had indicated with his head that Jimmy's presence was required. He removed the feed sacks from around his feet, pulled his boots on, and limped in the direction of the doublewide. He didn't have a clue why he was being summoned. It was Saturday, wasn't it? Don't these Mexicans understand about days off?

Maria handed him a coffee as he entered the kitchen. He wanted to know why Pedro had woken him. Maria looked at her brother before replying. "There much work need be done."

Jimmy didn't want to work today. "Tell Pedro I am too sick to work." Maria looked from Jimmy to Pedro before repeating what Jimmy said to Pedro in Spanish.

Pedro looked around the table at the other men. Suddenly they all started to laugh. Jimmy slammed the door as he left the house on his way back to the barn. Let the damned Mexicans go out and work. He was tired and hung over. Now he painfully remembered why he didn't drink beer. A man needed to know his limitations. Beer had never agreed with him, but whiskey did. He really disliked the fact that they had all laughed at him, probably because they thought he was some kind of pussy, because he didn't feel well. Mexican bastards, he would figure out a way to get back at them. He pulled his boots off. Then Jimmy began the painful process of rewrapping his frozen feet.

•　　•　　•

It was comfortable in the trailer. Tom could have easily slept in, but he was determined to get his second deer. He knew that he didn't really need another deer, but if he could give more venison to the Burnetts, that'd be great. He climbed out of bed and nearly tripped on Bella. She had moved from her usual spot and was closer to his bed. Maybe the heater had gotten too warm for her? He bent down and gave her a pat. She didn't acknowledge him. It was probably too early.

He turned the coffee on and listened to a news stream on his laptop. Nothing new in the world, it seemed. Suicide bombers continued to blow themselves and others up around the world. Global warming, or was it plain old Mother Nature, was still hotly contested.

Tom made his way to the cedar grove where he'd hunted yesterday. He was confident that the dogs wouldn't run this route again this morning. However, the deer would most likely still be bedding there. He sat down, leaned against a tree and waited. It had been a clear evening and now it was quite cold sitting on the ground. Hopefully, he wouldn't need to sit for long. Tom scanned the surrounding area and the first deer stood. They were creatures of habit. That was good for him, but bad for the deer. He patiently watched as more and more deer got up and stretched as the sun heated up their bedding area. A repeat of yesterday, minus the dogs, he hoped.

The big doe was on the move again and in the lead. Hopefully, she had the same plan as before. There was a slug in the chamber and Tom clicked off the safety. They were far enough away that the noise shouldn't be noticed. The deer walked up the game trail toward him, then turned southeast. They were still a bit far for an easy shot. He would wait a moment longer.

The biggest doe was visible through the tall thicket. She was sixty yards away. Tom raised the 870. He put the sight where he wanted and squeezed the trigger. The big doe jumped and waved her tail in the air as she bounded southward, toward the creek. He was sure he had hit her, but not so sure about how well. Tom suddenly wished he had taken some practice rounds.

●　　　●　　　●

Jimmy lay and shivered in the barn and then heard the van start. Maybe he should have gone with them. If he was moving around working, at least he would keep warm. It was too late now. Besides, he didn't want to work today. They paid him shit. Jimmy was so damned tired of being a slave to this bunch of Mexicans. Maybe he could go back to Mayville and take care of Woozy. She might be missing him. It had been a while. Maybe she was lonely, like he was. Probably not, he had beaten her pretty good. But he'd decided that it hadn't been his fault. She was to blame. She was the one that'd been wearing that slutty outfit. Yeah, going back to Maysville probably wasn't an option after all, but he knew that it was probably time to move on.

The sun was shining. He had a little cash in his pocket. He might as well wander over to the highway and stick out his thumb. Maybe he could catch a ride south to Florida. There surely wasn't any future working for these Mexicans.

He untangled himself from the damned feed sacks for the last time, pulled on his boots and laced them tight. He might have to cover many miles today. As he walked past the trailer, he thought he heard a noise. Was someone inside the doublewide? Jimmy wondered if that someone just might be sweet Maria. If it was, today might turn out better than he'd hoped.

He bounded up the steps two at a time onto the front porch of the doublewide. Jimmy opened the screen and gave a gentle rap on the door. No response. He was positive that he heard someone moving about inside. He knocked gently on the door again.

"Who you be?"

"Maria its Jimmy, I was hoping for another cup of coffee?"

Maria paused. Jimmy hoped that she was considering it.

"My brother say no one come in."

Jimmy cursed under his breath, Pedro, bastard. He tried the nice guy approach again, "Please, Maria, all I want is some coffee?"

Maria took awhile and replied firmly, "My brother say no one come in."

Jimmy held the screen open as he slammed his shoulder into the door. It didn't budge. Maria screamed. He looked around the porch for something to prop the screen open with. He found a table and propped it against the screen. This held it open.

He raised his boot and kicked the door. Maria screamed again, this time louder. Jimmy kicked at the door again and could see that the door frame was weakening. He raised his boot a third time and pounded it into the door. Maria now screamed non-stop. The lock barely held. Maria tried frantically to move a chair to block the door, but she was too late. Jimmy crashed through the door after he slammed into it again with his shoulder.

●　　●　　●

He shook his head in frustration as Tom watched the deer scatter. How could he possibly have missed? Well, he might not have, but he knew the shot hadn't been one of his finest. He had taken two bad shots in the past, one of them a lung shot and the other a gut shot. He was afraid that this shot was probably a gut shot, which meant he would have to do some serious tracking. If the blood trail was poor, tracking in a thicket would be nearly impossible. A lung shot would have been fatal, but there would still be some tracking to do. Tom leaned against the tree and waited to let the deer lie down somewhere and bleed out. Not the most humane way of getting a deer, but it might be his only option.

At least it was a sunny morning with little hint of a breeze. Tom moved to where the doe had been standing when he'd taken the shot. Fortunately, there was blood, unfortunately not a lot. Worse yet, there was no frothiness to it. He realized he'd probably delivered a gut shot.

Some people believe that hunting is cruel and shouldn't be allowed. Right now, Tom couldn't agree with them more. He cursed himself for the unnecessary pain he'd just inflicted on that doe. Now his goal was to find her and put her out of her misery. The doe was running downhill. Tom knew this was a good sign, but the blood trail was hit or miss. Three hundred yards later, he found a spot where the doe had rested. That was another positive sign. She was badly hurt. Tom knew the doe wouldn't live. He needed to find her.

He tracked her as she continued her downhill, southward run. She had laid down a number of times, now bleeding less and less. Tom hoped he found her soon. If he didn't, he might end up losing her trail. He knew the deer wouldn't go to waste in the animal world and that her death would keep other animals alive. But, he had been the one that had taken the shot that would end her life. It was his job to find her.

Finally, he spotted her up ahead, just shy of a creek bed. He checked her, she wasn't breathing. She was dead. He stood and looked down at her for a moment. She was beautiful. He felt terrible about the poor shot he'd taken. Tom vowed never to be so arrogant again, and never to hunt without practicing. He pulled his knife from its sheath. Then, he heard a woman scream.

●　　●　　●

Jimmy landed hard on the floor after the door gave way. Maria bolted down the hallway, and shut herself in the bedroom. Jimmy pushed himself up to stand and then yelled down the hall after her. "Maria, all you had to do was get me a cup of coffee. If you had, none of this would have happened."

The door was locked, but Maria knew it wouldn't hold. She scanned the room, looking for something to protect herself with. She could see the door knob moving as Jimmy tried to open it.

"Come on, Maria. Open the door. All I want to do is talk. Do you really think I want to hurt you?"

Maria desperately tried to open one of the windows. It was screwed shut from the outside. Jimmy gave the door a kick. Maria screamed as loud as she could. Jimmy kicked again and the door blew open.

She tried to run past Jimmy as he attempted to regain his balance that he'd lost after kicking open the door. But, she was too slow. He grabbed her arm and threw her down on the bed, hard. He held her down with one hand.

Jimmy smiled, "I've wanted you ever since the first time I saw you. And now I'm going to have you."

Maria was no match for Jimmy's strength. She still tried unsuccessfully to kick out and inflict some damage. Jimmy just laughed at her efforts. He ripped her top away and then began to tear at her jeans. Maria fought much harder now. The harder she fought, the more Jimmy smiled. "You're a whore just like all women. I'm the man that's going to give you what you need. I'm the man that's going to give you what you deserve."

Maria began to pray. She prayed like she never had before.

Jimmy laughed at her, "No amount of praying is gonna save you now, you slut."

Maria let out another loud scream. Jimmy backhanded her. He was absolutely wild as he fumbled with his belt and dropped his pants. All of Jimmy's weight kept her pinned to the bed. Maria desperately clawed at his exposed skin.

Finally, she lost the fight. He had won. Jimmy lay still for a moment. He breathed heavily as he lay on top of her and then he stood. He looked down at the young naked body lying before him. Once again, another slut got what she deserved.

He smirked, "You got exactly what you wanted, and exactly what you deserved." He bent down to pull up his pants. He paused, had he heard a noise? Jimmy started to turn ever so slowly as he heard another sound. Unfortunately, it sounded a lot like the ratcheting of a shotgun being loaded.

Jimmy Fugate was finally at a loss for words. The twelve gauge slug hit him chest high, penetrated his spine and exited through his heart. Recovery was not an option. Jimmy's knees buckled and he slumped to the left, and then fell face-down onto the floor.

Maria screamed one last time. Finally, she opened her eyes and watched a shadow, her savior, walk down the hallway. She had never stopped praying. It seemed to have worked. With much difficulty, Maria managed to pull herself upright. She wrapped her torn clothing around her naked body. On shaking legs, she walked into the bathroom and started the shower, staying there until all the hot water was gone. When finished, she dressed in the baggiest clothes she could find. Then she went and sat on the sofa to wait.

CHAPTER 25

She didn't move for hours. She sat with her knees pulled tightly to her chest. She sat there until her brothers and cousins and their friends came back from work, seven hours later. Her oldest brother, Pedro was the first one through the door. Maria sat and stared at the floor. As he looked from the busted door to his baby sister, Pedro had a terrible feeling that he knew what had happened, but he had no idea what was waiting for him down the hall.

Pedro looked at the mess of the man that lay on the floor in the bedroom. He rapidly directed the rest of the men to get moving. Maria sat on the sofa and waited. They took what they needed and were on the road south in 15 minutes. Maria, wrapped in a blanket, lay on the backseat.

Nobody spoke, they all knew the plan. They were going to Tennessee. There, they would stay with friends and then carry on down to Alabama. They didn't have many options. Pedro and two of his friends were the only ones in the country legally. They would find work in some remote location and work for whoever needed help, work for whoever didn't check too closely on their status. Maria would be okay. At least that's what Pedro hoped. He wondered how anyone could really be all right after what she'd been through.

•   •   •

Harold Ricks owned properties in both Nicholas and Fleming Counties. They weren't much, but it helped him make ends meet. He parked in front of the doublewide that he rented on a week to week basis. Harold always kept a close eye on his rental properties. He'd had some renters screw him over in the past, but, the Mexicans that rented the doublewide seemed to be all right people. They kept pretty much to themselves. But, Harold hadn't seen their van for two days now. He climbed out of his truck. He needed to check, to find out if anything was wrong. As he stepped onto the porch, he immediately found a problem. The front door had been busted up.

He knocked and the door swung inward, barely attached to the hinges. Well shit, they were gone all right. All the cabinets were open and their food was gone. It smelled like something was spoiled, also. They had paid the rent just five days ago, so it wasn't such a big loss. He walked around the house and noticed that nothing seemed to be missing. He had some old junky furniture in the place, because he rented it as a furnished unit. Since most of the migrant workers didn't have furniture, they looked for places like this.

He continued down the hall. He noticed that the smell got stronger. What would be rotting this far away from the kitchen? After Harold walked through the broken bedroom door, he wished he hadn't.

His hands trembled as he dialed 911. He had never had anything like this happen in any of his rentals. He was shocked to think that the Mexican group was involved in anything like this. In his wildest dreams, he never expected to find a dead man with his pants to his knees lying on the floor in one of his rentals. It was going to take a bit of work to get this place ready to rent again.

He walked back outside to wait for the police to come. He had watched enough cop shows to know that he didn't want to mess up any evidence or anything like that. Harold thought about that pretty girl, Maria, the one that had been taking English lessons. Seeing the dead guy with his pants to his knees worried him terribly, especially for that young girl.

●　　●　　●

Gordon Davis had been the Sheriff of Fleming County for twenty years and was highly respected in the community. He received a call to respond to the Ricks property on the county line for a possible homicide. Davis knew exactly where the doublewide was situated. The 911 call had simultaneously been patched through to Nicholas County, since the property was actually located in both counties. Davis was the first one on the scene. He had been informed that Wilson was on his way. Davis had heard some stories about Wilson, most of them not very flattering. He didn't like hearsay. He hated gossip. He would let the man prove himself.

Davis stepped out of his cruiser when he arrived at the Ricks' rental property. Harold Ricks was waiting in the front seat of his car. Visibly distraught, Ricks slowly climbed out of his car and walked up to greet the sheriff. A moment later, Wilson arrived. He'd never met Davis before. The two men introduced themselves and shook hands. Harold gave them a summary of what he'd found. He also explained why he happened to come to the doublewide today.

Armed with the information, Davis asked Ricks to wait outside until they were finished. Wilson watched as Davis put on gloves and shoe coverings before entering the house. Luckily, Wilson had similar supplies in his truck and he did the same.

They walked into the bedroom first to get a general idea of what had happened. Then, Davis suggested that they backtrack. They'd start at the front door and work their way to the bedroom. That would give them a better understanding of what had gone down. He recommended that Wilson take notes. Davis would recite what he saw as they walked through the house. After they finished, they could talk about anything that needed additional attention. Wilson was okay with the note taking assignment, for the moment anyway.

At the front door, Davis commented, "It looks like multiple attempts had been made to gain entry. There are boot marks at different locations on the painted finish, which indicates multiple kicks. The perpetrator used his right foot. The wood frame is also splintered higher up. So, the final assault on the doorway was most likely delivered by the perpetrator's shoulder."

Wilson was impressed with Davis' observations. Maybe there was something to be learned from the old guy, he admitted.

Davis continued, "The table on the porch was used to prop the door open so the perpetrator could freely attack the door. The chair inside the front door has slid several feet. See that line of dust on the floor? That shows where the chair had previously been. The victim probably attempted to move it to keep the perpetrator from gaining access. Unfortunately, it was an exercise in futility."

Wilson once again was impressed with the older sheriff's assessment.

Davis paused and asked, "What do you think of my reconstruction so far, Wilson?"

Wilson conceded, "So far, very convincing, Sheriff."

Sheriff Davis moved toward the bedroom door. He studied it a moment and continued, "This door's still locked, as it was before it was kicked in. The door also has a right hand in-swing, so it's harder to kick, especially for someone using their right foot. But, the frame was weak and it probably failed after a relatively easy blow."

Wilson looked at the door and nodded in agreement.

"There will most likely be the fingerprints of the man lying on the floor on both doorknobs."

Wilson was puzzled, "You mean you believe he was the last person to have touched the door knobs?"

"Probably, Wilson, but that's pure speculation."

●   ●   ●

Tom sat back on the sofa while he enjoyed a beer. He had finished cutting up the deer he'd shot over the weekend. The meat was packed away in the freezer. There were also two extra bags of venison for the Burnetts. He remembered that they had little space in their freezer. Maybe he would drive over to let them know that he had some more venison for them. He started for the door and noticed as Bella's head snapped in his direction.

"Come on Bella, you want to go for a ride in the truck?"

Tom was amazed at how quickly Bella could transition from a sleep state to one of total alertness. She stood with her front paws on the armrest and looked out the back window of the crew cab.

One of Bella's favorite things was to ride in the truck with the window down. She could smell all those smells she seemed to love; cows, horses, manure. Tom crossed into Fleming County. He noticed that there were two sheriffs' vehicles in the driveway of the doublewide where the migrant workers lived and where Jimmy had been. Both county sheriffs, Tom thought it doubtful that the Nicholas and Fleming County Sheriff departments would be working together.

Tom slowly rolled past the doublewide and thought back to the night when he'd seen Jimmy there. He had given Jimmy fair warning. The guy was obviously too stupid to take it. There was no point feeling sorry for him. He was a born loser, one that the system couldn't rehabilitate. He got what he had coming. Wilson would try to pin this on him. He was sure of it. But, as far as he was concerned, this was just a case of *delayed reckoning.* This day had been inevitable. He turned his attention back to the road and continued to the Burnetts.

Tom pulled the truck into the drive and jumped out, "Bella I'll only be a minute."

Linda Burnett answered the door and they exchanged hellos.

"Linda, I just stopped by to tell you that I shot another deer. I have two more bags of venison in my freezer and they've got your name on them. Whenever you need some more meat, you can either pick it up or I'll bring it to you."

"That's very kind of you, Tom."

"Oh, and this meat is from a doe, so it will be more tender. It won't require nearly as much doctoring up as buck venison does."

"That venison you brought over has been great. Chad uses some kind of special recipe. The kids even like it."

●　　●　　●

Wilson and Davis both stared at the man lying face down on the floor.

"Wilson, why don't you pull the guy's wallet out of his pants? Let's find out who he is."

Wilson read the name, "Jimmy Fugate, Maysville."

Davis scratched his chin, "Maysville, huh? What's a Maysville man doing down here in this migrant workers' home?"

Wilson seemed to think that was a pretty good question. "Maybe he had reason to be hiding down here?"

"You're probably right about that, Wilson."

Davis looked the body over a little more closely, "Let's see. Are you ready for some more of my observations?"

Wilson couldn't argue with that. The guy seemed to know what he was talking about. He grabbed his note pad as Davis poked around on the crusty wound.

"From the looks of the entry wound, I'd say that a twelve gauge slug was used and was the cause of death. And with the guy's pants down around his ankles, I'm assuming he was having a go at the young Mexican girl. Someone surprised him and now Mr. Fugate is in Hell, doing the devil's bidding."

Wilson scribbled away on his pad. "Do you think it was one of the Mexicans that shot him?"

Davis pondered the question, "No, I don't believe so. I believe if the Mexicans had caught this man doing that to their sister, shooting him would have been the kind thing to do. I believe the shooter was someone with another reason for being here."

Back outside, Wilson and Davis discussed what they had discovered.

"Wilson, do you feel confident that you'll be able to handle this investigation?"

Wilson was surprised at the question. He wondered why Davis was questioning his ability. "Of course I feel confident handling it," he indignantly snapped.

Davis was surprised at Wilson's reaction. "Wilson, don't get excited. I want to be sure you have the resources to bring this to a conclusion. Right now, I'm still working a homicide in Fleming County and personally I feel this might be more than my group can handle."

Wilson smiled at Davis, "Sheriff, I feel perfectly capable of handling this case. As a matter of fact, I believe I have a fairly strong lead."

Davis raised an eyebrow at Wilson's last statement. He was curious about Wilson's claim, but he didn't have time to get involved with this, as he was under the gun with his own active investigation. Wilson followed Davis to his cruiser.

As they shook hands, Davis added, "Wilson, if you need any help, and if I can give it to you, I will. All you need to do is phone me."

Wilson liked the man, "I'll do that, Davis." He watched Davis drive away, walked to his truck, and grabbed a roll of crime scene tape from behind the seat.

Ricks had been waiting for the sheriffs to finish their business. He walked over to Wilson.

"Sheriff, is there anything else you need from me?"

"Not at the moment, Mr. Ricks, but maybe you could give me a hand with this crime scene tape."

Wilson finished securing the crime scene. He sat in his truck and made some phone calls. It dawned on him just how busy he suddenly was. He had just been fretting about not having enough to do.

He pulled away from the doublewide and headed back to Carlisle. He was hungry and he had a lot of work to do. He slowed his truck as he passed by Padgett's trailer. Padgett's truck was in the driveway. He accelerated out of the Abners Mill hollow and made a left turn on Route 68. He thought about Padgett and nagging thoughts came back to him.

How is it that Padgett happens to live so close to where all the recent crimes have happened? What about those two meth labs that were torched, which resulted in Jack Estep's death and Albert Rankin's close call? And, what about Becky Adkins' Oxycontin that Padgett supposedly found? He really could have planted it on her. And, that poor young kid that overdosed? Could Padgett have somehow been responsible for that, too?

He remembered something he'd heard about Padgett's partner being killed by a drug addict. Maybe Padgett has a hard-on for druggies. Maybe Padgett isn't the great guy everyone thinks he is. Padgett seems to like to spend a lot of time in the woods. He could have found those two meth labs and taken the law into his own hands, like some kind of sick revenge.

Well, he was going to figure it all out. He had never liked Padgett, never did trust him. I'll be damned, he thought. He suddenly felt increasingly optimistic and very sure of himself.

"Padgett, I've got my eye on you."